INKED

A DANIKA FROST NOVEL

CONNOR ASHLEY

CHARLOTTE PAGE

inked entertainment

Danika Frost Series:

Chosen (Prequel Novella)

Inked (Book 1)

Burned (Book 2, coming 2020)

Also by Charlotte Page:

The Trial (coming 2020)

Also by Connor Ashley:

The Paranormal Containment Agency:

with Tatum Flynn

A Case of Blood and Shadow - (Book 1, coming 2020)

Betty Bedlam Series:

with Mark Henry

Damned - (Book 1, coming 2020)

Assassin's Revenge Series

with Carrie Harris

The Crown of Blood and Fire - (Book 1, coming 2020)

To my mum, Debbie. The strongest woman I know.
- Connor

To my loveable goof of a cat Ollie, who borrowed some of
Dani's healing powers just in the nick of time
- Charlotte

It was a perfect night for hunting.

Danika Frost slipped through the city streets, weapons tucked out of sight. A gun at the small of her back. Her sword hidden at her hip, the long blade magically retracted within the hilt. Though it was barely past seven, the autumn sky had grown dark, the moon new and missing from the sky.

Above her, a raven's cry split the quiet. The creature swooped low, barely missing Dani's head. She didn't bother ducking, instead giving the bird a sideways glare when it settled in the low branches of a nearby tree. "Did you find them?"

The bird cocked its head to one side. Silent.

"Save the lecture, Poe. Did you find them or not?" Dani kept her voice hushed. The streets were mostly bare, but she didn't need passersby to see her talking to a bird.

Third floor, second window. Poe's voice was crystal clear inside Dani's mind. *And I don't lecture. I inform.* The raven made an indignant noise and took off again, soaring into the sky. He landed on a building across the street from the seedy motel where Dani's target had rented a room for the night.

Dani rolled her eyes and followed, keeping to the shadows. Poe might be an ancient, demon-hunting spirit, but he was also the biggest nag Dani had ever met.

And tonight's hunt—for a cheating spouse rather than one of the many demons roaming the streets of Blackthorn City—was just the kind of thing Poe liked to lecture about. No matter how many times Dani explained that these cases were the only thing keeping her private investigation business in the black, Poe never failed to point out Dani's shortcomings. Mainly, that she wasn't hunting demons every second of her life.

When she reached the building across the street from the motel, Dani leaped and grabbed the bottom of the fire escape. The rusted metal didn't slide down like it was supposed to, forcing Dani to rely on her arm strength to get up the first six rungs, until her feet finally contacted the ladder and she could hurry the rest of the way up to the third floor.

With the delay, she barely had her camera out in time to capture her client's husband stumbling through the motel room door. He was an older white man, early fifties according to his wife, with graying hair and the beginnings of a beer belly jutting out over his belt.

The shutter clicked as Dani took photo after photo of the clandestine couple, her long-range lens capturing the pair in perfect detail. The husband's date was far too young for him, probably no more than Dani's twenty-three years, and severely out of his league. The woman was slender with generous curves, her golden hair cascading down her back. And the detached way she kissed the older man, the way she let him paw at her breasts, gave Dani the impression she wasn't a real girlfriend. At least, not one he'd landed for free.

Poe glided down to where Dani was photographing the affair, her cheeks burning as the couple discarded their clothing. Dani *hated* cheating cases. Her clients were never happy to find out the truth, but this—capturing intimate moments on her camera, searing the images into her mind for weeks after—was the worst part.

Must we watch them fornicate? Poe complained,

turning away from the scene with contempt in his beady black eyes. *These cases are beneath you, Danika. You have a sacred duty—*

"To rid the world of demons," Dani finished for him. The bird had been a broken record her entire life. "I can't do that if I'm homeless and starving. And you need a new refrain, old friend."

They'd had this fight often in the five years since Dani opened *Frost Investigations*, and though the business had pulled her from the brink of homelessness and given her something close to stability, Poe remained stubbornly opposed to the idea.

Dani turned her attention back to the motel room. The cheating husband was still wearing his pants—thank god—but he pulled out a pair of fuzzy pink handcuffs from his briefcase. To Dani's amusement, the woman managed to talk the man into wearing the cuffs himself. Dani snapped another photo.

Her latest client, Camilla, wasn't going to like Dani's results. She'd made it clear during their first meeting that she hoped her husband was working late at the office, as he claimed. But all of Dani's clients hoped as much. Hoped that their husbands or wives or even, in one case, a mistress, were just busy with work or volunteering. No one ever wanted to find out their loved one was unfaithful.

Though she hated the voyeurism, Dani had

learned that if she didn't catch her marks in the act, if she didn't show the full progression of their betrayal, her clients would find any excuse not to believe her— and in doing so, find any excuse not to *pay* her. And no money meant no meal.

Dani's stomach growled at the thought. She'd been trailing Camilla's husband since three that afternoon and hadn't eaten dinner yet. She'd kill for one of the burgers at Bloody Mary's, the drag bar above which she rented her apartment and office space. Or maybe a platter of their famous barbecue ribs. Her stomach grumbled again. As soon as she was finished here, she was heading straight home to see Mary, the bar's owner and star drag queen, for a hot meal.

Now, all she needed was for Camilla's husband to stick his dick where it didn't belong and—

"Poe, did you see that?" Dani pulled the camera away from her face and stared across the street into the motel room. There was something ... *off* ... about the woman. Something in the way her spine moved as she slipped out of her dress and straddled the older man. But even with Dani's heightened senses, she couldn't see well enough to assuage or confirm her sudden suspicions.

See what?

"Can you get a closer look?" As soon as the question passed her lips, Poe took off and flew closer to the window. Dani flipped through the pictures she'd taken so far that night, zooming in on the woman, looking for signs.

Her heart stopped when she landed on a picture of the woman's face. More specifically, on her catlike eyes, glowing with demon energy. "Shit." Dani brought the camera back to her eye, zooming in as tight as her lens allowed. The woman trailed her fingers down the cheating husband's hairy torso, then raised her hand. Her nails extended into razor-sharp claws, and before Dani could do more than curse, the demon buried those claws in the man's chest.

"Shit, shit, shit." Dani hung the camera strap around her neck and hurried down the ladder, dropping to the ground from two stories up. She landed harder than she'd meant to, the soles of her feet aching in complaint, but she was up and running a second later.

Danika? Poe sounded worried, but there was also a bit of righteousness in his tone now that they had a demon in their sights. That always improved his mood.

"I see it." She took off across the street, looking for a way to the third floor without having to pass the woman at the front desk. She didn't have time to explain herself or convince the woman to give her a key. If she didn't hurry, the man was going to be demon food.

The fire escape is around the corner, Poe said, swooping down to fly beside her. *If you just—*

"No time," Dani said and leaped into the air.

Her fingers caught the bottom of the second-floor windowsill. She shimmied onto the ledge and leaped again, grabbing the base of the cheater's window and using the brick facade to help herself onto the third-floor ledge.

Dani winced when she saw the scene inside. She was too late to save Camilla's husband. His organs were already missing, the demon now busy gnawing on his rib cage. Dani's earlier desire for barbecue made her stomach turn.

But she still had a job to do. She called back to Poe, who circled the sky. "Ready?"

Of course, I'm ready.

Dani shielded her eyes and shattered the window with a single kick. The sound alerted the demon, but Poe dove fast, slipping into the room and scratching at the demon's eyes with his talons. The distraction gave Dani time to maneuver through the shattered window and draw her sword.

The demon swatted at Poe, and when it looked up at Dani, it laughed at her weapon of choice. "Missing something?" A two-pronged voice slipped past the woman's lips, the soft voice of the human body—most likely long dead—and the throaty growl of the demon now driving the corpse.

Dani looked down at the hilt in her hand and smiled. She flicked it to the side, and the long steel blade slid into place, gleaming in the shitty motel lighting. Easily three times the length of the hilt, the blade was one of her colleague's more ingenious inventions, allowing her to carry the weapon in public without drawing unwanted attention.

Poe dove at the nearly naked demon again, who hissed and swiped its claws at him. Then it paused, frowning as it looked between Dani's sword and Poe. *"Ink Carrier."* The demon growled Dani's title like a curse.

"The one and only." Dani lunged, driving her sword toward the demon. It dodged out of the way, at the height of its speed and strength after consuming human flesh. The demon slipped past another arc of Dani's sword and caught Dani around the throat, raising her into the air.

"I wonder what you'll taste like," the demon mused, tightening its hold around Dani's neck.

Dani grabbed the demon's wrist, using the hold as leverage to kick the creature in the face. They both hit the ground, the air knocking from Dani's lungs. "Kiva," she wheezed, gathering air again. "Jasper."

A burst of pain stole Dani's breath as the panther tattoo peeled away from her back, the Ink pooling across the floor before solidifying into the mighty creature. Kiva's black fur shone in the soft light, her amber eyes checking over Dani before she pounced on the demon, mighty jaws closing around its bare leg.

The demon screamed, a bloodcurdling sound, and Dani instinctively covered her ears. As she did, Jasper unspooled from her left forearm, the onyx-scaled king cobra slipping along the floor toward the demon. He would wait for his turn to eat whatever remained when Kiva was done with it.

Though Dani didn't need her Ink—the three ancient spirits who lived in the tattooed patterns on her skin—to deal with a single demon, she knew they liked the chance to stretch their bodies. Being cooped up for days on end left them agitated, and it had been awhile since they'd taken down a demon.

"You'll pay for this," the demon wailed as Kiva released its leg and bit down on its torso.

Dani stepped forward, adjusting her grip on the hilt of her blade. "You almost had it. Just off by one teeny, tiny word. I'll *get* paid for this."

The demon's glowing eyes widened with fear. With a single blow, Dani severed the demon's head from its body and stepped aside to let Jasper swallow it whole.

Kiva padded over to Dani and nudged her nose into Dani's hand. *Are you all right, Little Warrior?*

Dani scratched Kiva behind the ears until the great cat rumbled with pleasure. "I'm starving."

From the outside, Bloody Mary's looked like any other bar. A neon sign welcomed patrons in flashing red light, illuminating the heavily muscled bouncer checking IDs as the primarily male clientele waited for their chance to get inside. The rotation of bouncers was a little more clean-cut than most places in Blackthorn, and they wore their pants considerably tighter too, which the line of waiting men seemed to appreciate thoroughly.

Henny Dreadful must be performing tonight, Dani thought as she approached. Of all the drag queens who performed at Bloody Mary's, Henny always drew the biggest crowd. The rowdiest too.

Though she sported a splattering of purple demon ichor on her black leather jacket, and looked like a hot mess compared to the men vying to get inside, James, that night's bouncer, smiled when he saw Dani and ushered her past the crowd. He planted a kiss on Dani's cheek. "Mary's in the kitchen," he whispered as he shooed her inside.

"Right where I'm headed. Thanks, James," Dani said with a wave. Though she loved the bar's patrons, she didn't make a habit of coming through the front door. She had her own private staircase at the back of the bar that led directly to a set of two doors—one for her apartment and the other for the office of Frost Investigations. But tonight, she couldn't bear to go another second without dinner.

Not bothering to stop at the packed bar to order her meal, Dani slipped into the kitchen where the queen bee herself supervised the kitchen staff.

"Any chance I could steal a burger before I head up for the night?"

At the sound of her voice, Bloody Mary whirled around, her blond wig teased a foot in the air and her severe makeup painted thick enough to be seen in the darkest corners of the bar. "There's my girl!" Careful to dodge the kitchen staff with her wide, padded hips, Mary strutted toward Dani dressed in her signature sequined gown of black and red that accentuated her big-girl curves. Mary towered head and shoulders over her, causing Dani to crane her neck once the drag queen got close. Then again, at over six foot without her heels, Mary towered over most people.

She made to hug Dani, but stopped at the last second. Behind the layers of blush, Mary's fair skin went white. "What the devil is all over your clothes?"

"The devil about sums it up." Dani gave Mary an apologetic smile. "Figured I should get something to go so I don't gross out the boys on the dance floor."

"Oh, don't you worry about them. You're always welcome here." Mary put together a to-go bag for Dani, including a double cheeseburger and an obscenely large serving of seasoned fries. Ever since Dani helped the bar's owner with some … personal demons … a couple years before, the bar and the apartment above had become a haven for Dani. Mary didn't ask questions, and she didn't harass Dani for being antisocial most of the time either.

"Thanks, Mary. I owe you one." Dani's stomach growled at the smell of food so close, and she fished out a fry from the bag, unable to wait a second longer. "I should get out of your hair. You've got a full house tonight."

"Don't be a stranger. You still owe me a brunch date." Mary kissed the air on either side of Dani's face, saving Dani's cheeks from the bright red lipstick she wore.

Dani slipped out the back door and reached inside

the bag for her burger. By the time she made it up her exterior stairs, she'd already finished half of it, the juice dripping off her fingers. If Poe hadn't already returned to her chest, he'd lecture her about her lack of manners. She could practically hear him anyway.

Your mother didn't raise you in a barn, Danika.

The thought of her mother stalled Dani's heart, but she shoved the memories away, focusing instead on how she could grab her key without getting burger grease all over her jeans.

The office door on Dani's left swung open, and her office manager Lana poked her head out. Ever the professional, Lana was dressed in smart black dress pants that hugged the curves of her hips and a burgundy blouse that complimented her fair skin. Yet despite the clean lines of her clothes, her blond hair had escaped an uncharacteristically messy bun, loose strands curling around her ears.

"Camilla's in your office," she whispered, glancing surreptitiously over her shoulder. "She refuses to leave until you speak with her."

Dani grimaced. Of course, the wife was there. Clients like her *never* waited until Dani called with updates. Since she was still covered in the remains of Camilla's husband—well, the insides of his killer anyway—Dani said, "I'd better change. Could you get the—"

"On it." Lana stepped out onto the stairway, heels clicking against the metal floor, and unlocked Dani's apartment door, using the spare key Dani had given her for emergencies.

"Thanks." Dani stepped inside and hit the light switch with her elbow, annoyed that her meal would likely go cold before she finished with her client. She unholstered her gun and set both her weapons on the table. "Is Spencer still here?"

"He left about an hour ago. Adrian needed a study break, so they went to find food."

"At least one of us has managed to keep a boyfriend." Dani sat her bag of fries on the other end of the table and lifted her camera from her neck.

Lana accepted the camera from Dani, but she gave her boss a skeptical look. "I'm pretty sure you can't complain about the lack of love affairs when you refuse to date." She flipped through the photos on the viewfinder and grimaced. "I assume you'll want copies of these for the wife?"

Dani nodded, grateful for the subject change. She was happy for Spencer and Adrian—who had been together since they were teens—but seeing them always reminded her of her own breakup and subsequent years of solitude. "Tell Camilla I'll be with her shortly. But don't show her the camera." Dani paused at her bathroom. "She'll want to look immediately, and there are things on there she shouldn't see."

"Got it." Lana turned on her heel and closed the apartment door behind her.

Alone, Dani stripped out of her ruined clothes, hopped in the shower, and scrubbed the last of the demon ichor from her skin and her bright, box-red hair. After ensuring she was clean of all demonic residue, she went in search of something appropriately formal for Camilla. Her older clients didn't appreciate Dani's usual style, expecting to see her in slacks and boring blouses instead of Dani's preferred jeans and soft T-shirts. Dani hated dressing for them, but it was yet another safeguard against clients refusing to pay.

If she looked like a serious professional, they were more likely to pay her like one.

Dani paused at her front door and took a deep breath, steeling herself for the conversation. It was never easy telling her clients that they'd been cheated on. Even less so when Dani knew their partner was demon food. *Like a Band-Aid.* Dani took another breath. *Quick and painless.*

Lana was waiting for her with the stack of photographs when she opened the door. Dani flipped through them, handing Lana any photo that showed the escort's demonic eyes. "You don't have to stay late. I'm sure Cassie would appreciate seeing you before she goes to bed tonight."

"My sister's sixteen. She stays up later than I do." Lana nodded toward her desk, where her laptop was still open. "I just have a few things to finish up, then I'll be out of here."

"Cross your fingers we get paid," Dani muttered under her breath before heading for her office door. She swung it open without knocking and crossed the room. She didn't acknowledge Camilla's presence until she was seated behind her massive desk. "It's past office hours."

Camilla sniffled and shifted in the seat across from Dani. In her midforties, Camilla looked like she'd stepped out of a high-end designer magazine, with a silk blouse, soft cardigan, and a knit skirt that hit just below the knee. Her chestnut hair was pulled back into a bun, streaked with thin lines of gray. "I know, and I'm sorry, but I couldn't go another night without the truth. Hal's secretary said he left work at three this afternoon, but he never came home. His phone goes straight to voicemail."

"I'm sorry to be the bearer of bad news, Camilla," Dani said, cutting right to the point, "but I don't think you'll be hearing from your husband again." She spread the photos out before her client, shot after shot of the dead man sucking face with a much younger woman, being strapped to a bed, the woman climbing into his lap.

Dani watched as her client looked over the photos, wishing she could tell the woman the whole truth but knowing she never could. If she told Camilla her husband was dead, she'd want to know why. And without being able to explain the existence of demons, or the lack of a body—Jasper had taken care of the remains—the police would either look to blame Dani or call her insane. Even having a friend on the force, Dani wasn't about to take that risk.

"Hal wouldn't leave me," Camilla insisted. "He may be stupid enough to cheat, but he wouldn't *leave* me. He'll be back tonight. Where did he go after … *this?*"

"He took his mistress shopping. He purchased new clothes, luggage, even a new phone. All signs point to them skipping town together." Dani reached out and brushed the photos into a pile, but before she could take them back, Camilla placed a hand firmly on top. "I'm sorry, Camilla. They're gone."

Camilla grabbed the edge of the photos and flung the entire stack off the desk. The images fluttered to the floor, and Camilla stood and grabbed her purse. "We'll see about that. I have lawyers. I'll freeze his assets until he can't rub two pennies together without my say-so."

Dani stood too, refusing to cede the higher ground to her client. "He'll be out of the country before you get a chance. Let him go. He doesn't deserve your worry, Camilla. You're too good for him. You deserve better."

"I don't need the advice of a *child*," Camilla snapped, turning for the door.

"Mrs. Anderson," Dani called, pushing every ounce of authority into her voice, even as she deferred to Camilla's surname.

The woman paused at the door.

"Per our agreement, final payment is due at the time of photographic evidence." Dani gestured to the sordid photos on the floor. After being stiffed one too many times, Dani started making clients pay half up front, but there was still the occasional jilted spouse that tried to weasel their way out of the second installment.

Camilla paused long enough, lips pursed so tight they practically disappeared, that Dani worried the new widow might try to avoid payment. Then, with a sigh and a sour expression on her face, Camilla dug around in her purse, pulled out her checkbook, and slapped the check on the desk. Dani didn't dare glance at it until the exterior door slammed shut.

When she looked, she was glad at least to see the correct amount staring up at her.

As much as she hated these meetings, getting paid enough to cover both rentals for a couple months made it worthwhile. Dani sat and leaned back in her chair, her hastily eaten burger sitting heavier than she'd like.

A soft knock on her door had Dani sitting up. "Lana? I thought I told you to go home." When she met her assistant's gaze, her whole body went cold. "What is it?"

"The hospital called," Lana said, worry thick in her voice. "They need you to come over right away."

Danika Frost stood frozen outside the massive building.

The hospital always struck fear in her otherwise stoic heart. She clenched her fist, angry with herself. She hunted *demons*, and yet she was afraid of a building. *No, not the building,* she realized, tears prickling. It was the woman inside, and everything this placed represented, that spurred her heart into double time.

It was her constant failure.

A mother she couldn't save.

Get on with it, Dani chided herself. She forced her

limbs to move and propelled herself forward until she crossed the threshold of the hospital. Despite her misgivings, it was a good hospital. Clean. New. A wonderful, caring staff. One of the nurses, who worried at her fingernails by a set of locked doors, spotted Dani and waved her over.

"I'm so sorry for calling this late," the nurse said, swiping a keycard over a scanner to unlock the doors. "Andrea's having one of her episodes, and the staff can't get anywhere near her."

"It's no trouble." Dani clenched her teeth and breathed slowly through her nose, a failed attempt to calm her ragged heart. After the first dozen of her mother's *episodes,* the staff had no choice but to move Dani's mother to a more secure area of the hospital. Andrea might be ill, but she was still a former Ink Carrier. She still held an echo of her enhanced strength. That made her dangerous, especially with her mind no longer her own.

Once they were through a second set of locked doors, frantic screams echoed off the walls. The nurse cast an apologetic look at Dani, as if Andrea's condition was the hospital's fault for not better helping her. Dani couldn't bring herself to give the nurse a reassuring smile, but it wasn't the staff's fault—they weren't equipped to treat a mind tormented by actual demons.

No, this was Dani's fault. For six years, she'd failed to find the demon who scrambled her mother's mind. For six years, her visits grew more and more infrequent until the guilt finally forced her back. Or one of Andrea's episodes did it for her.

"Next room on the left, Miss Frost." The nurse paused before the described door. "Again, we're so sorry to call you for this. It's not our normal protocol." She held out a syringe.

"My mother has never been one for normal, even before this." Dani accepted the needle. "I'll take care of things."

Dani palmed the syringe, twisting her arm so her mother wouldn't see, and approached the door. Through the small window, she could see her mother inside, destroying what was left of the room. "Demons!" her mother shouted. "I can hear them. I will find them!"

Andrea Frost threw herself at the door, the metal buckling against her strength. "My daughter needs me!" she shouted, unable to see through the one-way glass, not knowing Dani stood on the other side, watching. Even if she could see through the glass, there was no guarantee she'd recognize Dani. Some days she did. Some days she didn't.

When Andrea let out a frustrated scream and abandoned her assault on the door, Dani finally noticed the markings on the far wall, drawn in what looked like blood. They appeared to be demonic symbols, though some Dani had never seen before. Sevens with curled stems. Counterclockwise spirals that pivoted into a twisted *S*. Twisted hourglass shapes.

"Wish me luck," Dani murmured before reaching for the handle and slipping inside Andrea's room.

"She's not safe!" Andrea cried, tracing the symbols on the wall. "My baby isn't safe. I have to protect her from the demons. They're out there. They hide in plain sight, but I can see them. I can stop them!"

Dani flinched, but these rants had become common over the years. The doctors had diagnosed Andrea with a severe form of schizophrenia, assuming her obsession with demons, and the fact that she heard their voices, were all part of her illness. Unfortunately for the Frost women, it was all too real.

"I'm here, Mom," Dani said gently. "I'm safe."

Andrea whirled and looked Dani up and down. Dani crossed the fingers of her empty hand that tonight was one of the better nights. That her mother would recognize the daughter she seemed so worried about.

"Danika? Is that you?" Andrea's posture relaxed as recognition took hold, and Dani felt small under her mother's attention. Like she was seventeen again, part of her frozen in time at the moment her mother lost everything to the demon Dani couldn't catch.

"You have to relax, Mom." Dani inched forward, each step smooth and silent. "You're scaring the nurses."

"Nurses?" Andrea searched the room, as if seeing it for the first time. As if realizing she wasn't at home. Dani often wondered what Andrea expected to find when she searched like this. They'd moved often throughout Dani's childhood. What did Andrea picture when she thought of home?

"Never mind the nurses, Mom. I'm safe. You're safe. No one will hurt us." Dani was close now, close enough for Andrea to strike if her mood turned. If the demonic torment ripping apart her mind made Andrea forget who Dani was. "It's going to be okay."

Andrea nodded, but her eyes filled with tears. "I don't like it here, Danika." Her lower lip trembled, and she reached out for her daughter. "I want to go home. Please take me home with you."

"You know I can't, Mom." Dani's throat closed up, and she blinked away tears.

"Please?" Andrea tried again, voice pitched into desperation. "Please, Danika. I miss you. I want to go home."

Dani nodded. She didn't know what else to do. "I'll try, Momma. I promise, I'll try."

Andrea hugged her then, so tight Dani's back popped in several places. Dani raised her arms, but instead of returning the embrace, she slid the needle into Andrea's neck and pressed down on the plunger. A strong sedative flooded Andrea's body, and before she even swayed on her feet, the room was flooded with nurses. They helped Andrea back into bed while a doctor gave Andrea a second dose of something, probably the antipsychotic they thought would help the schizophrenia.

"We'll give you a moment," the doctor said. "You still have a few minutes before she's fully out."

"Thank you," Dani whispered, unable to meet her mother's betrayed look as the nurses finished securing the restraints. When they were alone, Dani perched on the edge of Andrea's bed.

"I don't want to sleep." Andrea tugged at her restraints, but the drugs had already sapped her strength. "He'll be there. He's always there when I close my eyes."

That caught Dani's attention. She finally looked at her mother, forcing herself to bury the shame that came every time she had to drug her own mother. "Who?" Dani knew who her mother meant, the demon who had done this to her, but she hoped—

despite the improbability of it—that her mother might know something. That somewhere in that fractured mind of hers, she knew the name of the creature who attacked her.

Andrea's eyelids grew heavy, her panic dulled by the drugs. "The demon," she whispered, words slurring. "He whispers to me, you know. Tells me all sorts of terrible things."

"What things?" Dani demanded, scooting closer to the head of the bed. "Mom, what does he say?"

"The world is going to burn." Andrea giggled, sleep dragging her under. "He's going to remake it in his vision. We're all going to die."

"How, Mom? How is he—" But Dani didn't finish her question. Her mother had fallen asleep, and there was no telling what truth, if any, had been in her words. Dani held her mother's hand, rubbing her thumb along Andrea's bruised knuckles. "I'm going to find him, Mom. I'll find him and make him fix you." She released her mother, squeezing her hands into fists. "And if he refuses, I'll tear him limb from limb until he changes his mind."

Dani stood and kissed her mother on the cheek. A single tear slipped down Dani's face, and she scrubbed it away, furious at the whole situation. At herself, for not being able to care for Andrea at home.

At the hospital, for not figuring out a better way to help.

But most of all, she was furious at the demons who had crawled into her world. At the necromancers who helped bring them to the human realm. Dani brushed her fingers against the hilt of her sword. At least she could deal with one of those things tonight.

At least she could go hunting.

The club pulsed with music, each concussive sound wave echoing up Dani's back. She moved without a care in the world, a cute boy dancing beside her. A part of her recognized him —recognized the dimple in his cheek, the bright blond hair, the easy confidence in every movement— but his name eluded her. It didn't matter. They were young and wild and free.

Dani spun, the boy raising her hand in the air to twirl her. The skin on her forearms was fresh and smooth, not marred by Ink or scars. *Why does that seem odd?* Dani shook the thought away, focusing on the boy. On the curve of his lips as he smiled. As he whispered her name. As he asked if she wanted to leave.

Outside, nausea slammed into her and she stumbled. The boy asked if she was okay, and then suddenly, she was. Her senses grew sharp. Strength flooded through every limb.

But then pain tore across her chest, and the panic followed quickly behind. Poe was stitching himself into her skin. The Ink had fallen to her. Which meant her mother—

Dani woke with a start, bolting upright in bed. A scream had built at the back of her throat, but she forced it down. Scars covered her right forearm, and Dani brushed her fingers over the other Ink, making sure they were safe.

Jasper, taking the form of a king cobra, wrapped gracefully around her left forearm. At her chest, a black and gray rendering of a raven marked Poe's resting place. And on her back …

Dani twisted to peer over her shoulder, but the panther tattoo wasn't there. Kiva wasn't—

I'm here, little one. Kiva's voice tumbled through Dani's mind, and the black panther strolled in from the other room. She licked Dani's face, washing away the tears Dani hadn't noticed gathering there. *You usually sleep better than this after a hunt.*

"I don't usually hunt after visiting Mom." Dani wiped the sleep from her face and pushed away the blankets. "Did you stay out all night?"

The panther seemed to shrug. As much as a creature walking on all fours could. *I needed some time away from the bird.* Kiva stretched lazily. *He chatters constantly when we're in the spirit realm.*

"Yeah?" Dani didn't know much about what happened to the Ink when they were in her skin. Whenever she'd asked, Poe said it was none of her concern. Kiva implied that it was beyond her mortal comprehension. And Jasper … well, he never said all that much about anything. His silences had grown heavier after they'd lost Silas. Since *she* had lost Silas. None of the Ink blamed her, but that didn't stop Dani from blaming herself.

I should get back. Kiva stretched again, looking for a moment like an overgrown house cat. *Are you going to be late for work?*

Dani glanced at the clock. It was already dangerously close to nine. "I'm the boss," she said at last. "Work begins when I decide it does." But she was already hurrying out of bed and heading for the shower. Dani called for Kiva to return, and as she slipped out of her clothes, a panther tattoo stretched across her back, nestling the Ink into her skin. It hurt every single time the Ink returned, the pain like an entire tattoo session experienced over the course of a few seconds. She never got used to the flash of agony in her flesh, but she'd learned to bear it without crying out.

It was a small price to pay for the other enhancements to her body. Speed and strength to rival that of the demonic world. Incredibly fast healing, which came in handy more often than Dani cared to admit. Better than perfect vision. Sharp hearing. Everything about Dani changed when she became the Ink Carrier. Everything.

Thanks in large part to her nonexistent commute, Dani managed to get ready and stroll into the office only a few minutes past nine. Lana was already there, the company checkbook and a stack of bills in front of her. She didn't look up from her work when Dani came in, but she did manage to utter a distracted "Hello" before signing off on the check.

In addition to scheduling clients, Lana handled everything administrative for Frost Investigations. She kept the lights on, the taxes paid, and made sure Dani paid *her* on time too. Dani would be lost, and deeply in debt, without her.

Desperate for caffeine, Dani took a detour to the kitchen turned break room. "Morning, Spencer."

"Morning, boss." Spencer stretched before hunching back over his latest experiment. Unlike Lana, Spencer opted for the more casual end of business casual, though his seemingly simple outfit of jeans and a soft knit sweater probably cost more than Dani's entire wardrobe.

Spencer may have broken away from his necromancer family and abandoned that kind of magic, but he'd escaped with his fortune intact. He was the other reason Dani had been able to afford the start-up costs of her business.

"What are you working on?" Dani placed her usual mug under the coffee machine, selecting a pod and brewing a single cup. Spencer had a series of daggers laid out on the table before him while strangely colored liquids bubbled merrily over Bunsen burners.

"I'm trying to make another blade like your sword. Something smaller and stealthier." Spencer glanced up from his work. He was rocking his natural colors today, dark curls framing his brown eyes. "It isn't going very well."

"Do I really need another blade? With the retraction spell, I can bring the sword anywhere I need to go. Between that and the bullets you make, I haven't had any problems." The machine sputtered the final few drops of coffee, and Dani brought her mug to the kitchen table. "You don't have to fix what isn't broken, Spence."

The reformed necromancer shot her a wounded look. "I tinker because I *care*, Danika."

"I know you do." Dani sipped her black coffee. On the far wall, her team had taped up a collection of newspaper clippings, surveillance photos, printouts from the internet, and scrawled notes that looked like something out of a conspiracy video. It wasn't much, but it contained every lead they'd ever followed on the demon who tormented her mother's mind.

Dani traced the dozens of dead ends they'd followed over the years. Every time she thought they were on to something, the trail went cold. Clues dried up. No one in the necromancer world would talk to them, not even to Spencer, the banished heir of the Owens family, who worshipped demons as gods.

"Dani? Have you seen this?" Lana called from the reception area, a tinge of panic in her tone. Dani and Spencer hurried out of the kitchen to where Lana was turning up the volume on her computer.

A white man in his fifties stood at a podium surrounded by microphones. His brown hair was impeccably styled, and Dani recognized him instantly. "Mayor Conrad," she grumbled. Nathaniel Conrad was one of the most prominent necromancers in Blackthorn, in part because of the time he'd spent as the city's mayor. He was the so-called *tough on crime* mayor, but crime wasn't actually down since he'd taken office. He just kept the other necromancer families in check enough that human citizens remained oblivious to the existence of demons. Oblivious, and enamored with their mayor.

The trio watched as Nathaniel Conrad thanked

the crowd for coming, which elicited cheers from the gathered supporters. He droned on about what a pleasure and honor it had been to serve the great city of Blackthorn, and how he counted on their support in his latest venture.

"Life in Blackthorn has never been better," the mayor crooned to his legion of delusional fans. "Crime rates are down. Employment rates are up. And as far as I'm concerned, Blackthorn citizens are the best and brightest this nation has to offer."

More cheers, loud enough this time to make Lana's speakers crackle. Dani hated him, Conrad and all his followers. They had no idea what kind of monster they'd elected. "He's so full of shit."

"He believes more of it than you'd guess." Spencer crossed his arms, but he didn't look away from the screen. Dani imagined it was a similar feeling to watching a car wreck. "Except he's not talking to the normal people of Blackthorn. He's referring to the five families."

The five families. Five distinct groups of necromancers, bound by blood and oath and magic, that ran nearly every facet of life in Blackthorn. Their influence had been spreading lately, pushing past the boundaries of the city and filling the whole state. In addition to the Conrad and Owens families, there were the Brennans, the most prolific organized crime family in America. They flooded the streets with drugs and weapons, not to mention the demons they raised. The Rivera family ran most of the banking industry, using their connections to launder money for the other families, keeping necromancers off police radar and buying off the officers and detectives who caught on to their schemes.

And finally, there was the Dasari family. They ran the city's nightlife, brokering deals between mortals and demons for a cut of the profit. Mortals like Lana, who Dani had saved from a horrible fate five years earlier.

Dani shook her head, pushing the Dasari family out of her mind. She didn't have the time, or the emotional reserves, to reopen those wounds.

On the screen, Mayor Conrad beamed, and the crowd cheered like their team had just won the state championship.

"Wait. What happened?"

"He's running for senate." Lana's pale skin had taken on a greenish undertone. "Do you think he'd be the first necromancer in Congress?"

Spencer laughed and ran a hand through his hair. The dark curls changed into deep auburn at his touch, one of the few types of magic Spencer still indulged in. "He'd be the first one from Blackthorn, but you can't tell me the government isn't already overrun.

Hell, there's at least one demon in every branch of government, and a solid third of the human assholes sold their souls to get there."

"That's not overly reassuring, Spencer." Lana swatted his arm, her other hand fiddling with the amulet she always wore around her neck. The amulet that kept Lana, and everyone around her, safe from the danger within.

"It's the truth."

Lana and Spencer launched into a debate about which politicians were literal demons, but Dani couldn't stop thinking about the wall in the kitchen, filled with her failures. About the injustices of men like Nathaniel Conrad gathering power at the expense of innocent people when her own mother had been hospitalized for *years* because she was trying to protect humanity. All the work Dani had done in Blackthorn—all the demons banished from Earth—felt useless, like trying to get a Band-Aid to fix a bullet wound.

Her mother needed her. She had to stay focused on what really mattered.

"We need to review the board again," Dani announced abruptly and headed for the kitchen.

"Dani ..." It was only one word, but Spencer's reluctance dripped off each syllable.

She whirled around. "I can't give up, Spencer. Not

when men like Nathaniel Conrad are vying for more power." Dani squeezed her eyes shut against the building tears. "I can't fix all this on my own. If I had my mother—"

"Of course we won't give up." Lana rose from her desk. "But I think Spencer's right to be cautious. Without new leads, we have nothing else to go on."

"And you're not alone, Dani. We're in this with you." Spencer rested his hands on her shoulders, his formerly brown eyes now a dazzling green. "But you can't stay stuck in the past. You need to move forward. You need even a tiny social life. Something to jog you out of this obsessive routine—"

"I'm not obsessed."

"—and with any luck, that change will bring new ideas. New leads. Something we can actually investigate."

Dani pinched the bridge of her nose. She hated to admit it, but maybe they were right. Going over the same puzzle pieces over and over and over hadn't done them any good. There were still too many holes to form a picture. They needed something new. And maybe, just maybe, the key to finding those new pieces was doing new things.

Before Dani could voice her agreement, there was a knock at the door.

"That must be our new clients," Lana said, sitting

back down at her desk. "They called first thing this morning about their daughter."

"Fine." Dani took another swig of her coffee. "But we're not giving up," she told her friends. "I'll … think about the social life thing."

"That's all we ask." Spencer kissed her on the cheek and disappeared into the kitchen.

Dani crossed to the front door to meet her new clients. Her mom's case might have to wait, but she wasn't giving up.

She'd never give up.

4

A middle-aged couple waited nervously on Dani's second-floor stoop. Bundled warmer than the weather required, Dani clocked the pair as being from a small town in a more northern state. Somewhere heavy-duty coats and scarves were already standard dress this early in the autumn.

Dani invited her potential clients in and led them to her office. "Is there anything I can get you, Mr. ..." She trailed off, leaving space for their names.

The man cleared his throat and helpfully supplied, "Hughes. I'm John. This is my wife, Anne."

"Danika Frost." She extended her hand. "Though I imagine you already know that." Dani relaxed into her chair and gestured for the couple to sit. "My assistant didn't have many details. How can Frost Investigations help you?"

"It's our daughter." Anne Hughes reached for her husband's hand, fingers trembling. "Ellie moved to Blackthorn a year ago for college, but we haven't heard from her in almost two weeks. We just got this note from the school." Mrs. Hughes pulled a worn letter from her purse. "They refunded our tuition check. Ellie never registered for classes this fall. She dropped out last semester and never told us."

"I assume you've tried calling?" Dani asked, and the silence in the room grew chilled. Anne's dark plum lips pressed into a thin line. "I know it seems obvious, Mrs. Hughes, but you'd be surprised some of the basic steps worried loved ones will skip. I have to go through all the routine stuff first."

Anne softened at that and leaned back in the chair. "We've done it all, Miss Frost. We called and texted. We stopped by her apartment, but her roommates haven't seen her in weeks either. They said Ellie was fine, and then one day she didn't come home from work. They thought she'd given up on city life and returned home."

"And if you're knocking on my door, I assume you've already struck out with Blackthorn PD?"

John nodded. "The police took our statements, but they haven't been any help. Do you know how many missing people there are in this city? Detective Hart says there's at least a dozen missing girls like our Ellie, and those are just from the last two weeks. He's the one who suggested we reach out to you, said you have a knack for these kinds of cases."

Dani fought to hide her surprise. If Nick Hart—one of the few truly decent cops in Blackthorn—sent the Hughes family to Dani, then their daughter's case was more dire than it appeared. Dani had worked with Nick a few dozen times over the past two years. At first, they bumped into each other when their cases intersected, but soon Nick learned to seek out Dani when mortal science couldn't explain what happened to his victims. The detective didn't know anything about demons or necromancers, but he could tell when something was off about a crime scene.

Had Ellie met a similar fate to Camilla's husband? Was she already demon food?

"If you met with Detective Hart, I assume he already had you check on anyone matching Ellie's description at the morgue."

"You think our daughter is dead?" Anne's voice came out high and thin, and she reached for her husband. John pressed his thick fingers against his closed eyelids, like he could push the tears back inside. They slipped down his weathered face anyway.

Dani should know better than this. Making clients cry never ended well for anyone.

She had to backtrack. And quick.

"Let's not get ahead of ourselves. If Nick thought that was a possibility, he would have said so." Dani made a mental note to remind Nick not to send weepy parents to her doorstep without a heads-up. She guzzled the last of her coffee and wished for a refill. It was too early for this. "Has Ellie ever run away before?"

"No, nothing like that," Mrs. Hughes said, but her husband gave her a look.

"What was that?"

"Nothing," Mrs. Hughes said. "There's *nothing*, John."

"Ma'am, I can't help your daughter if I don't know the truth." When Anne didn't respond, Dani focused her attention on John. "Mr. Hughes, if you know something—"

"Ellie never ran away from home, not in the traditional sense. But coming to school here … that felt like she was trying to escape." John ran a hand through his thinning gray hair. "We begged her not to come. We told her a city this size was too dangerous for a young woman on her own."

A young woman like you, John's expression said, though his voice did not. The way he watched Dani, concern creasing his forehead, made it clear that he thought Dani was *also* too young to be on her own in Blackthorn. She almost laughed. Blackthorn should be afraid of women like her, not the other way around.

Dani pushed the parents, prying into every part of their daughter's life in search of clues about what could have caused her disappearance. But either there was nothing noteworthy about Ellie Hughes, or her parents were woefully uninformed. As far as they knew, Ellie wasn't dating anyone, she'd worked as a receptionist at a company called Clean Smile—which a simple online search revealed didn't exist—and she didn't have any enemies.

"We even bought her a plane ticket to come home for the school break." Anne dabbed at her eyes with a tissue. "She'd seemed so excited about coming to visit, but last week we checked on the reservation. She'd canceled the ticket and put the refund on her card."

"Do you have access to her banking information?" Dani leaned forward. *Finally,* something she could use.

But John shook his head. "No. I mean, we do, but she emptied her account before she disappeared.

Wherever she is, she's using cash. The police said that makes her almost impossible to track down."

Dani nodded absently to herself, trying to put together the scattered pieces. There was almost nothing to go on, and what little the parents did know showed no signs of paranormal foul play. To Dani, it sounded like their daughter felt trapped. Perhaps her parents were overbearing. Perhaps she felt embarrassed about dropping out of school and thought the only way out was to take her money and run.

Poe wouldn't like it. He hated whenever Dani took on cases with no demonic leanings, but Dani's heart broke for the parents. And it's not like she could afford to keep her business open—or her mother well cared for—if she only took on paranormal cases. There were plenty of demons roaming the streets of Blackthorn, but humans were perfectly capable of hurting each other on their own too.

Besides, Spencer and Lana were right. A little time away from the demonic world, even to investigate a mundane missing persons case, might do her some good. Provide perspective.

"John. Anne." Dani stood and reached out her hand. "I'll take the case."

After a hurried breakfast, Dani made the ten-block trek to Ellie's apartment. A cool breeze swept through her red hair as the heat from the morning sun warmed her face. Though it was fully fall in Blackthorn, Dani managed to get away with just her leather jacket over her T-shirt. Overhead, Poe circled in the clear blue sky, a speck of irritated black feathers that followed her like a cloud.

I don't like this, Danika, the bird had croaked when she explained Ellie's case over her meal. *There's nothing demonic about a missing girl in a big city.*

"So, we should do nothing?" Dani had shot back. "What do you suggest? Tell the parents, 'Sorry that your daughter is missing, but since there's no sign that a hell beast is responsible, we don't give a shit.' Come on, Poe. Where's your empathy?"

It's not a matter of empathy. Poe had ruffled his feathers. *You are one person, Danika. You cannot be everywhere at once. Your time is better spent hunting.*

Now, two blocks from the address Ellie's parents had given her, Dani pushed the memory aside. She didn't know why she bothered trying to explain herself to Poe. The bird had been harping on her for the past six years, ever since she'd taken the Ink. Hell, he'd been a nag before that too, back when he was still her mother's burden.

If his energy wasn't so damn irritating when he

was part of her skin, she wouldn't let him out this often. But she'd learned quickly that his nagging voice was easier to ignore than the anxiety and sleeplessness he could cause when he was cooped up for too long.

Dani turned the corner and stopped before Ellie's address. The apartment building looked uninhabitable, the siding faded and crumbling. The brick window ledges had seen better days, eaten away by time and the elements. Dani tried the buzzer for apartment 513, but nothing happened. On a hunch, she tested the front door. It stuck at first but swung open, the lock broken long ago.

Inside, the building was in worse repair than the exterior. White paint yellowed with age peeled away from the walls like rotted demon skin. A series of mailboxes on the far end had gone rusty. Even the floor, which at one point might have been vinyl, appeared to be more dirt and concrete than linoleum. Surprisingly, the old building had an elevator, but there was a hastily scrawled *OUT OF ORDER* sign taped to it, so she climbed the stairs to the fifth floor.

This place told a far different story than the happy college life Ellie had spun for her parents.

Dani knocked on the door to 513. Mr. and Mrs. Hughes didn't have a key for Ellie's place, but their daughter did have two roommates. With any luck, one of them would be home, saving Dani the trouble of breaking in. She may have a friend on the force, but breaking and entering was still a crime.

Shuffling footsteps approached from the other side, and after a pause, the door swung open, catching on a chain lock. A young woman with pale skin and dark brown hair peered through the crack. She wore slippers on her feet and a robe closed over what looked like pajamas. "Can I help you?"

"I'm Danika Frost." Dani handed her business card through the crack in the door. The younger woman took it and flipped it over. "Ellie's parents hired me to find her. I was hoping to take a look at her room. Maybe ask you a few questions?"

The roommate sighed. "We already talked to her parents."

"I'd like to think I'm more thorough and objective than worried family members." Dani flashed her brightest smile, the expression forced upon her features. "I promise to get out of your hair as fast as possible."

"Fine." The door slammed shut, and metal slid together as the chain was undone. "Make it quick. I work second shift, so I need to get ready soon." The roommate waved Dani inside. "I'm Jenn, by the way."

"Thank you." Dani glanced around the small apartment. It didn't look like it was designed for three roommates—there were only two bedrooms—but the women had managed to make the rundown place look cozy. "How long has Ellie lived here?"

"About six months? She got kicked out of campus housing when she quit school. Katy knows her better than I do." Jenn headed for the kitchen where a now-soggy bowl of sugary cereal sat waiting for her. Dani followed. "Babe?" Her voice carried through the apartment. "Someone's here about Ellie."

The bedroom door opened, and a young Black woman stepped out. She wore dark gray slacks, a white button-up shirt, and sensible shoes. "Jenn, have you seen my apron?" The girl, who Dani assumed was Katy, swung through the kitchen. She kissed Jenn on the cheek as she passed by and stopped at the table to rummage through a basket of clean laundry. She pulled a maroon half apron from the pile, with the name of an Italian restaurant embroidered into it. One of the nicer places to eat in Blackthorn, judging by her outfit. Not that Dani was an expert, given that her usual spot was a drag bar. She was more of a grab-and-go kinda girl.

"I'm sorry to bother you both before work, but I'm trying to find Ellie Hughes. Do you have time for a couple of questions?"

"If something bad happened to Ellie, I guarantee

that boyfriend of hers was involved," Katy said, tucking her shirt into her slacks.

"Ex-boyfriend," Jenn corrected.

Katy scoffed. "Those two are never exes for more than five minutes. They're the epitome of on-again, off-again."

"Her parents didn't say anything about a boyfriend. Do you have his name?"

"Sean," the pair said in unison, matching disdain dripping from their voices.

Jenn leaned against the counter, scooping up a spoonful of brightly colored cereal. "Ellie's parents didn't want to hear about Sean. As far as they're concerned, their daughter's still a blushing virgin and couldn't possibly be dating a dirtbag like him." She took a bite of her breakfast, chewing with her mouth open. "The denial was strong with those two."

"Where did Ellie meet Sean?"

"At some club. Ellie bounces between a lot of different bars, bartending and waitressing. Since she met Sean almost a year ago, she can't seem to hang on to a job for more than a few weeks. She goes missing for days at a time, probably in some gross sex den." Katy shuddered. "That's why we weren't worried when she first went missing. It's not unusual for her."

"She sounds like a terrible roommate," Dani noted.

Katy shrugged and adjusted her blouse. "She paid

rent on time and cleaned up after herself." She kissed Jenn on the cheek again. "I need to go. Can you show her Ellie's room?"

After Katy left for work, Jenn led Dani through the living room to a closed door and pushed it open. "All of Ellie's stuff is in here. We figured she'd be back eventually. It doesn't look like she took anything with her, except maybe a few outfits."

Dani stepped into the room. It was messier than the rest of the small apartment, but not overly so. "Do you think Sean could have hurt Ellie?"

"I don't know. I never saw him hit her or anything like that. She did have a black eye about a month ago, but she claimed she fell at work. I never bought that excuse, but it was only the one time." Jenn leaned against the door frame with her bowl of cereal. "Sean's bad news, but I don't think he'd seriously hurt her."

"What does he do for a living?"

Jenn shrugged. "Hell if I know. He always seems flushed with cash, but he lives in the shitty part of Blackthorn."

"Is there a non-shitty part?"

That made Jenn laugh. "Fair point. But he lives on the lower end of Golding Street, south of Pickering."

Dani winced. "Yeah, that's about as shitty as it gets." The area Jenn described was a hotbed for drugs and prostitution. It wasn't the kind of place women with any other options chose to work. Pimps controlled those streets and took 80 percent of the profits. The young women, and men, were exploited in all kinds of ways.

It also happened to be run by the Brennan necromancers.

"I won't take up any more of your time. I'll take a look at Ellie's room and let myself out, if that works for you."

"Sure. I'm going to finish breakfast and hop in the shower. Don't steal anything." Jenn slipped away, and Dani waited until she heard the water kick on in the bathroom before she shut the door and crossed the room to open the window.

Poe swooped inside, and Dani called Jasper's name, the king cobra uncurling from her skin. She filled them both in on what she'd learned about Ellie's boyfriend. "There's no guarantee he's involved with the Brennans, but it's worth checking out. Help me look through Ellie's room for anything useful."

Jasper didn't respond—he rarely did anymore—but he joined their search and slithered under the bed. Dani and Poe got to work too.

Ellie's room was filled with memorabilia from her past. The bedside table held a framed photo of Anne and John Hughes, which nixed Dani's theory that Ellie wanted to escape her parents. Trophies from high school track meets were prominently displayed on the small bookcase, and there was even a yearbook lying open on Ellie's desk.

This didn't look like a girl who wanted to run away from her past. If anything, the room looked like Ellie was miserable with her present. There weren't any current photos of her on the walls, and nothing that indicated she had a boyfriend. It screamed of someone who wished to go back to a time when she was successful and safe and loved.

Dani took photos of everything, including the half-full bottle of Zoloft beside Ellie's bed. The depression and anxiety meds only made Dani more worried. Life in the big city clearly wasn't everything Ellie had hoped for. And if her roommates were right, this Sean guy had a not-so-small part in that life.

I took the case, Dani texted to Nick. Any insights you want to share?

The detective's response came lightning quick. You know I'm not supposed to share information with PIs, Dani.

She shouldn't be surprised by his response. Nick would never admit in writing that they shared information. Which they did. Often. Whenever they thought they could help solve a case, they were forthcoming with leads. As far as Nick was concerned, they were on the same side. His bosses disagreed.

Maybe I should tell the chief you've been sending clients my way.

Three dots danced at the bottom of Dani's screen. They disappeared and reappeared at least a half-dozen times. Then finally—

Meet me at the precinct in an hour.

Please tell me you're not working with that detective again. Poe perched on the edge of Ellie's mattress and cocked his head sharply to the right.

Dani stowed her phone in her back pocket. "I thought you liked Nick."

Poe clicked his beak. *I liked Rajan. But you had to go and ruin that one, didn't you.*

"None of that was my fault." Hot, searing anger burned through Dani's veins. "And I don't ever want to hear his name again, do you understand?"

You may be the Carrier, Danika, but you do not dictate what I can and cannot—

"Poe, return," Dani demanded, cutting the raven off midsentence. He burst into smoke and tattooed onto Dani's chest. She shook with the force of his return. Shook from the righteous fury that rocked through her. No part of what happened with Rajan Dasari was her fault. The Ink was supposed to be on her side, in all things. Poe shouldn't prefer that traitorous necromancer to her. It went against every-thing he stood for. "Stupid bird."

Shall I return too? Jasper's voice hissed through Dani's mind like wind through dried leaves. She'd almost forgotten he was there, silently searching the room.

Dani nodded and flinched at the pain in her forearm that accompanied Jasper's tattoo. She let herself believe it was that pain, not the forced memory of Raj, that left her eyes stinging as she left Ellie's room and headed for the police station.

Danika strode down King Street like she owned the place.

With two cups of coffee in hand—black for her, cream and sugar for the detective—she headed straight for the city's central police station. The key to getting in and out of the precinct without being stopped was looking confident about her place there. Nick knew she was coming, but if the chief noticed her first, he was likely to kick her out before she could harass Nick about sending grieving parents her way with no warning.

And before she got whatever helpful information Nick planned to share.

As she neared the station, a plethora of news vans sat waiting out front. Someone stood before a podium thick with microphones, gesturing to the old, gothic-style building behind him.

Dani groaned. "Mayor Nathaniel fucking Conrad." At the edge of the crowd, she could make out his speech, a diatribe of nonsense about how if elected state senator, he'd bring his same attention and support of law enforcement to the national stage, lowering crime rates across the country.

Crime in Blackthorn wasn't low. It was hidden. Which, like Dani, the necromancer turned mayor knew all too well. Unfortunately, most people couldn't tell the difference.

A white man two decades Dani's senior approached with a clipboard. His warm smile faltered when he took in her sour expression, but he didn't abandon his quest. "Are you registered to vote, ma'am?"

Dani paused and considered him, cringing at being called *ma'am*. She didn't notice any of the tell-tale signs of demonic possession—no strangely colored eyes, forked tongue, webbed fingers, or tail— but that didn't mean this man was strictly human. Some of the mayor's lackeys *were* human, of course, but Dani had learned the hard way to be vigilant around a necromancer's sphere of influence.

Finally, she nodded. "I am."

"That's wonderful!" The man lowered his clipboard, apparently no longer necessary since she was already registered. "Can we count on you to vote for our wonderful mayor and bring him to the national stage?"

"Not even if he was running unopposed," Dani said without missing a beat. "I hope Eisha Bell wipes the floor with him." Dani sidestepped the now-gaping campaign staffer and climbed the steps. Eisha Bell, a Black woman from the opposing party, was exactly what the state senate needed. She cared about serving people, not power, but she didn't let anyone push her around.

And, as far as Dani could tell, she didn't have any ties to the demonic realm. Which is more than Dani could say for any politician coming out of Blackthorn.

Inside the police station, there was a flurry of activity. Dani stopped by the main desk to sign in and wove her way through the chaos. Across the bullpen, Dani spotted Nick. Her heart gave a little lurch, which she ignored.

Detective Nicholas Hart was all light. His blond hair was shaved tight on the sides but left longer on top. Long enough that Dani could usually tell Nick's stress level from a single glance—the more frustrated he was with a case, the more he ran his hands through his hair and the taller it became. He peered up from his desk as Dani approached, his eyes the crystal-clear blue-green of the sea.

"Is one of those for me?" Nick asked, his voice a warm rumble in his chest.

Dani passed over the sweetened cup. "I still don't understand why you ruin perfectly good coffee with cream and sugar."

Nick swigged a long gulp and grimaced. "I think this one's yours." They traded cups and Nick took a tentative sip this time, his shoulders relaxing when he got the sweetened caffeine hit. "Did you make it past the zoo okay?"

"The press conference outside? Yeah." Dani sat on the edge of Nick's desk and enjoyed her own coffee, not caring that Nick had already sampled it. "Though I think one of the staffers had to scrape his jaw off the floor."

Nick sat up straighter. "Why's that?"

"A woman told him 'no.' I doubt he understands the concept." She took another drink and relished the burn against her tongue. "So, about this missing girl."

"Right. Ellie Hughes." Nick pulled a folder from the stack on his desk and flipped it open. "I doubt her parents mentioned her record when they came to you."

"Record?" Dani reached for the case file. She skimmed across the charges. "Two counts of soliciting and …" Dani turned the page and glanced at Nick, shocked. "Another for possession of cocaine? Her parents didn't say anything about this. Her roommates didn't either."

Nick leaned back and straightened the ends of his tie. His black suit jacket was draped over his chair, and he'd rolled the sleeves of his crisp white shirt up to his elbows, exposing his strong forearms. "I'm not surprised. Parents don't like to believe their children do these kinds of things, especially if they think it never happened under their roof. And I guess Ellie's roommates didn't know."

"Do you have anything on the boyfriend?"

"Sean McGrath." Nick reached for a second file and handed it to Dani. "Low-level crook with his fingers in just about everything. Allegedly. We haven't made anything stick yet, but we're investigating him for drug trafficking, running a prostitution ring, weapons charges, the works."

He was probably caught up with the Brennan necromancers too, based on his address and exploits, but she didn't mention that piece of the puzzle to Nick. Despite working together on some of Nick's paranormal-adjacent cases, Dani had so far managed to protect him from her world. She intended to keep it that way.

"This is great, Nick. Thanks." She closed the case file. "How soon do you need this back?"

"It's yours. I made copies." Nick's white skin, tan from spending time outdoors, flushed a soft pink. "Just don't tell my boss."

"I wouldn't dream of it. Chief Martinez is—"

"Heading right for us." Nick sat up straighter. "Hide that."

Dani tucked the files inside her leather jacket and tugged the zipper all the way up. "He'll still know I was here about a case." While she could find Ellie without the file, it would be easier if she had it. Plus, she didn't want Nick to get in trouble. She had to think of something before the chief caught her at his desk. "Kiss me."

"What?"

"We need to make this look like a social call, Nick." Dani wasn't sure where the idea came from, but she leaned into it. There wasn't time to come up with anything else. She bent closer to Nick, keeping one arm snug around her waist to hold the case file in place. "Kiss me."

Nick faltered, eyes tracking his boss's approach, and then in a sudden flash of decision, he reached up and cupped the side of Dani's face. His kiss was gentle across her lips, and Dani sank into his touch more than she expected she would. She pulled him closer and kissed him deeper. For show, of course.

"Detective Hart." Chief Martinez's voice was like a bucket of ice water crashing over them. "This is a police station, not a brothel."

Nick pulled away quickly and cleared his throat. "Sorry, sir."

The chief made a harrumphing sound, like he was a prudish schoolmarm. "Escort your lady friend out of the precinct. I don't want to see this kind of behavior in the office again."

"Of course, sir." Nick stood, his broad shoulders hiding Dani's face from the police chief as she slipped off the desk and headed for the door. "I'm sorry about him," Nick said at the exit. The mayor's speech had ended, and the stairway and sidewalk had died down to normal foot traffic.

"Don't be sorry." Dani placed a reassuring hand on Nick's bare forearm. "It was my idea. A bad one, apparently. I hope it gets you in less trouble than the files would have."

"I'll be fine." Nick drew a hand through his short blond hair and glanced at the place where her fingers lingered on his skin. "Do you want to meet up later?"

"To go over the case?"

Nick shook his head. "I thought we could get

dinner. Or maybe just drinks, if dinner seems like too much. Or coffee. We could do coffee."

Dani pressed her fingers to Nick's lips, cutting off his devolving date ideas. She let her mind wander briefly over their short-lived kiss. Her lips still tingled from his touch, and she found that she very much wanted to repeat the experience. "Dinner sounds great. Pick me up at seven?"

The detective grinned. "It's a date."

"A date," she agreed. Spencer and Lana would be so proud.

Back at the office, Dani threw herself into work to avoid thinking about Mayor Conrad. Or the police chief, who was probably on at least one necromancer's payroll. Maybe two. And *lady friend?* What kind of sexist bullshit was that?

She also tried—and failed—to keep from thinking about her kiss with Nick. She had a missing girl to find. She needed to focus on what mattered, not some silly crush.

"Ma'am, I understand that. But the girl I'm looking for is—"

"I don't care why you're looking for her," the woman on the other end of the line shot back. "We don't share information about the people here. Do you have any idea how brave someone has to be to check into a crisis shelter? What kind of hell they've escaped to be here? I'm not about to share information that could get these girls killed."

Dani massaged her temple with her free hand. This woman, who'd introduced herself as Malinda Bailey, ran a shelter for women and girls escaping abusive situations. Dani understood why Malinda wouldn't confirm or deny Ellie's presence, but that wasn't what she was asking for.

"Can you please just take down my contact information and, if Ellie shows up, give her the choice of contacting me? Her parents are worried sick. They just want to know that she's safe."

"How do you know her parents aren't the problem?" Malinda said, her voice as cutting as Dani's blade.

"I don't," Dani conceded. "Which is why *Ellie* should be the one who decides whether to call me. Isn't that part of your mission? Helping women find their agency and make their own choices again?"

There was a long pause on the other end of the phone. "Fine. You can give me your number, and if this girl shows up, I'll *consider* letting her know."

"That's all I ask." Dani repeated her contact information for the shelter's director and let her phone drop to the desk. She'd already called every hospital in Blackthorn, all the rehab and homeless shelters, and even the closest police stations outside of the city. The women's shelter had been her last hope, and she still had nothing to go on.

Spencer sang through the office as the front door clicked shut behind him and Lana. "We have lunch!"

Dani's stomach growled at the mention of food, and she joined her team in the kitchen where Lana was grabbing napkins from the cupboard. "You two are my heroes." Dani accepted a carton of chicken lo mein from Spencer and popped the lid. The fragrant steam filled her senses, and she grabbed a pair of chopsticks. "Any luck with the girls on Sixth?"

Sixth Avenue was a popular spot for some of the independent prostitutes in Blackthorn, entrepreneurial sex workers who had managed to stay free of the local pimps. They kept an eye on the city, and despite staying away from necromancers, they knew more about the true happenings in Blackthorn than most humans. They were also fond of Spencer, who invited them to his parties without any expectations, providing space where they could let their hair down without creeps hitting on them.

"Our girl Ellie has definitely been working the streets. Destiny hasn't seen her in a few weeks, but she and Ellie attended some of the same parties this summer." Spencer picked up a steamed dumpling and plopped the whole thing in his mouth. He scanned over Sean's case file again. "I got the impression this boyfriend of hers is more boss than partner."

Dani swiveled the file to face her. "Which means I definitely need to speak with him." She hated this part of the job, dealing with flaming pieces of garbage like Sean. With any luck, she'd have an excuse to punch the asshole. "Nick said he's into just about every criminal enterprise in Blackthorn. Any chance he runs with the Brennans?"

"Oh, so Detective Hart is 'Nick' now, is he?" Lana dropped her fork into her vegetable fried rice. "I think Boss Lady has a crush."

"About damn time," Spencer said, and pointed his chopsticks at Dani. "That man has had it bad for you since day one."

Dani fought the urge to correct her friends. Sure, Nick had asked her on a date, but it wasn't all that serious. Right? "Focus, you two. We have a missing girl on our hands. I need to know if Sean might be part of the Brennan gang."

Dealing with a single sleaze bag was one thing, but if Ellie's beau was in with the Brennan necromancers, things could get ugly. They wouldn't be thrilled if Dani interfered in their business. Not that it would stop her.

"What's his surname?" Spencer asked.

Dani checked the file. "McGrath. Sean McGrath."

"I don't recognize the name, but that doesn't mean much. I've been out of the loop almost eight years now." Spencer bit into another dumpling. "The Owens family doesn't exactly love the Brennans anyway. Dear old Dad thinks their line of work brings shame to our 'dark lords.'" He scoffed, clearly disagreeing with his father's view. Spencer often said that his family's reverence toward demons was one of the worst things about them. The worshipping played a big part in his decision to cut them out of his life. "It's possible I wouldn't know about McGrath even if I was still in the inner circle."

"Okay, then. I go in expecting demonic trouble and hope to be pleasantly surprised that he's not a necromancer." Dani leaned back in her chair and picked at her lo mein. "Lana, can you round up a list of potential bars that might have hired Ellie? You can ask Martin if he knows any places that pay part-timers under the table."

"Martin?"

"Bloody Mary," Dani clarified. "Martin is the man behind the makeup."

"Right. Of course. I haven't seen him out of drag in ages." Lana added a line to her growing to-do list. "Anything else?"

"For now, no. I'll go try to get a lead out of the boyfriend."

"What about me?" Spencer asked.

Dani looked up from the kitchen table, and her attention caught on the research board affixed to the far wall. She followed the trail of dead ends. They'd tracked every possible lead over the past five years trying to find her mother's demon. The board on the wall was a constant reminder of why Dani worked so many long hours. Of why she pushed through exhaustion and put up with condescending clients.

It was also a constant reminder of her repeated failures.

"I need you to go over everything we already know about the reaper demon who attacked my mother. There has to be something we're missing."

"Dani ..."

"If you tell me it's hopeless, Spencer, I swear on my sword I'll let Jasper eat you."

Spencer held up his hands in mock surrender. "I wouldn't dare." The soft smile fell from his face and he reached for Dani, holding her hand in his. "I know how much this means to you. And if it's what you want, I'll chase this demon until the day I die. But I don't want you to have false hope. You can't let this keep you from living your life."

"I know." Dani squeezed his hand once before

releasing him. She set the rest of her lo mein on the table and stood. "I should pay Sean a visit sooner rather than later." She turned her back on the memory of her failures and flashed a grin. "As it turns out, I do have a social life. I don't want to be late for my date with Nick."

6

Sean McGrath lived in a run-down building that reminded Dani of the apartment she'd had when she first moved to Blackthorn. The floors were stained with a dire cocktail of piss, blood, and vomit, and the walls had seen better days too. The paint—previously white or cream or maybe beige—had been stained an array of muddy colors by decades of cigarette smoke and bare, sweaty skin as drunk tenants leaned against the walls for support.

Dani climbed the stairs to the third floor and searched for room 309, Sean's last known address. When she reached Sean's door, the rusted metal nine was missing, but the outline was still visible through the caked dust. She knocked and grimaced at the stickiness of the door against her skin.

No one answered, and she tried again, this time

kicking the base of the door with her leather boots instead of touching the paint with her hands.

Inside, shuffled footsteps preceded the clinking of empty glass bottles. Dani kicked the door again, and a man's voice shouted back, "Fuck off!"

"Open the door, Sean." Dani kicked again, hard enough to rattle the door against its hinges. "I'm not going to ask again."

Sean let out a slew of muttered curses, quiet enough that a normal human probably wouldn't have heard him, but with Dani's enhanced Carrier senses, she made out every last one. She was embarrassed for him. He didn't even have the brain power for creative profanity.

Several locks flipped and the door opened a crack, still attached by the chain. Sean peered out, and Dani winced at the sight of him. Long, unkempt hair fell over his face, his pale skin shiny with grease and broken up by patchy stubble and more acne than Dani had seen on a man in his late twenties. All angles and sharp lines, Sean's narrow face matched his skinny frame, and there was a glazed-over hunger to his eyes that made Dani's skin crawl.

Through the gap in the door, Sean looked Dani up and down, his sour expression melting into a lazy grin. "Now, what do we have here? How can I help, sugar?"

What Dani wanted most in that moment was to punch the gross look off his face, but she generally tried to save violence as a last resort. "I'm looking for Ellie Hughes."

Sean raised a pierced eyebrow, the metal bar winking in the dim yellow light of the apartment. "You're not a cop." There was no question in his tone. Dani didn't know what gave her away, but she wasn't exactly eager to be lumped in with Blackthorn's corrupt police force anyway. Besides, *not* being a cop was often an advantage in dives like this.

"You're right. I'm not." Dani fought the urge to step back when Sean smiled more fully, revealing teeth yellowed by years of nicotine. "But Ellie's parents hired me to find her. For reasons incomprehensible to me, Ellie apparently dates you from time to time. Have you seen her?"

A scowl creased Sean's oily face. "You shouldn't listen to rumors." He backed away from the gap and slammed the door in Dani's face.

Dust rained down from the ceiling and coated Dani's jacket. She cursed and brushed the debris away. She didn't have time for this nonsense. Sean's dismissal only made her more determined to speak with him, and she wasn't about to let a closed door get in her way.

Dani gathered her balance and kicked out like she

was attacking a demon. Her boot connected with the dead bolt, and the door flew inward with a crash that echoed off the bare walls of the hallway. Metal tore from the wooden door frame as a variety of locks ripped loose and the handle smashed into the inner wall.

Dani stepped into the room, crumbled plaster raining down on her. The haze momentarily blocked her vision, and she only saw Sean lunging for her, fist raised, at the last second. She ducked, her enhanced speed allowing her to dodge the blow with ease. Dani pivoted as she stood, grabbing Sean's still-outstretched arm and pinned it behind his back. She slammed him face-first into the wall and pressed tight until he cried out in pain.

"Let's try this again, shall we?" Dani leaned close but regretted it the moment she got a full inhale of his stale smoker's breath and unwashed hair. She grabbed the door and swung it closed to keep onlookers to a minimum.

"I don't have anything to say to you." Sean wriggled in an attempt to break her grip, but his wiry strength was no match for hers. "Let go of me."

"Is everything all right?"

A soft voice floated through the apartment as Dani tightened her hold. A petite white woman stood in the doorway to what was most likely the bedroom, judging by her oversized T-shirt and lack of pants.

For a moment, Dani tried to picture the girl with a little more meat on her bones and more life in her eyes, but even with those adjustments, this girl clearly wasn't Ellie. Her face was too narrow. Her nose hawkish instead of thin. Blue eyes instead of brown.

"It's okay, Amy," Sean said, calm despite his face being pressed hard against the wall. "Just a little misunderstanding."

The girl—Amy—looked from Sean to Dani and nodded absently.

"Go back to bed. I'll be there soon."

Amy wandered back into the room and closed the door behind her. Either run-ins like this happened often around here, or she was too high to tell how much danger her greasy boyfriend was really in.

Dani squeezed Sean's wrist until he winced. "Looks like you've moved on quickly."

Sean glanced over his shoulder as much as he could, given the position of his arm. "Amy and I have a special history."

Dani let out a snort of disgust. "And what would Ellie say if she knew? From what I've heard, though the reasons are deeply unclear to me, Ellie loves you. Doesn't it bother you that she's missing?"

"I—" Sean hissed in a breath and bit down on his

lip. "Listen, if I promise not to hit you, will you let me go?"

"Gladly." Dani released Sean and wiped her hands on the backs of her jeans. "But if you continue to waste my time, your wrist won't be the only thing that hurts. Got it?" She waited for Sean's half-hearted nod. "What do you know about Ellie?"

"Not much." Sean crossed the room and grabbed a beer from the fridge, popping off the top with the edge of the counter. He drank deep from the glass bottle and wiped his mouth on the back of his shirt-sleeve. "Besides the fact that she was *stellar* in bed. There wasn't much she'd say no to, especially if the price was right."

"Makes sense," Dani said, careful to track the man's every movement, especially with the heavy bottle in hand. "That you'd have to pay, that is."

"Please. I've got girls lined up around the corner for the chance to hop on this ride."

Dani doubted it, but she didn't have time to argue the point. "Ellie's been missing for weeks. Do you have any idea where she might have gone?"

"How should I know? She probably ran back to that Podunk she came from. Ellie wasn't cut out for city life." Sean drained the rest of the bottle and set it on one of the few empty spots on the counter. A cocky grin tugged at his lips. "Though I doubt those country boys will know what to do with her now that she's been with me."

He was wrong, in so many ways. Ellie hadn't gone home, but Dani didn't need to tell Sean that. He clearly didn't give two shits about her, forgetting her as easily as a broken toy. At least Ellie seemed to have gotten her sense together and left him. If only she'd bothered to tell anyone where she was going.

Sean sauntered closer, his gaze trained on Dani's cleavage as he licked his lips. "I bet I could teach *you* a thing or two."

Crack.

Sean hit the ground, clutching his face while Dani shook out her hand. Blood dripped from Sean's nose, and if his screaming was any indication, Dani had broken it.

Dani crouched beside the vile excuse for a man. "I'm tired of your bullshit, McGrath. I want a list of every bar Ellie worked at and every corner you made her turn tricks. I need to know about any repeat clients who took a special interest in her."

"There wasn't anyone!" Sean cried from his place on the floor. "Ellie said she wanted out. That she wanted to go back to bartending. I don't know anything."

"Bullshit." Dani grabbed her phone and pulled up a notes app. "I need a list of bars."

Sean's teeth were red with blood as he spewed out a series of names. When he was done, he crawled to the coffee table and wiped his face on a used napkin. "Fucking psycho."

"This is me on a good day." Dani secured her phone in her pocket. "If I find out this list is incomplete, or if you warn anyone that I'm coming, you'll find out just how psychotic I can be."

<hr>

The first two bars on Sean McGrath's list were a bust.

Sure, they were sketchy enough to pay staff under the table, but no one had seen Ellie in weeks. The third and final bar was in one of the worst parts of town. Known only as The Bar, it was a hot spot for trouble. Blackthorn PD had all but given up on the place, a sight of constant fights and where the bathroom drug deals had migrated to just beneath the lip of the bar.

It was brazen enough that bartenders must have known it happened, but since it was technically out of sight, they kept it out of mind.

If Dani weren't, well, *Dani*, she might be worried about stepping foot in a place like that. But with Kiva inked to her back and Jasper on her left arm, she was more than safe from a bunch of bikers and addicts.

Poe, ever restless, was out tonight. He swooped low, into Dani's sight line, then perched on a blown-out streetlight outside the bar.

The raven tilted his head at her, his beady eyes full of disapproval.

"Save it, Poe. I'm not in the mood." It was still early, only about five, so the bar shouldn't be *too* full yet.

Poe ruffled his feathers. *I haven't said a word. It's not as if you'd listen to me anyway.*

Danika ignored the bird and pushed open The Bar's front door. Despite laws against smoking inside, the bar was hazy with smoke, and judging by the pungent smell, it wasn't all tobacco. Dani scanned the bar, and her initial assumption seemed correct. Only a half dozen or so patrons congregated in the watering hole, a couple pairs sitting at wobbly wooden tables and the rest hunched over the bar, nursing warm beer.

All eyes turned to Dani when the door slammed shut behind her. She garnered a few scowls, but after a beat, everyone went back to their drinks, losing themselves to quiet conversations or to their own thoughts. Dani pulled a photo of Ellie from her back pocket and approached the first table.

"Have either of you seen this woman?" she asked the pair of older men with arms full of faded tattoos.

"Nope," the mustached man on her left said.

Dani frowned. "You didn't even look."

"Don't have to." The man lifted his beer and took a long drink. "Ain't that right," he asked his companion.

The other man, bald and bearded, nodded. "Yup."

"Thanks," Dani deadpanned, cursing herself for having the tiniest modicum of hope. "You've been a big help."

She slipped away from the first table, but as she neared the second with her photo, the woman pulled a thick knife from her belt and laid it on the table. Dani didn't bother asking if either of them had seen Ellie. She wasn't about to get any answers there.

One lead. That's all she needed. One lead, and she could get the hell out of this place and get ready for her date with Nick. She hadn't been on a date in *ages*. Not since she broke things off with Raj, who she once believed to be the love of her life.

Instead, that man brought nothing but disappointment and misery.

Part of her didn't want to bother with dating. She had more than enough to keep her busy, and with the Ink, she was never alone. But Nick was a good man, and Poe was forever harassing her about *continuing the Frost line*.

If she didn't produce an heir before she died, the

Ink would die with her. There'd be no one else to keep the balance of humanity from falling to demons.

Dani pushed that particular thought aside and slid onto one of the barstools, dropping Ellie's photo in front of her. On the other side of the bar, a woman in her early twenties appraised her with cautious eyes.

"We don't give out information here, if that's what you're after." The woman tucked a bit of bleached-blond hair behind her ear, the rest of it up in a ponytail.

Dani pulled out her wallet and set a twenty on the counter. "Do you have whiskey?"

The woman scooped up the bill. "Double shot, coming up."

While the bartender poured the drink, the two other patrons at the bar peered over their glasses at Dani, seemingly surprised by her drink of choice. One even raised his own glass of amber liquid in sloppy salute. When the double shot landed in front of Dani, she tossed it back in a single gulp and pushed the empty glass across the bar.

"Another."

Dani handed over another crisp twenty for good measure. She was wildly overpaying for the drink, but that was the point. With any luck, the extra green would soften the bartender's heart. When the glass was full, Dani knocked that back as well, hissing a bit as the whiskey bit the back of her throat.

"Any of you seen her around?" she asked in full-on tipsy mode, despite it being too soon for the alcohol to take effect in a normal person. But Dani wasn't a normal person. She couldn't get drunk even if she wanted to, and damn did she want to at times.

The men at the bar eyed the photo, but they both shook their heads.

"Bummer." Dani spun the photo around and slid it in front of the bartender. "What about you?"

The bartender's eyes widened as she stared down at Ellie's smiling face. She did a decent job returning her face to neutral, but it wasn't fast enough to hide the split second of recognition. "Nope, never seen her."

"That's too bad." Dani lowered her voice so only the bartender would hear. "If I don't track her down soon, I don't know if we'll find her alive." She kept her voice nonchalant, like Ellie's survival didn't matter to Dani one bit. "Guess I better be heading out."

Dani slipped off the stool and sauntered across the bar. The small hairs on the back of her neck stood at attention, every pair of eyes tracking her departure until the front door clicked shut.

From above, Poe ruffled his feathers. *About time, Danika. That bar is no place—*

"Wait!" The bartender rushed out the back door and hurried down the alley to Dani. In the fading sunlight, she looked even younger than she had inside. Something had left her with rail-thin arms, shaking hands, and premature worry lines. "I know her. Her name's Ellie, right?"

"Yeah," Dani replied, careful not to say too much, letting the bartender fill in the silence.

"She was here when I started. She showed me the ropes, pointed out the worst of the creeps and who to avoid. I liked her." The young woman pulled a pack of cigarettes from her pocket and lit up, her hands shaking. "Is she okay?"

"No one has seen her in weeks." Dani let her words settle over the bartender, left time for the young woman to rush to conclusions. "Her parents hired me to find her. Do you have any idea where she could be?"

The bartender chewed her lower lip. "I haven't seen her in over a month ... but we worked this one gig together. The place was creepy as hell, but it paid well. Not well enough, as far as I was concerned, but Ellie said she needed the money. I know she went back at least once or twice. Maybe she's there?"

What could possibly be worse than the shithole they'd just left? "Which bar was it?"

"It was a club, actually." The woman took another

long drag from her cigarette and dropped it to the sidewalk, stamping it out with her shoe. "Obsidian."

Above her, Poe squawked, causing Dani to flinch.

The girl took that as a sign. "You've heard of it?"

Dani gave a sardonic nod. "Yeah, I've heard of it."

Of course it was Obsidian. Of fucking course her investigation would lead there. She cursed herself for ever taking this case.

The woman glanced back at The Bar, scrawny arms wrapped tight around herself. "I should get back."

"Thank you," Dani said. "I know Ellie's loved ones appreciate it."

Only once she was alone did Dani let the frustrated growl rise in her throat. She wanted to hit something. Right now.

Dani stomped her way home, temper rising with each block. Halfway back to her apartment-slash-office, her phone buzzed against her thigh. It was Nick.

I hate to do this, but I caught a case. Can we reschedule?

Dani typed back a response, letting the detective know she was busy with her own case too. So much for getting a social life.

But then Dani grinned and ran her fingers along

the hilt of her sword. There was more than one way to let off steam.

While far from a date with a sexy guy, a night of righteous violence was just what she needed right now. She'd punch and hack away all thoughts of Obsidian, and everything that came with it. At least for the night. It was only a matter of time before the case forced her to go back there, but for now, she had demons to kill.

Poe was going to be thrilled.

7

The one night Danika Frost *wanted* Blackthorn to be overrun with demons, she couldn't find a single one.

Darkness had finally fallen over the city. In the graveyard, without any streetlights to illuminate the way, Dani tried to see the stars. Unfortunately, the city's smog kept them hidden from view. She sighed. Beside her, Kiva prowled across the cemetery lawn, the panther's jet-black body little more than a shadow passing each gravestone.

"Are you sure you saw the demon dart in here?" she asked Poe, who flew overhead.

What kind of question is that? I'm always sure. He soared higher into the sky. *Unfortunately, the creature seems to have disappeared ...*

Of course it had. Wherever it was, her target was out of range of her demon-hunting instincts. Most of the time, she could sense when a demon was close, especially lower-level creatures like the one she hunted. It must be faster than Poe guessed. *Estimated,* the bird would probably remind her. The raven never *guessed.*

Dani swiped her sword through the air and bit back a tirade of choice words. Why did Ellie have to work at Obsidian? Why couldn't she have stayed at The Bar? The chances of Dani running into Raj when she went to investigate the next day were higher than she could stomach.

What's wrong? You're especially tense. Jasper shifted his perch on Dani's shoulders, elongating the final word into a hiss.

"I'm fine."

Jasper stretched out his body and swiveled his head back to stare at Dani, his piercing yellow eyes and slit irises seeing through her bravado. He shot his forked tongue out and licked her face.

You're not fine.

Dani caved and let her whole body deflate. Before she knew it, the truth spilled out.

"It's the case I'm working. There's a missing girl."

You find lots of missing girls. Why is this one different?

Jasper nuzzled his cool head against Dani's cheek. She reached up and stroked the king cobra's scaled body.

"Her last known location is Obsidian."

At that, Kiva stopped walking and glanced back at Dani. Poe harrumphed, making his feelings on the matter perfectly clear.

He thought Dani's stress was irksome and misplaced.

No wonder your heart is heavy, child. Kiva's warm voice filled Dani's head. *Could you send the chameleon?*

Dani suppressed a laugh. She didn't think the families of those buried in the cemetery would appreciate her humor, even if the space was currently empty. "Spencer isn't a chameleon." Dani understood why the Ink thought of him that way though. One of Spencer's demon-given magics was a powerful glamor that he used to change his hair and eye color whenever the mood struck.

And Kiva made a good point. Spencer and Rajan were still friends, despite the fact that Spencer worked full time for Dani. If she asked Spence to go to Obsidian for her, he'd do it in a heartbeat. But asking him felt like admitting weakness, and Dani had been raised to hone every weakness into strength.

She had to be the one to go.

If her mother understood what was happening, she'd make Dani go on principle.

Before Dani could explain her reasoning to Kiva, the wind kicked up, bringing the putrid scent of rotting fresh to Dani's attention. She crinkled her nose and adjusted her grip on her sword, shifting into a ready stance. The demon must be close. From the smell, the body it stole must be wearing thin and nearly used up. Which, Dani realized, explained why it was roaming through a cemetery. It needed a fresher corpse.

At your two o'clock, Poe said shifting his course to the east.

Like mortals, demons were always at their most dangerous, their most reckless, when they were desperate. And a demon on the verge of losing its human host? Those were the most desperate of all. She'd have to be careful.

The path through the cemetery bent right, and Dani crouched behind a statue. Up ahead, around the rough stone of her hiding spot, she found what she'd been looking for all night. Something to hit. Really hard.

Bits of rotten skin and flesh fell off the demon's stolen body as it dug with frantic fingers at the freshly covered grave. Dani grimaced. Hitting the juicy ones was too gross to be satisfying. The universe seemed intent on keeping her from getting any sort of release tonight.

Figured.

"Everyone ready?" Dani asked her trio of ancient demon-hunting spirits. A chorus of affirmations rang in her head, and Jasper slid down to the grass, his body lengthening to its full size. Her blade caught the weak light, shining up at her, sharp and ready for action. "Now!"

Poe dove first, piercing the night with his screech. The demon snapped its neck up in the bird's direction in time for Poe's talons to scratch across its face. One of the eyeballs slipped from the socket and fell to the ground.

Dani smirked and strode across the cemetery to the demon. "You might take the prize for the grossest, most incompetent demon I've faced this year."

She sliced her sword at the corpse's head, but the demon moved with surprising speed. He slipped under her blade and dove at Dani, catching her around the waist. Thick, black claws extended from his fingertips. Dani tried to twist away, but she still caught the edge of the talons across her back. They ripped through her jacket and shirt to split open her skin in long shreds that burned like fire.

The pain caught her off guard—it had been ages since a demon broke skin—and she tripped over a short headstone, landing hard on her bleeding back. She cursed herself for going into a fight distracted.

Cursed Raj, too, for turning up in her life when she least expected it.

"Looks like I don't need to keep digging," the demon said, its voice like gravel. Each word seemed to struggle to escape the blue, chapped lips of the corpse, so far along in the decomposition process that part of the body's throat had caved in on itself.

The demon stalked toward where Dani lay on the ground, her back still in agony.

Kiva leaped over Dani, her huge black paws snapping the demon's clavicle. It screamed as it struggled, but it was no match for Kiva's size and strength.

Dani pulled herself back to her feet, adjusting her grip on her sword. She approached the struggling demon, now missing one eye and its ribs cracking one by one under Kiva's weight. "You know," Dani said, raising the sword, "I think you're right. There's no need for you to dig anymore."

She sliced the corpse's head from its body and severed the demon from its tether to the human world with a satisfying crunch. Kiva nudged her cold nose against Dani's back, and she lifted her shirt, exposing the cuts. They should have started healing already, but something prevented Dani's skin from stitching back together.

Demonic infection, Kiva said, swiping her tongue across Dani's back as Jasper unhinged his jaw to consume the beheaded corpse. As the panther cleaned the wounds, the burning subsided and then disappeared, leaving only the heat of Dani's own quickened healing.

Kiva nudged her side with the top of her head when she was done. *You must be careful, little one.*

Indeed, Poe added, landing on the nearby gravestone. *Especially since you have yet to produce an heir.*

Dani groaned. Not this again. "I have been a little busy, Poe." *And it's not like there's been any takers these past couple years,* she added to herself. Dani wasn't exactly keen to have children—she was only twenty-three, after all—but Carriers didn't have the longest life expectancies. The longer she waited, the less time she'd have to train her daughter. And if she didn't continue the Frost line, the world would lose the Ink and there would be no one to stand in the way of demons or the necromancers who raised them.

Procreation was the last thing Dani wanted to think about while Jasper feasted on a rotting corpse in front of her.

"Come on," Dani said when the snake had finished. "We should get back home."

Jasper didn't even wait to be recalled. He burst into Ink, full belly and all, and stitched himself back into Dani's left arm. She hissed in a breath at the sudden pain, her heart aching for the lingering echo in the scar on her right arm.

"Do you want to walk to the edge of the cemetery before you return?" Dani asked, but the panther didn't respond. Instead, she turned south and sniffed at the air. "Kiva, what is it?"

I smell death. She sniffed again. *It's human.*

8

Danika followed Kiva through the cemetery and allowed the panther to prowl the city, keeping to the shadows of backstreets and alleys along the way.

"Can you tell how many?" Dani whispered, careful not to draw unwanted attention to the great feline. The streets in this part of town were usually deserted this late at night, but Dani didn't want to risk a wayward pedestrian overhearing them.

Kiva sniffed the air again, hackles raised. *One. Possibly two.* She glanced at Dani, her warm golden eyes full of concern. *There's a lot of blood.*

Two more blocks, Poe called from up ahead. *There's a body on the ground, but I can't tell who it is. I'm going in for a closer look.*

"Poe, wait—" But of course, the bird didn't wait.

Dani took off at a sprint with Kiva at her heels, covering the two blocks as quickly as she could. Flashing lights made her stop before turning the corner. Poe didn't bother mentioning the huge police presence already setting up a perimeter around the body. "Kiva?" she asked, and before she could issue the command, Kiva slipped from the shadows and inked herself along Dani's back.

Dani gripped the brick wall beside her as the pain rippled across her skin. If the panther was a normal tattoo, it would have taken several sessions and many long hours to get the work done. Instead, all that pain concentrated into a few agonizing seconds. Though she had Carried the Ink for six years, it still made Dani's knees weak whenever Kiva—the largest of the Ink—returned to her skin.

She sucked in several deep breaths, adjusted her jacket to mask the slash marks that now ran down the back, and stepped out from around the corner. Good thing she hadn't worn her mother's leather jacket out tonight. Had the demon ruined that, Dani would have forced a necromancer to raise the demon again just so she could kill the thing a second time.

Blackthorn PD was out in full force. Flashing lights bounced off the surrounding buildings, old dilapidated shells with boarded-up windows. Crime scene techs in navy-blue windbreakers swarmed the area, some photographing the scene while others collected samples of blood and other fluids from the street and sidewalk. The place smelled of piss and death, Dani's least favorite combinations of city stenches. A woman with neatly braided brown hair worked to secure the scene, roping off the entire section with yellow police tape.

Dani scanned the cordoned-off area for a friendly face, someone who would let her get close enough to see if the dead body was her missing girl. For Ellie's sake—and that of her parents'—Dani hoped not.

At least the police chief wasn't there. She didn't expect to see him at a crime scene, but Nick had complained about him being a micromanager before, so she hadn't ruled it out.

She found Poe perched at the edge of the nearest building, too far away to speak with him without being overheard. Dani tried to wave him over, but the bird flapped his wings as if in a shrug.

The police shooed me away like I'm some common animal, came Poe's voice in her head. *I can't see his face.*

His face. Not Ellie, then.

The policewoman finished securing the scene and ducked underneath the tape, dismissing drunk passersby trying to get a closer look. Dani didn't know the woman. Not that it mattered much. It wasn't like she had enough clout around the police station to get an invitation into crime scenes. Not without—

A hand touched Dani's shoulder, and she whirled around. She almost smashed her fist into his face before she recognized the man before her. "Nick," she said, breathless and embarrassed at her overreaction.

He held up his hands. "Remind me never to surprise you."

"A girl can't be too careful," Dani replied, motioning over to the mess beyond the yellow tape.

"Scoping out the crime scene, Miss Frost?" Nick stood a little closer than necessary and grinned down at her. Dimples appeared at the corners of his lips, and as she breathed in the masculine scent of his cologne, a flutter of longing traveled through her. She couldn't help but wonder what he looked like under that crisp white shirt of his. Wide shoulders filled it out nicely, and his narrow waist told Dani he logged plenty of hours at the gym each week.

Poe cawed in the background and broke Dani from her wandering thoughts.

"I wanted to make sure it wasn't my missing girl," she replied, giving herself a shake.

"With any luck, it's one of mine. Come on. I'll get you in." Nick led her to the edge of the perimeter and held up the tape for her to duck under. "Miss Frost is a consultant," he said before the policewoman on guard duty could object. "She's with me."

Beyond, the dead body sprawled across the dirty alley. Nick let out a low whistle when they came to a stop. "Well, it's definitely not Ellie."

"Is he one of yours?" Dani asked while the forensics team took photos around them, bagging up evidence and laying numbered placards beside a discarded empty wallet and a bloody knife.

"He looks familiar," Nick said as he slipped on a pair of latex gloves. "Collins, let me see the wallet."

Dani bent down and examined the dead man. Blood pooled around his head, his skin gaunt with a morbid pallor that hinted he'd been dead a while. His throat splayed open in a vicious slash, thanks to the presumed murder weapon beside him.

Dani's attention moved beyond the body and took in the surrounding asphalt and brick walls of the alley. "Shouldn't a wound like that bleed more? I don't see any blood spatter."

Even the man's suit was relatively blood-free.

"He was probably killed somewhere else and dumped here." Nick flipped through the wallet. The cash and credit cards were gone, but the man's driver's license was still inside. "Yup, he's one of my missing persons cases. Ricardo Nuñez, forty-five. He's been Mayor Conrad's assistant campaign manager since the last election. Almost didn't recognize him."

"How long has he been missing?"

Nick handed the wallet back to the tech Collins. "Not long. His fiancée reported him missing last night."

Dani stood, her attention still on the dead body. "I think it's safe to assume the neck injury is the cause of death."

"Probably, but we won't know for sure until after the autopsy." Nick guided her away from the body and lowered his voice from prying ears. "I'm sorry about earlier, by the way. My work can be a bit unpredictable."

Dani's brow crinkled. "Sorry about what?"

Nick stood, his six-foot frame towering over Dani by several inches. "Rescheduling dinner last minute. I promise it wasn't a case of cold feet."

"Oh. Right." She'd forgotten about the canceled date the moment she heard the bartender mention Obsidian. "I don't know," she said, slipping off her jacket. It was suddenly far too warm next to him despite the late hour and the cool autumn night. "There's something exciting about having our first date at a crime scene, don't you think? It could make for a fun story to tell our friends."

Dani winced as soon as the words fell from her

mouth. What the hell was wrong with her? They hadn't even gone to dinner yet and here she was talking about them like they were destined to be the kind of couple that wouldn't shut up about how they met. Dani wished the ground would open up and swallow her whole.

"Uh, Detective, I think you should see this," Collins called, saving Dani from learning Nick's reaction to her pitiful attempt at flirting.

"I'll be right back." Detective Hart cleared his throat and walked back over to the body.

This time, Dani didn't follow. She was too busy deciding how to make a swift exit. The body wasn't Ellie, and if she left now, she might be able to salvage some kind of dignity the next time she saw Nick.

The techs and medical examiner grabbed the body and helped flip Ricardo over onto his stomach. The fabric of his suit had been ripped away, revealing a large open wound on his back.

"What the hell is that?" Nick asked.

"Scarification is getting big in the body mod world," Collins said.

Dani frowned and hurried to Nick's side, all embarrassment forgotten as she peered down at the wound.

Someone had carved a circle into Ricardo's back and etched a series of intricate symbols inside.

"Nah, I'd say whoever slashed his throat did this to him."

"Why?" one of the other techs asked Nick. "It's weird, sure, but I've seen worse shit in this city."

While the trio continued discussing the markings, Dani kept several truths to herself.

It wasn't a knife that made those markings. It wasn't a gang sign or some hipster form of body modification.

The sigil carved into the skin meant one thing: Ricardo Nuñez had been marked by a demon.

———

By the time the crime scene techs finished their work and the medical examiner carted away the body, Dani had made a decision.

"I'm heading out," she told Nick. "There's a lead on Ellie that I want to track down before it gets too late. Can you send me a photo of that symbol when you have a minute?"

Nick's brow furrowed. "Does it have some significance I should know about?"

"Not sure yet." She wasn't about to explain demon sigils to Nick. He'd managed to stay out of her world so far, and she wanted to keep him free of it as long as possible. "But if I find anything helpful, you'll be the first to know."

He nodded. "If I can't get ahold of the tech photos, I'll see if I can grab a shot while I'm at the morgue."

"Good luck with your case," she said, stepping over the pool of blood. She wasn't sure if she should kiss him or shake his hand or just walk away. Given her idiotic comment about using a crime scene as a date, maybe she should disappear and never see the man again.

Thankfully, Nick raised his coffee cup in salute. "You too. Not that you need it. If anyone can find Ellie, it's you."

Dani sure hoped so. To do that, though, she needed more leads, which meant following the trail to Obsidian whether she liked it or not. Ellie needed her, and she wasn't about to let her emotions get in the way of saving the missing girl. She said goodbye to Nick and left him to his own investigation.

Though she could have hailed a taxi, Dani chose to walk the fifteen blocks to Obsidian, calling back Poe along the way. The bird's irritation buzzed within her, and she used it to keep focused on the job instead of dwelling on the memories that had flooded back since the bartender mentioned the club.

For the first few blocks, her mind went over the possibilities surrounding Ricardo's death. Nick would work hard to find the murderer, but he wasn't likely to find a human culprit for such a crime. Whoever dumped Ricardo's body wanted to make it appear like a mugging, but it wasn't some desperate human who attacked the poor man.

A demon sigil like that meant Ricardo had been used as a host, and if he'd only gone missing last night, the demon must have been exceptionally strong for the body to give out so soon.

Dani needed to prioritize her duties. While evidence of a demonic possession meant Dani would have to meddle with Nick's investigation into Ricardo's death, she had to stay focused on Ellie for now. Unlike Ricardo, Ellie might still be alive, which put her at the top of Dani's to-do list. The dead could wait until Dani tracked down the girl.

When she finally reached Obsidian, business was booming. A line ran down the entire block, at least a hundred hopefuls desperate for their chance to get inside the exclusive club. Dani strode right past each and every one, ignoring their shouts of protests. At the door, she tried to duck past the bouncer and under the rope, but the woman blocked her path.

"Not so fas— Dani? Is that you?"

Dani gave the bouncer a sheepish smile when she recognized the dark-haired, brown-skinned woman. "Hey, Amara."

"Don't you 'Hey, Amara' me. It's been ages, girl. Where have you been?" Amara, a Dasari necromancer like her cousin Rajan, pulled Dani into a tight hug. Amara was a couple years younger than Dani, and they had grown friendly during the years Dani dated Raj.

Not that she, or anyone else in Raj's family, knew that Dani was the Ink Carrier.

At first, she'd hated going to Obsidian, hated the reminder of that part of Raj's life. Over time, though, she came to appreciate the advantages of being undercover at the club. It was the easiest way to learn more about the five families *and* any new demons on the scene looking to cause trouble.

Dani extracted herself from the hug. "You know me, always busy. Is that cousin of yours around?"

"Yeah, the workaholic is here almost twenty-four-seven," Amara said. "Go on in. Give him hell for me."

"Always," Dani promised, and slipped into the club.

Walking into Obsidian was like stepping through a veil into another world. A pulsing bass thudded against Dani's eardrums. Bodies pressed together as they writhed to the music on the crowded dance floor, and a shudder worked down her spine when she spotted her first demon.

In a man's tall and muscular body with a shaved

head, the demon appeared normal enough as he danced with a young brunette, but when he bent to kiss her neck, a long blue tongue snaked out and flicked along her skin.

Lifelong instincts had Dani's fingers inching toward the sword at her waist, but Obsidian wasn't a place to take down demons. Not when a solid 50 percent of the patrons around her were either demons or necromancers. Not when she'd managed to hide her identity as the Ink Carrier from all of the Dasari clan.

Except for Raj.

Dani scanned the club for the leader of the Dasari necromancers. The first time Dani had come to Obsidian, Raj's father, Hasan Dasari, still ruled the club. Back then, it was rare to find any of the other necromancer families operating out of Obsidian. But as Dani surveyed the bar area, she noted that informed consent for demonic dealings wasn't the only change Raj had made after his father passed.

Of course, the club was full of the Dasaris. The extended necromancer clan not only made deals in the club but also supervised the humans who worked the bar. Some, like Amara, ran security until they'd proven themselves ready to broker their own deals.

Dani passed one of the small private rooms stationed around the club, the expensive silk curtain left open. Inside, a man in a smart tailored suit drew an orange sigil on the table in the center of the small room. Another man, who wore his expensive suit like he dressed in one daily, stared at the sigil as a tiny demon materialized. It had a vaguely human shape, except instead of skin, green scales covered its naked body. Dani seethed as the necromancer accepted a briefcase of cash and brokered a deal.

The club was too noisy to hear what the man bartered away beyond the money, or what he hoped to gain in exchange. The necromancer pricked his client's finger with a needle and allowed beads of blood to drop over the summoning. The sigil marking consumed the blood and turned a glowing red. Then, the demon laughed and disappeared in a puff of smoke, their bargain complete.

At least that deal didn't include possession.

After another scan of the room didn't reveal Raj, Dani took a seat at the bar and ordered a beer. Dani didn't notice any demonic signs from the human who served her—no forked tongue, tail, elongated teeth, or other aspects—and she had to wonder why a young woman would agree to work in a place like this. Perhaps she wasn't yet aware of the kind of clientele Obsidian catered to. Most humans couldn't see demons—good people like Nick who had no cause to believe in their existence—but those in the know eventually developed the sight.

Dani pulled out the photo of Ellie and slid it across the bar. "Is she working tonight?"

After a brief look at the photo, the bartender shook her head. "Haven't seen her in a week or two."

"Any idea where she is now? Did she quit?"

"Not sure. We weren't close. Let me know when you're ready for another," she said before tending to someone at the other end of the bar.

Dani froze when she recognized the man's angled face, bald head, and eye patch that she knew covered an empty socket.

Caleb Owens. Spencer's uncle.

And the man responsible for the scar on her right arm.

Dani abandoned her beer before her grip shattered the glass. She stumbled away from the bar, as fear and rage and violence beat in equal measure with her drumming heart. She wanted to kill him. To tear the necromancer into a thousand tiny pieces for what he'd done to her, what he'd done to *Silas*. The fourth Ink. The Ink she lost.

The Ink he took from her.

She should have known better than to think Raj could help her. How could he let the Owens family inside his club after what they'd done to her? How could he let *Caleb* past the doors alive?

How could he—

Dani crashed into someone tall and solid. She started to push herself away, an apology already loaded on her tongue.

"Danika?"

She froze. She knew that voice. Knew the touch of the hand that now rested on the small of her back.

Their eyes met, and the breath escaped Dani like someone had sucker punched her in the gut. Or stabbed her in the heart, which was closer to the truth.

"Rajan."

9

A hundred emotions coursed through Dani, and each one echoed back at her from Raj's tortured expression. There was surprise. Hurt. Longing. Betrayal. And beneath it all, a current running deep through each: hope.

Raj wore an impeccable tailored black suit, his long dark hair swept back from his face and secured with a leather tie. He was clean shaven, and his brown eyes sparkled under the club's lights. Somehow, in the years they'd spent apart, he'd grown even handsomer.

"Sorry," Dani said, fighting the quaver in her voice, "I was just leaving."

She turned to go, but Raj's hand caught her just above the elbow. A gentle touch, more question than command, and even over the pounding bass she heard his soft, "Wait."

His voice was choked with emotion, and Dani turned back to him. Raj nodded across the club to where a VIP section sat empty behind velvet ropes. "Can we speak in private?"

A thrill of nerves flapped in her stomach like soaring ravens. When Raj pulled way, she swallowed down her fear and nodded. She wasn't scared of Rajan Dasari, leader of the Dasari necromancers. She was afraid of the strange flutter in her heart. Afraid of *Raj*, the man who had captured her heart so completely that after years away, she was still working to put it back together.

Raj led her to the VIP section, and as they passed beyond the velvet ropes, the air around Dani seemed to shift. The pounding bass faded to nothing, and Dani shot Raj a concerned look.

"No one will be able to hear us in here." Raj tapped the air at the edge of the rail, and it shimmered like the ripple of a pebble in a pond. "Take a seat."

Dani remained standing and crossed her arms. She refused to be impressed by the demonic magic keeping their conversation private. All she could think about was the cost, and of Caleb Owens sitting at the bar on the other side of the dance floor. Fresh anger boiled inside her. "How could you?" she snapped.

"How could I what?"

Dani stabbed a finger across the sea of demons and their soon-to-be victims. "Why is Caleb Fucking Owens here?" She pulled up her sleeve to reveal her scar. To remind him of what that monster did to her, but as she did, unwelcome memories rushed over Dani. Raj's fingers tracing the bumps of the acid-burned skin. His lips pressing against the scar.

Dani's grief echoed back from his expression. "It's not what you think, Dani."

"It never is with you, is it?"

Raj sighed and ran his hands over his hair. "Can we start over? It's been a long time."

"Two years." It was an impressive amount of time considering how intertwined their worlds were. They were fighting on opposite sides of an eternal supernatural war after all.

"Twenty-six months, actually." Raj's expression was so naked and vulnerable that Dani had to look away. She sunk into one of the soft leather chairs. Raj quirked a half smile. "Not that I've been counting."

Feelings that Dani had long since buried tried to rise to the surface, but she wasn't there on a social call or to see if there were any flames left between them to rekindle.

"How have you been?" he asked when she didn't respond. Raj leaned forward and braced his forearms on his thighs. The muscles in his arms strained against his jacket, and Dani couldn't help but remember the comfort of being wrapped up in his embrace. Of strong hands and wandering fingers that knew her body better than she did.

There was a time when she craved his smile. When she'd lie awake at night in his arms, his bare chest warm against her skin. She'd felt safe then. Loved.

Dani cleared her throat and shoved the memories aside. "I'm fine."

"Spencer says your work has really picked up. He's proud of you."

Dani shrugged. Though she'd never say so to Spence, though she'd never ask him to cut off anyone from his past, she hated that the men were still friends.

"What about your mom?" Raj asked, a note of caution in his tone. "Has there been any change?"

Ice curled in Dani's veins. He did *not* get to ask about her mother. Not anymore. Not ever again. Her lips pressed into a thin line. If looks could kill, Rajan Dasari would be a dead man.

Her lack of reaction finally shuttered something in him. He sat back in his chair and the emotion slipped off his face until only the perfect necromancer mask was left. "I assume you're here on a case?" he asked, sounding bored now.

"I'm tracking down a missing girl," Dani said. She pointedly ignored the twinge of hurt in her heart at his sudden change. She pulled Ellie's photo out of her pocket. "My sources say she worked here. I wouldn't have come otherwise."

Raj flinched, and Dani hoped he could feel the truth of her words vibrating along his bones. That was one of the magics he'd bargained for: Raj could always tell when someone was lying to him. Luckily for Dani, he could only sense an outright lie, not a lie of omission. He reached out and took the photo from Dani's hand, careful to avoid brushing against her fingers.

He examined the picture and nodded after a long look. "I recognize her. Elizabeth or something?"

"Ellie," Dani confirmed. "Does she still work here?"

"She was only a temp. She picked up a few shifts here and there, but we hadn't brought her on full time yet. A lot of humans don't take well to this place."

"And did Ellie? Did she handle your ... *clientele* okay?"

"As far as I know, yes. She seemed to be acclimating well. I can find out more if you—"

"When was her last shift?" Dani interrupted before Raj could offer a favor. She didn't want to owe him anything.

"Dani … I don't keep track of every temp who comes in and out of this club. I have people for that." He tried to sound apologetic, but all Dani could hear was an excuse. The reminder of the wealth and power he'd amassed as a necromancer. "I don't recall seeing her for at least a few weeks though," he said.

She couldn't catch a break with this case. "Did she make any deals while she was here?" she asked, thinking of the pixie demon she'd seen earlier.

Raj stiffened in his chair. "What are you implying?"

"It wouldn't be the first time a necromancer took advantage of a young woman's desperation." Lana had been possessed in this club five years ago and was Dani's first-ever case. Helping Lana and her sister Cassie had birthed the idea for Frost Investigations and was how she came to meet Spencer.

Raj too.

"Any bargains made within these walls take place between consenting adults." Raj's tone took on a dangerous edge. "Everyone knows the risks coming in."

"The desperate don't care about costs, Raj. They can't possibly understand what'll be required of them." She stood, the sparks of their old arguments reigniting. "If you'd ever wanted for anything in your life, you might know that."

"Right," Raj said, rising to his feet until he towered over her, "because my childhood was nothing but sunshine and rainbows. Like burying my father at twenty-three and running all of this is easy."

"Trust me," Dani said, heading to leave. "You don't want to compare childhoods."

Raj blocked her path. "Try being brown in America, Dani. No amount of money washes that away."

Dani paused, stalled for words. Raj wasn't wrong, but that was not at all the point she was trying to make. She looked up and held his gaze. "Name *one thing* you want but don't have."

His expression softened. His posture deflated, gaze falling until it lingered on her lips.

The look only lasted a second, but it was enough to send heat rushing to Dani's cheeks. Coming here was a mistake. She shouldn't have reopened these old wounds. Kiva had been right. She should have sent Spencer.

She pulled her business card from her back pocket and tossed it onto a nearby table. The python in the logo winked up at her.

"If you hear from Ellie or remember something pertinent, have someone call me."

Dani ducked around Raj and stepped out of the VIP section. The ear-shattering music returned to full volume as she made her escape across the dance floor.

When Dani made it back to her apartment, she slipped out of her leather jacket and took a long shower to wash away the day. The cuts on her back from the graveyard demon had faded to nothing, but the fresh wounds on her heart weren't as easily healed.

She stood in front of her closet, wrapped tightly in a soft towel, and reached for her comfiest pair of pajamas. But when the fabric slipped over her fingers, she pulled back. Her mind was racing too much to sleep. What Dani needed more than anything was a stiff drink.

Several of them.

If she drank enough, she reasoned, maybe she'd finally feel some of the alcohol's effects. Dani dressed in jeans, a clingy black tank top, and her favorite leather boots, pinning her hair up on top of her head. She hurried back downstairs and slipped in through the kitchen entrance to the bar.

The pair of cooks barely acknowledged her presence as she passed through, both too busy turning out some of the best barbecue in the state. Dani had been around long enough that all the staff knew her by sight and, thanks to Bloody Mary, they never questioned or judged when Dani came in looking a hot mess.

Bloody Mary poured out a line of shots for a group of guys, playing barmaid for the evening, and slammed back one for herself. "Hey, sugar," the drag queen said, her voice deep and red wig teased to the sky. She pressed a kiss to Dani's cheek and then grabbed a napkin to wipe away the smear of gold lipstick. "Your friends are in tonight."

"Yeah?" Dani found Spencer and Lana sitting at the far end of the bar. She wasn't surprised to see Spencer—he was a regular in Blackthorn's gay scene, Bloody Mary's included—but Lana usually went straight home after work to watch over her kid sister. Dani turned back to the drag queen and bar owner. "Could you send over several shots of whiskey? And maybe some wings?"

Mary winced. "That bad, kid?"

"Worse," Dani quipped before slipping out from behind the bar.

Lana waved her over. "Dani! How was your date?" Her words came out slurred, and she swayed a little on her seat.

Dani took the empty barstool next to Spence, who had glamoured his hair into a vivid white instead of his natural brown curls. "How drunk have you gotten her?"

Spencer shrugged, but there was a mischievous glint in his eye. "Only a little."

"No Adrian tonight?" Dani checked the dance floor for Spencer's longtime boyfriend but couldn't spot him in the crowd.

"Nope. He's off studying for exams. This final year of med school can't end soon enough." Spencer took a swig of his beer as Bloody Mary dropped three shots in front of Dani. He raised an eyebrow when Dani downed the first two shots in quick succession.

"Unless you have a way to make me actually feel this," Dani said, grabbing the third glass, "no judgment from you."

Lana motioned for a refill and whistled low. "Was your date really that bad? Is the detective a terrible kisser? I can ban him from the office for you."

Dani groaned and let her head rest against the bar.

"Aren't you supposed to be watching Cassie? Interrogate your sister about *her* love life."

Cassie was the reason Dani and Lana first met. Five years ago, when Cassie was an eleven-year-old dying of cancer, the young girl had hired Dani to find her missing guardian. Now, thanks to a demonic deal that Dani and the Ink helped renegotiate, with Spencer's help, Cassie and Lana were both thriving.

"She's at a sleepover tonight. Which means I have plenty of time to harass *you* instead." Lana tipped back the last drops of her red wine and motioned for more. "Now, spill."

"There's nothing to tell. Nick had to reschedule." Dani picked herself up and inhaled the aroma of chili-covered nachos that a couple was eating farther down the bar. Her stomach grumbled up at her in complaint.

"You're not this upset over some boy canceling your date." Spencer considered her. "Is it the case from this morning?"

"First of all, he didn't cancel. He caught a case of his own and postponed." Dani didn't know why she bothered making the distinction, but she felt compelled to all the same. "But yes. Things got … complicated."

Bloody Mary delivered the wings—boneless and

chargrilled, just the way Dani liked them—and Dani explained her night as she ate.

"And would you like to know the crowning piece of shit on my craptastic night?" Dani asked. "Ellie used to work at Obsidian."

"Oh no." Lana covered her mouth with her hand, her wine glass forgotten.

"Did you see him?" Spencer asked, and Dani nodded. He cursed under his breath and called to Bloody Mary for another round. "I take it things didn't go well?"

Dani knocked back the shot the moment it was set in front of her. "Nope."

Lana reached across Spencer and held Dani's hand. "Do you want to talk about it?"

"Not particularly." Dani squeezed Lana's hand, and somehow her friend's touch loosened the lump in her throat and the words spilled out anyway. "He hasn't changed, not a damn bit since we broke up. Did you know he still lets your uncle into the club?" She turned to Spencer in time to see the shock there. "Fucking Caleb Owens, sitting at the bar without a goddamn care in the world. And Raj *knew*. He fucking knew he was there and let him stay."

Dani rubbed at the scar on her arm. She could still hear the screams from that night as the necromancer's potion burned Silas, her beloved python, from her skin. On the coldest days, she swore she felt that same chemical heat against her skin, could smell the charred flesh. And Raj, who was there when it happened, who helped heal some of that pain, let the monster responsible inside his club.

"Hey, now. You're okay." Spencer gently took hold of her wrist and pulled her hand away from her scars. "Come on. Let's dance. Lana?"

Lana slipped off her stool and came to stand on Dani's other side. There was no use arguing with them. Dani climbed down and let her friends drag her onto the dance floor. The music grew louder at the other end of the bar and a heavy bass echoed inside her ribs. Dani let the music burrow into her bones, let the drums move her body until she was drunk on the movement, on the touch of Lana's hand as she spun Dani in dizzying circles, on the press of Spencer's chest against her back.

Dani danced until the only thought in her head was the rhythm of the music and the beat of her heart. She danced until she forgot all about Rajan Dasari.

Until she forgot about the scar on her arm.

The world raced past Danika as she sprinted down

the sidewalk. Her speed felt unnatural, her limbs moving faster than ever before in her life. Poe's frantic wings flapped above her, leading her to some unknown place. Panic clutched at her chest. Her mother. Something terrible and awful and—

She screamed as white-hot pain seared down her back. Dani stumbled, catching herself on a stone wall as Kiva rippled across her back. Both of her arms bore the Ink—Jasper on her left arm and Silas wrapping around her right. It was too soon. Inheriting the Ink meant only one thing. Her mother could *not* be gone.

When the pain subsided, Dani called Kiva's name. Her voice came out broken and pitiful, but the panther answered her call.

Come, Little Warrior. Your mother needs you.

Dani gasped and woke in her bed. The sheets were tangled around her legs, her body slick with sweat. "Fucking nightmares," she swore, rubbing her forehead. She reached for the warmth of Kiva's fur, but all the Ink lay locked within her skin.

All but Silas.

Dani ran her fingers over her scars. As terrible as the recurring dream was, at least her Ink was whole. She missed Silas with all her heart. A part of her had been ripped away the night Caleb Owens murdered her affectionate and cool-headed python.

And her ex-boyfriend thought Caleb was fine company to keep.

She wasn't sure if she could forgive Raj for that, not that he seemed all that eager to earn her forgiveness. As she got ready for her day, she refused to think of him. Refused to remember his smile or the feel of his touch. Of how he knew precisely how long they'd been apart, or the possibility that he'd thought about her at all since their breakup.

Dani stopped by her office, where she was surprised to find Lana and Spencer. Lana had all the lights dimmed as low as they'd go, which left shadows around the bags under her eyes. Spencer wore his sunglasses and massaged his temples, his natural brown curls free from product.

"You two could have called in sick," Dani said, careful to keep her voice quiet.

Spencer groaned. "And admit defeat? Never."

"Suit yourself." Dani made a detour for the kitchen and pulled a soft ice pack from the freezer. The blast of cold air brought her back to her nightmare and the chilly fall night when her life fell apart. She shoved the thoughts away, grabbed a bottle of painkillers, and returned to the main room with a quick glance at their board of dead ends. She should visit her mother

…

Dani placed the bottle of pills on Lana's desk and

handed Spence the ice pack. Unlike the Ink Carrier, necromancers were fully capable of getting drunk, and suffering the consequences the next day.

"You're an angel." He removed his sunglasses and placed the ice on his forehead.

"I know." Dani's phone buzzed, and she found a message from Nick.

Just left the morgue. Medical examiner says Ricardo was dead before his throat was slashed. No cause of death yet. Call me when you get a chance?

Another text came through, this one with a photo of Ricardo on a slab at the morgue. The demon sigil was even bigger than Dani remembered, taking up almost his whole back.

Here's the photo I promised.

"Hey, Spence?" Her voice must have been louder than she meant because both of her colleagues hushed her. "Sorry, but can you take a look at this?" She held out the phone with the image pulled up.

Spencer removed the ice from his eyes and squinted at the image. "A demon sigil?" He reached for the phone and zoomed in to examine the marking closer. "Is this the dead guy from last night?"

"Yeah. Nick's working the case. Do you recognize it?" Each sigil was unique to the demon it raised, like an otherworldly fingerprint.

"It doesn't look familiar. Forward me the photo and I can look into it." He leaned back and put the ice over his eyes again. "After this headache goes away."

Spencer was more than the creative genius behind demon-banishing bullets and her retractable sword, but he rarely talked about his necromancer past. His knowledge often came in handy, but he kept as far away from actual demons as possible.

"I appreciate it, Spence."

When Dani was still dating Raj, he told her that Spencer possessed a rare and powerful demonic power, one forced on him by his parents when Spencer was thirteen. Raj said it gave him a deeper connection to demons and the demonic realm, but that it was awful for Spence. Dani never asked her friend about it, figuring Spencer would tell her if he wanted her to know.

She was careful not to push him too far, and she tried to limit favors.

Dani knew a thing or two about unwanted power.

That thought made Dani feel ungrateful. It wasn't that she resented being the Ink Carrier, not exactly. The Ink were family to her, and she couldn't imagine her life without them. But there was a time she envisioned a different life for herself. If she'd been born into some other family, she would have gone to college. She would have been a nurse or a doctor and helped heal people instead of decapitating demons.

"You know what? Let's call it a day. You two go home." Dani shot Lana a pointed look. "*Both* of you. I don't want to see either of you until tomorrow."

"But—"

"No 'buts,' Lana. Go home. Watch some trashy TV. Sleep all day." She pulled her office manager out of her chair and hugged her tight. "You deserve a day off."

Once Lana had shuffled out of the office, Dani grabbed her jacket.

Spencer groaned as he stood and slipped his sunglasses back on. "Where are you going?"

"To see my mom."

"Don't you normally go in the evenings?"

Dani rarely visited the hospital during the day. She liked to go when the ward was as quiet as possible. Something about seeing the other families visiting made the guilt cut deeper for not going more often.

Dani zipped her jacket. "I'm checking the morgue for Ellie today, and Mom is on the way so ..." She shrugged and fought back the creeping inadequacy that plagued her. For six years, her mother's mind had been tormented by what happened to her, and Dani hadn't been able to do anything to make it better.

Andrea Frost had been an excellent Ink Carrier.

One of the best, according to the Ink. Even Poe said so, which was high praise indeed. Faced with something similar, her mom would have gotten to the bottom of things years ago. Being Andrea's daughter made Dani feel like she was living under a huge shadow. The weight of expectation hung over Dani's shoulders like a constant companion.

"Good luck," Spencer said as she left.

Whether her friend meant the morgue or the hospital, Dani didn't know.

Her phone rang as she neared the hospital, the sky above opaque with angry gray clouds. Raj came to mind as she recalled handing him her business card. She shouldn't have given him her new number, even if it was for a case. A relieved sigh escaped her lips when she read the caller ID.

"Hey, Nick."

"Is this a good time to talk?"

Dani crossed the busy road and headed down the final block to the hospital. "I have a few minutes. Thanks for the photo, by the way."

"That's actually what I'm calling about." Nick paused. "The medical examiner is running a tox screen, but I've got a weird feeling about this one. It feels like a 'you' case."

"A 'me' case?" Dani teased, even though she knew what the detective meant. When a paranormal-adjacent case hit his desk, Nick often called her for aid. Most of the time, she could help get to the bottom of things without exposing him to the city's demonic underbelly. Sure, a lot of the cases ended with Nick finding the murderer already dead—usually a demon done in by Dani herself—but it worked for them.

"Please? I did get you those files."

Dani scoffed as she ducked into the hospital, Nick unable to see the smirk tugging at her lips. "I seem to recall Ellie's parents getting my name from you, Nick." There was a pause, and Dani's shoes clacked against the tile floors as she made her way to the psychiatric ward.

"You know I don't ask for help unless I'm sure."

"I know. I just like making you squirm," she said, and he laughed. "Listen, I gotta run. I'll call you back when I'm free." She hung up and paused a few doors down from her mom's room. The familiar guilt returned with a vengeance and gnawed at her ribs like a feral demon.

Soft voices filtered into the hall as she approached the room. A nurse, most likely. Dani hoped her mother wasn't having one of her episodes.

But when she reached the doorway, her heart stopped.

Raj sat by her mother's bed.

Rajan Dasari sat beside Andrea Frost, her hand clasped in his while he whispered something that Dani couldn't hear. Andrea smiled as he spoke, and then her attention moved from the necromancer and came to rest on her daughter.

Raj stiffened when he spotted Dani standing in the doorway, his face agape. He shouldn't be here. Tears burned in her eyes until she had to look away.

She couldn't do this. She couldn't fight or fall apart in front of her mother. Dani turned on her heel and stormed out of the room. The hallway sped past as she headed for the far stairwell. If she couldn't see her mother, she could at least go to the morgue and look for Ellie. She could—

"Dani, wait!" Raj's voice chased after her.

The first tear spilled over her lashes, and Dani scrubbed it away. She didn't wait for Raj, but his shoes squeaked across the tile floor as he ran to catch up with her. Dani's hands squeezed into fists, and she wished she'd brought her sword.

"Please, Dani." Raj fell into step beside her. "Let me explain."

"Explain *what*, Raj?" She whirled on him, her voice thick with emotion. "In what world is it okay to use *my mother* to get back at me? My visit last night was not an invitation to come waltzing back into my life."

"I didn't know you'd be here." He ran a hand through his hair. It was loose today, the ends curling against the nape of his neck. "You don't normally visit in the morning."

Dani stopped short. "How could you possibly know that?"

Raj paused a few steps ahead, head bowed. A deep sigh expanded his back beneath the crisp gray suit. "I never stopped visiting Andrea. I've been here every week since we … Well, since you and I stopped being a 'we.' The nurses said you only visit late in the day."

"I don't understand. The nurses never mentioned you. They're supposed to tell me if someone visits my mother."

He fussed with the platinum cuff links, not meeting her gaze. "I asked them not to. They wanted to tell you, but I … I donated money to help with the east wing renovations."

Dani knew she should be furious, but the warmth filling her had a gentler edge. "Why would you do that?" She could barely breathe around the lump of emotion stuck in her throat.

"You know why, Danika." Raj reached out, but he seemed to think better of touching her and let his hand drop. He was closer than he must have realized, though, because the backs of his fingers grazed Dani's arm. Her heart clenched as realization washed over her.

Raj kept visiting because he cared. He visited her mother every week for over *two years* because he cared about Andrea. Because he cared about Dani.

But how could he care about the Frost women and still do all the terrible things he'd done? How could he run an establishment like Obsidian at night and make sure his ex-girlfriend's sick mother wasn't lonely in the morning?

Tears threatened again. "I can't do this right now." Dani shoved past him on her way to the morgue. "I'm on a case."

Raj kept pace with her. "Anything I can help with?"

She glared at him. "Money can't solve every problem. Some things require actual work." Dani hoped the jab would send him away, but Raj only pressed his lips into a thin line and followed her downstairs to the morgue.

When they emerged from the stairwell, Dani headed straight for the main doors, but a man in uniform stopped her. "I'm supposed to check the Jane Does for my sister," Dani said, the lie falling effortlessly from her lips.

The security guard shook his head. "There aren't any family visits scheduled for today."

Dani's mind whirled through alternate options to get inside, but Raj rested a hand on her back. "Let me." He stepped forward to talk to the guard, and Dani caught the scent of his cologne. It was the same one he wore while they were together, a crisp scent that always reminded Dani of first snow.

Buried memories took center stage in her mind. Lazy Sundays in bed. Raj wrapped tight around her while flames crackled in the fireplace. Whispered promises kissed into her skin and strong hands massaging knots out of her aching muscles. Of magical nights spent—

No. That life is over. Dani shook the images out of her head. She didn't have time to linger on memories of a life she wouldn't have again. She had a missing girl to find, demon sigils showing up on campaign managers, and the unending search to find the creature that hurt her mother.

She didn't have time for a broken heart.

Not again.

The security guard nodded and reached forward to shake Raj's hand. Raj opened the door and turned back to Dani with an easy smile that lit his entire face. "After you, Miss Frost."

Dani wiped any trace of emotion off her face and stalked through the open door into the morgue. A blast of cool air sent a chill through her as she took in the tables of bodies covered with sheets. Raj followed her inside. "You know, a 'thank-you' is customary when someone does you a favor."

"Do I even want to know what you promised that man in exchange for letting us in?" Dani asked, searching the room for the pathologist. Before Raj could respond, the man walked in through the back and Dani rushed to him. This time, she stuck closer to the truth and told the doctor she was a consultant with Detective Hart. The pathologist complied—Nick having mentioned to the doctor that Dani was working with him—and looked through his inventory, pulling out all the unidentified bodies for the past two weeks since Ellie had gone missing.

As the pathologist pulled body after body, the sheer number of the dead weighed heavily on Dani's already bruised heart. So many people without family to claim them or with families who didn't know where to look. And these were just the women.

"Are there usually so many?" Dani asked as the pathologist lifted the sheet of the first body in the lineup. The woman looked Latinx, so definitely not Ellie.

At the shake of Dani's head, the pathologist repositioned the sheet and slid the woman back in her refrigerated drawer. "Stiffs in general or unidentified ones?"

"Both, I guess." Dani checked the next one. She was at least the right age and race, but she didn't look anything like the photos Dani had of Ellie. "Not her either."

They moved on to the next body. "Numbers have been up a little the past month or so. I could pull a report for your detective if you want."

"No, that's okay." They moved through three more bodies, none of them Ellie, but each one hitting Dani hard anyway. These girls were young, their lives cut way too short.

"This one came in this morning. I haven't had time to examine her yet, but I'd estimate she's been dead around a week." The pathologist pulled down the sheet of the final body. Dani shook her head again, but as she turned away, something strange curling around the girl's shoulder caught her attention.

"Wait." Dani bent to look closer at the mark.

"What is it?" Raj asked over her shoulder.

Dani ignored him. "Can you turn her over? I want to look at this here."

The pathologist grabbed the dead woman's shoulder and turned her onto her side. Dani cursed and pulled out her phone, opening the image Nick had sent earlier.

She called the detective. "Nick? Hey, it's Dani. I'm at the morgue. Can you get back down here? There's something you need to see."

The markings were identical.

Detective Nicholas Hart arrived in precisely ten minutes like he promised. He entered the morgue with an ease and self-assurance that made Dani wonder how much time he spent in the cold room. His navy suit jacket fit well, but next to Raj's perfectly tailored, custom suit, it was clearly off the rack.

Nick looked from Dani to Raj, and suspicion flickered across his face. He settled on a professional smile. "I don't think we've met. I'm Detective Hart."

Raj eyed Nick's outstretched hand and reluctantly shook it. "Rajan Dasari," he said, and Dani noted how the men's knuckles turned white as they each squeezed harder than necessary.

"Dasari?" Nick turned to Dani, a question in the

rise of his brow. "The same Dasaris who run most of the clubs in Blackthorn?"

"The very same." Raj straightened his back. He was still shorter than the detective. "I'm afraid I can't say I've heard of you though." He eyed the detective, wary of any cop who wasn't on his payroll.

Nick ignored the jab. "Is there a reason the club kid is in my morgue?"

"That's a great question. Raj?" Dani smiled sweetly at her ex, the expression cloying and false. "Why *are* you still here?"

The pathologist cleared his throat, cutting off the pissing match between the men. "Did someone want to look at these bodies before they need to go back into refrigeration?"

"Of course." Nick's entire posture transformed. Gone was the man who was interested in Dani and suspicious of the handsome club owner he'd found her with. In his place was a detective, focused solely on his case. "What did you want me to see?"

Dani approached the girl on the table, still positioned on her stomach. "This marking here. It looks—"

"Just like the one on Ricardo," Nick finished. Dani breathed in the masculine scent of his cologne as he stood close, his shoulder brushing hers. "Have any others come in with markings like this?"

The pathologist turned to his computer and searched the hospital database. "Now that you mention it, there was one two weeks ago. A John Doe, homeless as far as the cops who brought him in could tell. Bill, the other pathologist here, did the autopsy."

He brought up an image of a malnourished white man, his skin tanned and dirty, with sunken cheeks and unkempt hair. The pathologist flipped through medical photos until he found one of the man's bare chest. The demon sigil had been burned through skin and hair.

"It's the same," Nick said as Raj stayed quiet in the background.

"Looks like Bill noted similar markings on another of his patients from four weeks ago. Said it was some kind of deliberate scar tissue. Designed like a tattoo."

The next set of images were of a prostitute known only by the pseudonym Candy. This time, the sigil lay branded into her thigh.

Nick frowned. "I think it's safe to say these markings aren't some kind of fad sweeping the city."

Dani turned back to Raj and asked the silent question. Raj shook his head, confirming he didn't recognize the sigil either. Whoever it belonged to was burning through bodies fast. At least four people in as many weeks. Three of the four victims with no family or friends to miss them enough to come looking for them. Was Ellie out there somewhere, her body the latest vessel for this demon? Or was she already used up, and they just hadn't discovered her used corpse yet?

Nick pulled out his phone and took photos of the sigil. "Are all the marked victims unidentified?"

"So far as I know. Except the one you came in about this morning." The pathologist swiveled in his chair and checked his clipboard. "Rick something, yes?"

"Ricardo Nuñez," Nick confirmed. "He wasn't a runaway. I spoke with his fiancée this morning. She reported him missing after he didn't come home from the office two nights ago. He'd been working long hours, but she said he always called if he was going to be home late."

"When did she see Ricardo last?" Dani slipped easily into the investigative habits she'd picked up over the past five years.

"That morning before work. I had my partner speak with Mayor Conrad's chief of staff. She said Ricardo left work promptly at seven." Nick bent closer to the woman's shoulder, careful not to touch her body. "Any idea what kind of tool made those markings? Is it some kind of heated metal?"

Behind her, Raj snickered. He and Dani both knew

exactly what had made those markings, and it sure as hell wasn't a heated blade.

"We haven't found a match," the pathologist said. "No official cause of death yet either, for any of them."

"Strange," Nick mused. "It might be worth talking with Conrad to see what he knows."

Dani squeezed her hand into fists. "Count me in."

"I don't know if that's a good idea, Dani," Raj said, warning threaded through his tone.

"I don't recall asking your opinion," she snapped.

But Raj didn't take the hint. He closed the distance between them and kept his voice low. "You don't want to be on Nathaniel's bad side."

It wasn't Mayor Conrad—rising political powerhouse—that Raj was warning her about. It was Nathaniel Conrad's hidden self that seemed to have her ex-boyfriend worried, the head of the ruthless necromancer family who controlled even more of the city than the Dasaris.

Across the table, Nick scoffed. "On a first-name basis with the mayor, Dasari?"

Raj crossed his arms. "Our families are aware of each other, yes."

"And what?" Nick circled the table until the men were standing toe to toe. With his additional height, Nick stared down at Raj. "You think I can't keep

Danika safe while questioning a high-profile politician who knows better than to threaten the police?"

"What I *know*, Detective, is that you don't have the faintest idea what kind of trouble you've stumbled upon," Raj shot back, and it took all of Dani's considerable resolve not to smack the pair of them. "Why do you even need Dani's help? Can't solve your cases without a private investigator doing all the work?"

Dani grabbed Raj's arm and yanked him back a step. "All right, that's enough. From *both* of you. Raj, outside. Now." She released him, and Raj shook out his jacket. He glared daggers at Nick but headed for the door. "As for you," she said, turning on Nick, "I don't need anyone's protection. I'll be right back."

She left Nick stammering an apology and followed Raj into the hall.

Raj whirled on her the second she reappeared. "Who is this joker? Why are you helping a cop who doesn't know the first thing about your world? About *our* world? Fuck, Dani, he probably thinks the symbols are some new gang sign."

"Nick is a good man and a good detective." Dani led the infuriating—and infuriatingly handsome— necromancer farther down the hall toward the stairs. "I happen to like that he doesn't know about demons."

"Which means he'll never know who you are." Raj spun to face her, and Dani nearly crashed into him.

As it was, she was close enough to kiss him. "He'll never know the *real* you, Danika. Doesn't that bother you?"

"Why should it?" she asked, but her voice came out a breathless whisper. She knew she should step away, but her feet stayed rooted, like some magnetic force held her in place.

"Because he clearly likes you." Raj moved nearer, his hands hovering so close to hers that if she breathed too deeply, they would touch. His voice dipped even quieter. "He'd be a fool not to."

Dani's eyes fluttered closed, but behind her lids all she saw was the sigil seared into the victims' flesh. She came back to herself and stepped away, shaking her head. "None of this is your business. You should go."

"But I—"

"Go, Raj." When he still stalled, Dani sighed. "Unless you know something about the string of dead bodies, there's no point in you being here." The words cut across her tongue, and she flinched as they made impact. Despite his apparent confidence, Raj's shoulders slumped. He stared at her with those beautiful deep brown eyes, an expression she found so hard to resist. But she wouldn't apologize, no matter the emotion written all over his face, so strong it threatened to overwhelm her.

Dani stepped back and gave herself a shake. She had a case to work, and the sooner she got to the bottom of Ellie's disappearance, the faster she could focus on tracking down the demon who hurt her mom.

Thanks to the string of branded dead bodies, Dani now had two cases on her plate. The Ink Carrier couldn't ignore something like this, existing case or not. She'd need to juggle the missing persons job alongside finding out who, or what, the sigil belonged to.

The latter required she talk to Nathaniel Conrad, and as much as she hated to admit it, there were limitations to working with the detective.

There was no way the mayor would reveal anything meaningful to Nick. Not when the detective had no idea of the hidden world that existed in Blackthorn. Necromancers didn't make a habit of outing themselves and went to great lengths to stay underground.

Dani needed real answers. Whatever demon possessed those bodies had a *lot* of power. Too much to ignore. She couldn't allow a demon that strong to tear through innocent people. Dani wouldn't shirk her responsibility to hunt down the monster, even if it meant working with the one man she wanted most to avoid.

Besides, Raj's ability to spot truth from fiction could come in handy should the mayor decide to be less than helpful, even if Dani despised how Raj came into such a power.

"Look," she said, a fresh headache pounding against her skull, "if you really want to help, set up a meeting with Conrad. I'll go with you instead of Nick, if that's what it takes."

He perked up at that, the slightest grin tugging on the corner of his soft lips. "I still think it's a terrible idea, but if you insist on going anyway—"

"I do."

"Then I'd prefer to be there with you."

"Just set up the meeting." She stepped back toward the morgue. "I don't want to see you again until it's arranged. Understood?"

Raj grinned wider. "It'll be just like old times."

He disappeared up the stairwell before Dani could correct him. This would be *nothing* like old times.

Frustrated, Dani returned to the morgue. Nick and the pathologist were theorizing about the connection between victims. Nick smiled at her when she came in alone, but instead of asking after Raj, he stayed focused on the case.

"I think you're right about visiting Mayor Conrad. Ricardo is the only victim who had solid ties to the community. He's different from the rest."

Dani nodded, but her heart wasn't in it anymore. She only half listened while Nick spun various theories, her real attention focused on the computer screen. It had a blown-up version of the sigil, and something about it niggled at her memory. Something about it was familiar, something more than just a lifetime spent staring at similar demonic marks.

One piece in particular, a crescent moon with an arrow piercing the center, stuck in her mind. She knew she'd seen it somewhere before …

A touch on Dani's arm made her jump.

"Sorry," Nick said, stepping back to give her more space. "I called your name a few times. I'm done here, unless you have any other updates?"

"No, I don't have anything else." She ran a hand over her face. It wasn't even lunchtime, and yet she felt like she'd lived a thousand years since waking this morning.

She bid the detective a quick goodbye and regretted sending her staff home early.

Because she needed them.

And it couldn't wait.

An hour later, Dani stood outside Spencer's massive house with a bag of takeout in one hand. Spencer lived on the edge of Blackthorn, where the city gave way to sprawling estates and vibrant green lawns. Crime was nonexistent in the neighborhood, except for the pockets of bored housewives with more money than morals, who traded prescription pills like they were vanity stocks.

She rang the doorbell and elaborate chimes clanged throughout the interior. When the resonant sounds finally faded to silence, even Dani's enhanced hearing didn't pick up anyone inside. She was about to ring again when footsteps approached.

The door opened wide, but it wasn't Spencer on the other side.

"Hey, Dani." Spencer's boyfriend, Adrian, greeted her. His dark hair was cropped short, and he wore slim-fitting jeans and a thick sweater. Deep purple circles sat under Adrian's eyes, and Dani remembered what Spencer had said about med school. It looked like Adrian wasn't getting much sleep, and not for fun reasons. "I take it you're here for Spence?" Adrian asked.

"I feel like an asshole, but yeah. I am." Dani raised the bag of Thai cuisine. "I brought food though."

"He's a little worse for wear," Adrian warned as he led Dani inside.

The house was impeccable as always, reminding Dani of the homes in those interior design magazines they left out in the waiting room of her dentist's office. A far cry from her little apartment. Spencer had chosen clean tones of gray and white for the décor, the freshness accentuated with natural light shining through large windows and the aroma from bouquets of lilies found in every room.

They walked past the living room, where they had all spent many nights eating popcorn and bingeing movies on the plush sofas while bathing in the warmth from the grand fireplace.

Dani's shoes clicked against the gleaming hardwood floors, which always seemed freshly polished, no matter how recently Spencer had hosted one of his wild parties.

"Spence said you sent him home to recover."

Dani followed Adrian up the large winding staircase to the bedrooms, the walls covered with artwork from painters she didn't know the names of. "I did, hence feeling like an asshole. I wouldn't have come if—"

"If it wasn't an emergency. I know the drill." There was no judgment in Adrian's tone. He knew enough about what she and Spencer did at work to know it was important. Though he knew about necromancers and demons, that wasn't part of Adrian's world, and he didn't want it to be. He was a safe space for Spencer to come home to, someone the former necromancer could talk to about his work and then relax into the beautifully mortal world Adrian inhabited.

When she was being honest with herself, Dani was more than a little jealous of their relationship. It was the happy middle she didn't think she could ever find, caught between Rajan, whose entire life was wrapped up in the demonic world, and Nick, who knew nothing of the paranormal.

Yeah, definitely more than a *little* jealous.

Adrian inched open the door to the master bedroom. "We have company, babe." He paused in the threshold while Spencer groaned something unintelligible from underneath the blankets. "Give me a second," Adrian whispered to Dani before slipping inside the room and closing the door behind him.

Dani waited in the hallway and tried not to eavesdrop on the men in the other room, a challenging prospect with her heightened senses. Inside the bedroom, the mattress creaked as it compressed under Adrian's weight, blankets ruffling as they were pulled away. Adrian murmured gentle encouragements to his boyfriend, finally ending with "There's food."

"Okay, okay. I'm up," Spencer said, the bed shifting again. He groaned. "Why didn't anyone warn me that hangovers last so much longer when you're twenty-five?"

"I'll bring up some more painkillers," Adrian promised. His footsteps approached, and the door swung open. "You can go in. He's awake. Mostly."

"Sorry. Again." Dani grimaced. "I know you two don't get much time together these days."

Adrian shrugged. "I was on my way to the library anyway. It was good to see you." He pressed a brotherly kiss to Dani's cheek and slipped down the stairs.

She still felt like an asshole, but there was a reason Dani had come. She pushed into the room and found Spencer sitting up in bed, leaning against the cushioned headboard. "Are you up for Thai food?" She held the bag aloft.

"Always." Spencer reached for the bag and pulled out the box of pad thai, passing the red curry back to Dani. "So, what brings you to my sick bed?"

Dani snorted a laugh as she opened the curry and rice. "Remember that demon sigil I showed you this morning?"

Spencer nodded and shoved a forkful of rice noodles and chicken into his mouth.

"There are at least three other dead bodies with the same mark. All pretty fresh."

"Fuck."

"My thoughts exactly." Dani explained about the

three bodies—a homeless man, a prostitute, and the girl on the slab with the sigil on her shoulder—while Spencer ate. "Whatever is doing this has to be powerful. It's burning through bodies like they're nothing. Raj didn't recognize it either."

"I'm sorry?" Spencer almost choked on his food. "Raj was there?"

A knock at the door cut Dani off before she could respond, Adrian returning with a bottle of water for each of them and a couple of painkillers for Spencer. Dani focused on her curry while Adrian and Spencer shared a quick goodbye, envy tugging at her heart-strings. She wanted so desperately to find love like theirs, but she didn't have the time or space for it.

She wasn't entirely sure a love like that existed for her. Or if she even deserved it.

When Adrian left, Spencer returned to the conversation, his curls now a fiery red. "So. Raj was in the morgue?"

Dani wished she could disappear into the soft mattress. "Not just the morgue," she said. Despite being friends with Spencer for five years, she was never a hundred percent sure what she should tell him about Raj, since the men had been friends since childhood. Even though Spencer reminded her frequently that their relationship wasn't tied to Raj, she still felt bad shit-talking his best friend.

"Come on, Dani. What's going on?"

"He was in Mom's room," she admitted, noting the lack of surprise on Spencer's face. "You knew he still visited."

Spencer paused and chose his words with care. He opened his mouth at least three times to respond before he set his container of pad thai on his knee. "I didn't want to say anything. Raj didn't want to stop visiting, but he didn't want you to feel weird about it. He wasn't doing it for you."

"I know," Dani said, and she was surprised to find that she believed it. If Raj wanted to use the visits to get back into her good graces, he wouldn't have gone *two years* without saying something. Now that she'd had the time and space away from him, she could see that.

It'd be so much easier if he were all bad, if there weren't parts of him that melted her heart while the rest of him shattered her to pieces.

Dani cleared her throat and pressed her fingers under her eyes to stop the tears. "The sigil," she said. "If you and Raj both don't recognize it, any idea which of the other three families might be behind this?"

"It might not be a family." Spencer pulled out his phone. "It could be someone who broke away from the families. A loner, or someone new to town." He dialed a number and set the phone to speaker.

"Who are you calling?" she asked at the same time the phone picked up and a sleepy Lana answered.

"Spence?"

"Sorry to disturb you, Lan. Boss Lady needs us." Spencer set the phone on the bed between them.

Dani scowled at Spencer. "Sorry, Lana."

"It's fine," Lana said, the sleep in her voice already wiped away. Lana was nothing if not professional. "Are you at the office? I can come in."

"We're at my place," Spencer said. "Can you leave us on speaker while you drive?"

"You don't have to come in, Lana." But Danika could already hear the faucet running as Lana brushed her teeth.

Spencer filled her in on what they'd discussed so far while Lana got dressed and headed their way. "With a demon this out of control, I'm inclined to think we have a lone necromancer in our city," Spencer said, sitting up more fully now that his meds seemed to have kicked in. "If one of the families sanctioned this, the demon shouldn't be burning through bodies this fast. Unless …"

Dani set her now-cold curry on the side table. "Unless what, Spence?"

"If the summoning necromancer can't control the

demon, even with family backing, we're not talking some minor-level demon here."

"I'm here. I'll be right up," Lana said, still on the phone fifteen minutes later. Her car door slammed, and the line went dead.

Dani had never wished for a rogue necromancer so hard in her life. Necromancers who weren't tied to a family—necromancers who broke away, like Spencer did, but continued to raise demons—were dangerous and unpredictable. Without a family to back them up, they compensated by raising more powerful demons in an attempt to make up for the family they'd lost. With no group to share the heavy burden of the demonic bargains, loners gave up more than most in exchange for power and influence. They were reckless and often fell prey to the very demons they raised, sacrificing their entire souls in the process.

Yet they were still one person. A single necromancer acting alone was far easier to face than an entire, organized family.

If the alternative to a rogue was a demon so powerful that one of the five Blackthorn families couldn't contain it? Dani shuddered at the thought.

"We need to identify the sigil. We need to know what kind of demon we're dealing with," she said, desperation leaking into her tone.

"I'll hit the books."

"That won't be fast enough. At this rate, we could have another body tomorrow."

The door swung open and Lana stepped into the room, looking more put together than earlier that morning. "I may have an idea."

A surge of hope warmed inside Dani. "What are you thinking?"

"If Spencer and Raj don't recognize the sigil, I know someone who might." Lana slipped off her jacket and set it on the leather armchair in the corner before taking a seat.

"Who?" Dani and Spencer asked in unison.

Lana crossed her legs and rested her fingers on the amulet at her throat. "Pam."

13

"Absolutely not," Dani said as Spencer bit out a strangled, "Are you fucking kidding?"

Lana looked at them both, unconcerned. "Pam knows more about the demonic realm than any of us. She'd be a good resource."

"We're not going to ask a *succubus* for help," Dani insisted. Nothing good ever came from involving demons in her work, especially not one like Pam, who unspooled chaos like a fine thread. She'd seduce everyone in a two-mile radius if given the chance.

Lana squared her shoulders. "Normally, I'd agree with you, but we don't have a lot of time. The bodies are piling up faster than you can track this thing on your own, Dani. If you just talk to Pam—"

"Lana—"

"We can assume the demon has already moved on

153

to another host if Ricardo was dumped last night," Lana said, cutting off her objection. "If we don't figure out who's burning through bodies, the morgue is only going to fill with innocent people."

The room fell silent, and Dani cursed herself. Lana was right, but that didn't mean Dani wanted to do this. Letting them talk to Pam would cost Lana. In more ways than one. Dani hated to do it, but she couldn't argue with Lana's logic.

This new demon posed a huge problem for Blackthorn. Dani and her team had to figure it out before it got any worse. Before the distraction cost Ellie her life. Assuming she was still alive.

"Pam will want something," Dani warned, "for helping us."

"You can't seriously think this is a good idea." Spencer threw back the blanket and climbed out of bed. He raked a hand through his hair, turning it a blue so dark it was nearly black. "After everything we went through to bury Pam where she couldn't hurt anyone, so she couldn't hurt *Lana*, you want to let her out?"

"It's not Dani's decision to make. It's mine," Lana cut in. "I *want* to help. So, stop arguing and help me set up."

Fifteen minutes, and nearly as many arguments, later, the three of them had migrated to the secret top floor of Spencer's home. Dani still wasn't thrilled about the plan, and she could tell by the tension in Spence's shoulders the feeling was mutual.

"Ready?" Lana asked, sitting wrapped in restraints.

"As ready as we're going to get," Dani replied as Spencer secured the locks. "Last chance to change your mind." She kept her voice soft, the question for Lana alone, and let her hand hover over the amulet at Lana's throat.

The ornate pendant, a thin disc covered with swirling magic symbols, hung on a golden chain. Years ago, the amulet had absorbed Caleb Owens's liquified left eye. The Owens necromancer was many things to many people. He was Spencer's much-loathed uncle. Pam's summoner.

And the man who burned away Silas from Dani's arm.

"It's going to be okay," Lana said, trying to soothe Dani when Lana was the one who deserved support right now. "I trust you. I know I'll be safe."

Dani wished she shared Lana's unwavering faith, but she'd make sure Pam behaved. She wasn't about to let the succubus hurt her friend again. "We'll get you back as quickly as we can," she promised, and removed the amulet from around Lana's head.

The moment the amulet lost its connection to Lana, she slumped back in the chair, eyes rolling back in her head. She was unconscious for less than a second before she stirred again and tried to bolt.

Chains bit into Lana's skin, and she hissed. "What the hell is this?"

"Terrible to see you again, Pam." Dani pocketed the amulet and stepped back, surveying the succubus as she rose to power inside Lana. Without the magic of the amulet Spencer made five years ago, Pam would have constant control over Lana's body.

"*Finally*. I thought I was going to die of boredom trapped in here." Pam pouted her lips and slumped back in the chair, staring down at the black slacks and cream sweater. "I mean, seriously. Who dresses like this?"

Dani always thought Lana dressed rather stylish, if a bit reserved. She was professional and more put together than Dani could ever hope to be. But knowing Pam, she wouldn't be happy unless she was dressed for the club.

Beside her, Spencer crossed his arms, unamused. "How much of the last five years have you seen?"

"Five *years*? No wonder I'm so hungry." Pam pulled again at the chains that bound her, but Dani wasn't concerned. Spencer spelled the metal to withhold demonic energy. Pam wasn't going anywhere.

"Focus, succubus." Spencer massaged his temples

as if the succubus had reignited his headache. "How much have you seen?"

Pam bat her lashes at the pair of them. "If one of you gives me a kiss, I might just tell you."

"Not interested," Dani and Spencer deadpanned at the same time. Neither made a habit of kissing demons.

"Pity." Pam licked her upper lip seductively, hungry eyes roving all over Spencer. "I bet your energy tastes amazing."

Spencer groaned. "I'm way too sober for this."

"Let's focus," Dani said, drawing Pam's attention back to her. "I have more important questions for you."

If Dani knew anything about succubi, Pam was probably too bored with Lana's life to pay much attention to it. That's if the amulet even let her see anything at all. Most demons aren't interested in sharing a host's body—they want to be in complete control. At least until they use it up and move on to someone else.

For a demon to possess a living human instead of a corpse, they needed that person's permission—they needed to strike a *deal*. Only the most desperate would agree to the time-share bargain Lana and Pam had before Dani met them. But with Cassie's cancer diagnosis, Lana had been as desperate as they come.

She would have agreed to anything to save her little sister, including giving Pam permission to control her body.

Pam fluttered her lashes again, all innocence. "And what might those be?"

"We need to know who this belongs to." Dani pulled up the photos on her phone and showed the sigils to the bound succubus.

But Pam wouldn't even look at the screen. Instead, she twisted Lana's face into a mockery of a grin. "And why should I help you? All you'll do is lock me away again."

Dani forced herself not to smack Pam across the face, knowing Lana would be the one to feel it later. Pam had a knack for getting under people's skin. "What do you want?"

"Control of my body again, of course." Pam shrugged as best she could while being bound.

The absurdity of the request, despite how expected it was, made Dani bark out a bitter laugh. "I'm not letting you control *Lana's* body." Pam had done enough damage the last time she was allowed to roam free.

Pam pouted. "It was worth a try."

"If you want a *bargain* ..." Dani paused to let the tantalizing word sit in the air between them. Once a bargain was struck between human and demon, no one, not even the strongest necromancer or demon on this plane of existence or any other, had the power to break it. "You need to propose something more reasonable in exchange for the name."

Pam practically vibrated with excitement. "The Ink Carrier wants to bargain? Do you have permission from the host?"

"Yes, Lana gave me permission to make a deal on her behalf," Dani replied, hating herself for ever agreeing to this.

Pam considered her for a moment, mischief all over her face. "Well then, to help you in your quest, I want a year of control."

"Two hours."

"Six months."

"Three hours."

"One month."

"A day," Dani said, nearing the limit of what Lana agreed to before they woke the demon inside her.

Pam smiled, like she could sense Dani's bargaining powers nearing their end. "A week," the succubus said smugly, tipping up her chin.

Squaring her shoulders, Dani went in with an offer she hoped the succubus couldn't refuse. "Three consecutive nights, from sundown to sunup. No one from my team will tail you, but you must be back at Lana's house before the sun rises." Dani grimaced at just the thought of how much trouble and debauchery a demon like Pam could get into in that length of time. Dani planned to give Lana at least two weeks off from work to recover from Pam's three-night binge of shenanigans.

"Interesting," Pam said, enunciating each syllable. "What's the catch?"

"The bargain won't be complete until the demon is banished." Dani glared at Pam. "And you can't kill anyone, or do anything to alter Lana's physical form."

"Well, that's no fun."

Dani ignored Pam's complaints. "Do we have a deal?"

"Ugh, fine." Pam sagged in her chair. "The bargain is set."

An ice-cold power gripped Dani's spine. It came on so fast, so unexpectedly, that it stole her breath from her lungs.

"You all right?" Spencer, who had remained quiet while Dani set this bargain, rested a hand on her back.

"I'm fine." But she shuddered again as the power of the bargain swept through her.

"You did good," he whispered, though Dani couldn't help but think of what her deal would cost her friend. It had taken Lana months to get over the first time Pam ran amok with her body. Despite that,

Lana had agreed to give up five nights. At least Dani had been able to spare her two of them.

"Did I just take your bargain virginity, Carrier?" Pam laughed, the sound high and brittle. "I'm honored."

Dani shook off the last of the cold and opened her phone. "Enough. Now, tell me who made this."

Pam's gaze finally flicked to the phone, and her whole demeanor changed. Her smile fell, skin going ashen as all of her usual mischief vanished.

"Well?" Dani prompted, Spencer's warm hand still a steadying presence at her back. When Pam didn't answer right away, just went back to staring at the sigil, Dani realized something that send a fresh wave of chills down her spine.

The succubus was afraid.

"You should leave this one alone, Ink Carrier," Pam warned, sounding much more like Lana than she ever had before.

"Why?" Spencer asked.

"This is no lesser demon you're dealing with." Pam's bottom lip trembled. "This is old magic. Ancient, and far greater than anything you've come across in your lifetime."

"We need a name," Dani snapped, ignoring the hairs that stood on end at the back of her neck.

"He's gone by many names over the last millennium" Pam made to speak, but it was like fear closed her throat. When she forced out the words, her voice was harsh and cutting like razor blades. "Bet'uel, Tzuri'el, and Menachem. Esias, Uthyr, and Ozi. But most of my kind call him the Soul Stealer."

The Ink grew tense and stirred underneath Dani's skin.

Quiet settled over the room like frost, prickling everything with cold. "The other succubi call him that?" Dani asked, a deep-seated fear crawling inside her.

"Not just succubi," Pam said. "All demons. Whoever raised him must not have known. Because if he's here, you're all fucked, and not in the fun way."

"I need his name," Dani insisted, though every instinct told her to call to her Ink.

Pam shook her head.

"We made a deal, demon. One you must abide to. I need his name. His *true* name."

When Pam finally spoke, her voice was barely audible in the silent room, each word sounding like it physically hurt her to utter.

"Verloc Djurian Rlenheim."

14

Verloc Djurian Rlenheim.

The name seared itself in Dani's mind. After they returned Lana's amulet and locked Pam away, Dani and Spencer led Lana downstairs to rest. Lana insisted she was fine—and she probably would be—but their combined guilt and worrying was enough to convince Lana to rest for a while.

Dani wanted to apologize a hundred times for the bargain she'd struck with the succubus, despite the whole thing being Lana's idea. As foreign as it felt—even after five years working together—Dani *was* the boss. She was the Ink Carrier and should be able to do her job without forcing her staff into demonic bargains.

Nevertheless, the deal with Pam had given them vital information.

All demons went to great lengths to keep their true names hidden. The wielder of a true name wasn't given complete control of the demon, as many fairy tales would have people believe, but it did make several things possible. Key among them? The ability to trace the demon to the necromancer who brought it into this realm.

There was a catch though—there's *always* a catch.

Dani needed another necromancer to perform the spell.

After a series of quick goodbyes, Dani left her friends behind. Outside the air was cool, the sun still high in the sky. Dani checked that no one was near, then called for Poe.

The raven released from her skin, a tugging pain at her chest, and soared into the sky—the cloud of ink solidifying into the bird's corporeal form. For several blocks, they traveled in silence, Poe riding the wind while Dani walked down the sidewalk at a brisk pace. Eventually, Poe perched atop a branch at the end of the block. He waited until Dani neared before cocking his head to one side. He wanted to know why she'd released him.

"Did any of my ancestors run into a demon

known as Verloc Djurian Rlenheim?" Dani asked as she passed under Poe's branch. She tried to remember the other names Pam said—Ozi and … *something.* It didn't matter. The true name would get her what she needed.

Poe swooped past like an angry storm cloud. *Not that I remember,* his voice rang out in her head. *And I remember* everything.

"Of course you do." Even if Poe didn't recognize the name, it was still possible one of her ancestors had faced the demon. According to Kiva, each generation of Carriers tended to slay first and ask names later.

Shall I recount all your childhood misadventures, Danika? What about the time you stole your mother's—

"Poe, that's *enough,*" she said, and immediately felt bad for yelling at him. But she didn't have any emotional room left for a trip down memory lane, especially not one that centered around her mother.

The mother she'd failed to protect so many times.

Her current destination didn't help her mood either. "According to my sources," Dani said, avoiding mention of Pam to prevent yet another of Poe's infamous lectures, "Verloc is the demon tearing through bodies like they're a midafternoon snack. I need to find out who raised him."

Poe flew past, the wind off his wings buffeting her face in a gentle rebuke for snapping at him. *Why not ask the chameleon?*

"Spencer isn't a necromancer anymore. I won't ask him to break his vow."

Unlike the other four necromantic families in Blackthorn, the Owens clan were especially hard on their young initiates. Spencer never told Dani what his parents had done to him, but she knew they *gifted* him with a terrible power that nearly ate away his soul. The second Spencer turned eighteen, he took on one final ability—the power he uses to understand magic like science and create demon-killing inventions like banishing bullets and Dani's retractable sword.

But whatever his parents did to him left a mark, and Dani would never ask her friend to interact with the demonic world. Never.

Unfortunately, that only left her with one option.

Dani turned up the next street, and Poe landed on a roof a few buildings ahead. He twisted his head, surveying the area of the city they'd passed into. *Are we visiting Rajan, then?*

"I am," Dani clarified. "You're welcome to return or stalk the skies."

And why can't I visit with Rajan too?

She forced herself to count to three before

responding. "This isn't a social call, Poe. It's a negotiation—with a *necromancer*. I need him to do me a favor, which means he'll probably want something in return." Dani would never understand how Poe justified his adoration for Raj, especially since he hated every other necromancer in existence.

It was baffling. And more than a little frustrating.

Poe ruffled his feathers. *Well then, I'd better come along to ensure you don't bargain away too much.*

Dani didn't bother arguing. It was easier to let Poe do what he wanted when he got like this. When she had first inherited the Ink, Dani took each one of Poe's jabs personally, letting them make her feel inadequate and useless. Growing up, whenever Andrea asked Poe to teach Dani, he was an impatient tutor, but Dani never felt like a disappointment. So it had come as a shock to Dani's system when the bird grew snappy and irritable once she became Ink Carrier, picking at her every flaw.

Over time she'd learned it was simply the curmudgeon's attitude. Kiva had explained that it was his way of showing he cared, which was true enough. When push came to shove, Poe was the most protective of her Ink and threw himself into danger to save her at all costs. Knowing what she knew now, the cranky old bird's barbs only stung a tiny portion of the time.

At the intersection, Dani paused. Obsidian lay one

block to the east, Raj's luxury home to the west. Given the time of day, Dani made a left as there was a good chance Raj hadn't gone into work yet.

Unbidden, memories of lazy mornings in Raj's bed came back to her. Her heart swelled to remember his bed-tousled hair and the sleepy grin that curved his lips before he pulled her body to his and pressed kisses to the curve of her neck. She never forgot who or what Rajan Dasari was, but she had always felt safe in his arms.

But seeing his massive home come into view sent stabs of nerves prickling against her skin. Things were different now. If what Pam said about Verloc proved true, Dani was hunting down an enemy unlike anything she'd faced before, and she couldn't be sure which side Raj would ultimately choose. Which side of her family's generational war he would be on.

Poe got to the house first and perched on an ornate light post in the yard. He waited, uncharacteristically silent, as Dani stepped up the pristine stone walkway to the front door. Once upon a time, Dani had her own key to this door. When she and Raj split, he didn't believe she was serious until she had come to the house while he was at Obsidian, removed every trace of herself, and left the key behind on the kitchen counter.

Raj had called a thousand times after that. He wanted to fix things, but he couldn't understand the lines Dani had to draw for herself. It would have been easier had something big happened to make her end it. If Raj had cheated or betrayed her, he might have understood why she left.

Instead, it was a thousand tiny things, each one driving a wedge further between them, until Dani had to be honest with herself, had to be honest about her role as Ink Carrier. Walking the line between good and evil wasn't a choice for her.

Dani ascended the stairs and raised her first to knock before she changed her mind and left.

The door swung open before she got the chance and Raj, still dressed in the same gray suit from that morning, stood on the other side. He held his phone in one hand, like he was about to make a call. Confusion pulled at his brows when he spotted her. "Danika? What are you doing here? Did something happen?"

"Things are fine. I just need ..." Dani faltered as her mind filled with all the things she used to want from him—a friend, a lover, a sounding board for all her insecurities and her deepest fears. "A favor," she finished.

Raj considered her. "Two favors in as many days?"

A teasing note threaded through his tone, but when she didn't respond, his smile faded. "I was just about to call you. We have a meeting with Mayor Conrad."

Before Dani could reply, Poe swooped down from the roof and perched on Raj's shoulder. To his credit, the necromancer didn't flinch as the bird pecked affectionately at his ear. *Are you sure you don't want to get back together?* Poe asked, his voice audible to Dani alone.

"I'm sure." She glared at the traitorous bird, but at least Raj knew better than to ask what Poe had said. During the years they'd dated, he got used to the way Dani communicated with the Ink.

But you're running out of time, Poe insisted. *Without an heir to Carry the Ink, we'll be lost if you ...* Poe trailed off, which was such an unusual occurrence that Dani almost forgot to be upset about Poe's obsession with her reproduction. But he just couldn't let it go. *If Raj isn't suitable, there's always the detective.*

"I am *not* having this conversation. Poe, return." Dani bore the pain while her raven did as ordered. As soon as he was secure within her skin, his frustration echoed through her, paired with his anxiety about her lack of offspring.

Thankfully, Kiva's calming presence kept it from getting too unbearable.

"You okay?"

"The dumb bird knows how to ruffle my feathers." She was *not* about to go into the details of her and Poe's conversation with Raj of all people. "You said the mayor was willing to meet with us?"

"Yes." Raj closed the door to his house and locked up. "He said he could meet with us today."

"Really?" Dani hadn't expected the mayor to see them so soon. His schedule should have been full of meetings and appointments for his campaign trail. "How did you pull that off?"

Raj's slick black Jaguar sat waiting for him in the driveway, and he opened the passenger door for Dani. "Nathaniel owed me a favor. Said he could squeeze us in for a quick chat."

Dani didn't ask what Raj had done to earn a favor from the Conrad necromancer. She didn't want to know. Instead, she slid into the front seat, the leather warm even through her clothes, and tried to figure out how to ask the man she used to love for help without owing him something in return.

They rode in silence all the way to the edge of Blackthorn, cramped city streets giving way to a spacious neighborhood even more affluent than the one where Spencer lived.

Dani debated whether she should call Detective Hart to come with them, but that morning's meeting between Nick and Raj hadn't exactly gone well. She trusted Nick to remain professional, especially with the mayor, but she wasn't eager for a repeat performance of their posturing.

Raj drove slowly down the winding path to the estate, wheels crunching over the finest gravel. They passed luxurious lawns with the greenest grass Dani had ever seen. Several gardens were carefully placed along the grounds, many dotted with custom sculptures. As they neared the entrance, they passed a rather large marble statue of a winged creature. Others might mistake the creature for some ancient god or forgotten angel, but Dani recognized the creature for what it was: an Andras demon.

The lavish wealth of it all—and the mockery of a politician blatantly displaying demonic symbols around his home—made her sick. And when she laid eyes on the hulking mansion, she could hardly contain the fury building inside her.

"We need to play this smart," Raj warned when her knuckles cracked. He came to a stop in front of the house, and a man in a well-tailored suit walked down the steps to greet them.

The butler, because of *course* the mayor had a full staff for a house like this, led them inside. They moved through rooms filled with expensive art, traveling over tile floors that shimmered with gold. Shelves along the walls were filled with photographs of the mayor with political figures and low-grade celebrities, debate team trophies from his years at university, and strange artifacts that she couldn't even begin to guess at their purpose or origin. It took all of Dani's considerable restraint to keep herself from knocking over every ornate vase that they passed on their way to Nathaniel's study.

"Rajan!" a booming voice said the moment they entered the mahogany-paneled room. Mayor Conrad looked to be in his late forties, perhaps early fifties, with light brown hair streaked through with gray at the temples in a way that made him appear distinguished rather than old. He wore a navy suit with an American flag pinned to his lapel, like he was about to go on national television at any moment, with a veneer-white politician's smile spread across his tanned face. "How good to see you again."

Raj returned a warm smile. "Always a pleasure, Nathaniel." The men shook hands, and though it wasn't quite the same show of dominance Dani had witnessed in the morgue, it was clear the men were sizing up the competition.

Witnessing Raj interact with the other necromancer sent a shudder of annoyance through Dani. She hated the false, political politeness on display as they laughed and caught up on trivialities, like they were good friends. Instead, their families were locked in a constant battle for more power and control over Blackthorn. Sure, alliances sprung up from time to time between the families, but it was near impossible to keep up with the shifting allegiances. None of them ever really trusted any of the others, always looking for their chance to come out ahead.

Raj and Nathaniel probably had some mutual business venture for them to be this excruciatingly polite. The display acted as a reminder that Raj was now the head of the Dasari family. His necromantic power, along with his responsibilities to his family, had only grown stronger since his father passed away. Being in charge meant he knew everything that went on among his own clan, and that he would be the one making deals and alliances with the likes of Nathaniel.

"Conrad," Raj addressed the mayor by his surname like they were college buddies, "allow me to introduce my friend, Danielle Winters. She's the reason I set this meeting."

"Miss Winters." The necromancer held out his hand, and though Dani didn't want to touch him, she complied, fighting the urge to squeeze until his fingers broke. Instead of the firm handshake she expected, Mayor Conrad pressed a kiss to the back of her hand. "Rajan seemed quite insistent that I carve out a few minutes for you," he said when he released her. "How can I be of service?"

"I'm looking into one of your staffers, Ricardo Nuñez." Dani reached into her back pocket for her phone, subtly wiping the unwanted kiss off her hand in the process. "I'm hoping you might know something about his death."

"Ricardo?" Mayor Conrad asked, pronouncing the name like he was unfamiliar with it.

Dani pulled up the photo of the dead man. "He works on your campaign."

The mayor feigned distress at the sight of the dead body, though Dani doubted the sight was anything new, especially for a necromancer of his influence. "I'm sorry, Miss Winters. I'm sure you're right, but I have so many people helping with my campaign. I can't possibly remember them all, let alone their names." He flashed another smile, a predator baring its teeth. "I'm sure you understand."

"What I understand, *Conrad*, is that a man is dead." Dani shoved the phone back into her pocket and wished, not for the first time, that she'd brought her sword with her. Threatening the mayor might not be the smartest move, but it sure as hell would be satisfying.

"The mayor is a busy man," said a voice behind her. Dani turned and found a mousy-looking man with shabby brown hair and a rodent-like nose. He introduced himself as the mayor's assistant. "I already spoke with the police about Ricardo's death this morning. Mr. Nuñez was part of the campaign team, not Nathaniel's actual campaign manager, so he didn't have any real contact with the mayor. He was at work until seven that night and went home, as far as any of us knew."

"And that's the last you saw him?" Dani asked.

"Yes," the assistant said. "That's the last time I saw him."

Dani turned back to Raj, hoping for confirmation for what she felt in her bones. That the assistant, probably another necromancer or a wannabe, knew more than he was saying. But instead of confirming her theory, Raj shot her a warning look.

Which likely meant his ability to sense lies from truth was picking up on the blatant lie.

"Can anyone verify that you didn't see Ricardo after seven?" Dani pressed. "Do you have an alibi for that night? What about you, Mayor? Where were you the night Ricardo was killed?"

Mayor Conrad turned a satisfied shade of furious

red, but before he could respond, Raj stepped in. "Dani, that's enough." He placed himself between her and the mayor. "I'm sorry about her, Nathaniel. She gets a little overprotective of the victims she investigates."

"I understand." The mayor straightened his tie. "And I appreciate a woman with some spark, but I'm afraid I can't be of more help. I'll make sure my assistant sends Ronaldo's family everything they need to cover funeral costs. It's the least I can do after all his hard work on the campaign."

"Ricardo," Dani snapped, the edge in her voice as sharp as her sword. "His name was Ricardo."

"Of course. Ricardo."

Dani bit back a retort, afraid she might say too much. Bringing up the sigil on Ricardo's back would raise questions about who she was, and that was attention she'd rather avoid.

Despite what the mayor might pretend, he didn't give a shit about his dead staffer. The shady little assistant was likely coming up with some spin on the staffer's death to make his boss look good. News of Nathaniel's donation to Ricardo's family would make it to the newsrooms to bolster his image for the senate campaign.

At least it was one less worry for Ricardo's family,

even if the intention behind the donation was selfish and left a sour taste in Dani's mouth.

"We really should be going." Raj shook the mayor's hand again. "Thank you so much for taking the time to meet with us. I'm sure you're very busy."

Nathaniel let out a deep, smug laugh. "You don't know the half of it. Between the campaign, tonight's fundraising gala, and my responsibilities as mayor, this little meeting already has me running late for the rest of the day."

"Then we'll be out of your hair." Raj placed a hand on Dani's lower back and steered her out of the room.

But Dani wasn't about to be manipulated that easily. People were dead thanks to a demon that raised a deep-rooted fear in Pam, a demon Dani would have said wasn't afraid of anything.

Four victims marked with the same sigil on their corpses, and those were just the ones they knew about. There was no telling how long the demon had been burning through bodies like they were daily outfits to discard once worn. Or how many would meet the same fate as Ricardo, who went out to work one day and never returned home.

People like Ellie. A girl alone in the city with no one but a pimp for a boyfriend and parents back home who knew nothing about her real life.

Ellie who matched the homeless man and the

nameless prostitute in that no one would really miss her. Or even notice she'd gone missing until her parents grew worried from out of state.

It never occurred to Dani until now that both cases might be connected.

Dani spun out of Raj's grip and turned back to face the mayor and his assistant. "I forgot to mention. I'm a friend of Ellie's. She asked me to say hi."

Mayor Conrad froze, the mask of warmth falling from his face before he quickly replaced his fake smile. It only took him a moment to realign his facade; politicians were the best liars and bullshitters out there. But Dani caught it. The mix of shock and recognition.

"You know, Ellie. Ellie the—"

Nathaniel held his hands out for her to stop. "I'm sorry, Miss Winters. I'm very busy."

The necromancer eyed his assistant, who opened the door for them to leave.

"Tell your friend I said hello."

Without another word, Conrad sat back down behind his desk and fussed over some paperwork like they were never there.

"Come on, Dani," Raj whispered in her ear before she could respond. He grabbed her by the arm and had to practically drag her out of the Conrad estate.

When they were safely tucked back in Raj's car

and off the Conrad property, she whirled on him. "What the hell is wrong with you?"

"Me? You're the one who nearly got us killed." Raj took the next turn too fast, and the tires squealed against the asphalt. "You can't go into a meeting guns blazing, spewing accusations and suspicions like they're the damn air you breathe. That doesn't work with people like Conrad."

"People like *you*, you mean."

And it was true. That meeting proved every fear she had when she was dating Raj. His refusal to leave necromancy, his insistence that he could toe the line and still manage to bring good into the world, was corrupting him. It was slower than it might have been if he fully embraced the same path his father had, but Raj inched so incrementally toward the side of demons that he didn't even notice that they were becoming enemies.

It broke her heart, even as it enraged her.

Raj pressed harder on the accelerator. "I was born into this life, Danika. You should understand that better than anyone. The pressure I'm under. How it feels to have your entire life laid out before you were even born. I wouldn't have chosen this, but I have to play the cards I was dealt."

Dani did know. She understood the weight of obligation, but there was always a choice. She could choose to ignore her duties and keep the Ink locked within her skin. She could give up on this life. She could let the world be overrun by demons.

Instead, she embraced her destiny, because she believed the world was worth saving, even if it meant sacrificing her own dreams to do so.

Was that what Raj was doing too?

"The mayor and his assistant were lying," Dani said, ignoring the shades of truth in what Raj told her.

"I know." Raj said the words simply, but Dani took his agreement to heart. One of Raj's demon-giving powers, the one she resented the most while they'd been together, was the ability to detect lies with near-perfect precision.

"Then why didn't you say something while we were there? We could have used that—"

"To what, Dani? Piss off a master necromancer, in his own home, without backup?" Raj let out an exasperated sigh. "I would never put you in that kind of danger."

Dani fell silent after that. She didn't have any energy left to argue with him.

As they returned to the city, her mind kept slipping back to her earlier thoughts. As much as she tried to focus on what it meant for her case that the mayor was indeed lying, having a piece of her past sitting next to her in the driver's seat caused Dani to think of her future. Of the future Poe pestered her about, one where she was supposed to produce an heir for the Ink as quickly as possible.

But Dani wasn't ready to be a mother. Hell, she didn't know if she *ever* wanted to have children. She wasn't sure she could subject another soul to this life.

How could she raise a child, knowing all the while *this* was their future?

Dani placed a hand on her stomach and stared out at the darkening sky. That fear, that uncertainty, was the reason she sought a doctor for long-term birth control shortly after she started dating Raj. She wasn't ready to risk pregnancy. Wasn't sure if she would curse a child with this kind of life.

She wasn't even sure what would happen if an Ink Carrier and a necromancer had a child together.

The five-year expiration on her birth control would be up soon, but she had hoped her mother would be well before then. She wanted her mother there to counsel her through this choice, to help her decide if she was ready to become a mother herself. To continue the Frost line so the Ink could pass to her daughter when she died, just like they had for generations of Frost women.

When Raj pulled over in front of Bloody Mary's, he killed the engine. "Dani, I—"

"Don't bother." Weariness had replaced her anger.

She reached for the handle and opened her door. "I made a mistake when I asked for your help. I don't want you in my life anymore."

Raj watched her, and his dark brown eyes shimmered with tears. "You're lying."

"I don't care." She slammed the door, turned toward the bar, and didn't look back.

Dani paced her apartment, mind whirring with all the epic failures of her day. It was hard to believe that finding Raj at her mother's bedside wasn't even the worst of it. All of it flashed through her head—the sigils at the morgue, using Pam to identify them, the name Verloc Djurian Rlenheim meaning nothing to the Ink.

At least she hadn't asked Raj to use the demon's true name to find the necromancer who summoned it. There was no way she wanted him that involved now, not after how he'd acted around the mayor. But that left her with next to zero leads.

Except … Nathaniel Conrad knew Ellie, even without her surname. The necromancer might not have admitted to anything else, but there was no denying the fear that flitted across his face at the mention of Ellie. Especially since Raj's power picked up the lie—even if he wouldn't *do* anything with that information.

But what did Conrad expect her to say? Ellie the barmaid?

Ellie the *escort*?

Dani grabbed her jacket and slung it on. There was still a man—if he could be called that—who might have information for her.

Sean McGrath's place looked as beaten down as the first time she'd been there, and Dani wasted no time with pleasantries when she got up to his floor. She aimed a kick at the lock, and the door burst open, chains snapping and wood splintering from the force behind it.

Ellie's ex-boyfriend-slash-pimp startled from his place on the couch and sent an avalanche of empty beer bottles crashing to the floor. Sean whirled around, his hands coming up in fists like the world's worst boxer, but his face drained of color when he spotted Dani. "What are *you* doing here?" he asked with far less bravado than Dani guessed he intended.

At least he seemed to have learned his lesson after their last visit.

"Why didn't you tell me about Mayor Conrad?"

Sean had the audacity to look confused. "What about him?"

"Cut the bullshit, McGrath." Dani reached for her sword, the poor excuse for a man watching her every movement. Good. He should fear her.

"I don't—"

Dani tightened her grip but didn't pull the weapon loose. "I've had a hell of a day, and my patience for fuckery is nonexistent."

Sean measured the distance between Dani and the door. He shifted his weight. Then with a sudden burst of speed, he dove around the couch. Dani sighed at his pitiful attempt at escape. She drew her sword, flicked the magically hidden blade into place, and threw.

The sword arced through the air and embedded itself into the wall, mere millimeters from Sean's head.

"One last time," Dani said as she approached the trembling man. "The mayor."

His knees buckled, and Sean sank to the floor, crawling away from her. "I work with a lot of politicians," he admitted. "I'm the supply guy."

Dani yanked her sword from the wall and rested the flat of the blade across her shoulder. "What kind of supplies?"

"Whatever they ask for. Drugs and information, mostly. But sometimes ..." He trailed off until Dani tapped the tip of her blade against his ankle. "Girls.

Sometimes I send girls to the mayor's parties, up at that big mansion of his."

"Girls like Ellie?" Dani pressed.

Sean nodded, bottom lip quivering. "Ellie was his favorite. He asked for her every time, even paid double the normal rate to get her."

"Do a lot of your clients have favorites?"

"It's pretty common." Sean pulled himself back to his feet and appraised her. "I bet you'd be worth even more, depending on what you're willing to do."

"If you'd like to keep *all* your favorite body parts," Dani said, voice silky smooth, "don't say that kind of shit again." She twirled her blade and pointed it at the man's crotch, her meaning clear. "Now, you're going to tell me everything you know about Mayor Conrad or I might chop off a few pieces anyway."

Sean muttered profanities under his breath, but when Dani inched the blade closer, he yelped and held up his hands. "Fine. It's all the typical politician shit. Exclusive parties where the most VIP members get access to all kinds of drugs and booze in the back rooms. And girls. Conrad and his ilk pay a *lot* for their privacy, so if any of this gets back to me—"

"That will be the least of your problems, McGrath. Promise." Dani paced the filthy apartment, past stacks of crusty takeout boxes and empty bottles. Cigarette butts littered the stained carpets, peppered with ash and burn marks.

It made sense that Conrad paid for discretion. He'd built his image as a good man and loving husband. If voters knew their upstanding family man took advantage of young, desperate women, his popularity would plummet.

At least, Dani hoped it would. With politics lately, she was never sure just what voters were willing to forgive in their white male candidates.

"When was the last time Ellie worked one of the mayor's parties?"

Sean stumbled to his feet and leveled an uneven shrug at her. "I don't know. Maybe two months ago?" He squirmed under her intense stare.

"What happened that night?" she demanded.

"Nothing out of the ordinary." He bit at the corner of his thumb, and Dani didn't need Raj's ability to know that Sean was lying.

It would be fun to let one of the Ink out to intimidate this fool—Kiva would have the best effect—but Dani couldn't take the risk of Sean running back to Conrad with stories of living tattoos. She'd manage to hide her identity as the Ink Carrier from most of the necromancers in Blackthorn, and she intended to keep it that way.

Instead, she aimed with her sword and dug it into

the wall again, so close to Sean's manhood that the fabric of his shorts threaded where they touched the razor-sharp metal. Sean's eyes bulged out of his head and he heaved with frantic gasps.

"One more lie, and I start chopping. What happened at that final party?"

Sean stared down at the sword, then shook his head. "You wouldn't hurt me."

Dani withdrew the blade from the wall and lashed out to slice across his neck. The cut was shallow, but a line of red still welled up along his skin. She didn't say anything else. She didn't have to.

Sean touched his neck and swayed when his fingers came back red. The *supply guy* spilled his guts.

"I told Ellie to record them screwing," he said, holding his bleeding neck like it was a gaping wound instead of a nick to the skin. "I even gave her the video stuff to do it with. The mayor is into some freaky shit. Rough as hell too. I knew he'd fork over a lot of cash to bury footage like that. What with the election and everything."

"You blackmailed your own client?" Dani raised an eyebrow at him. "You do realize you royally screwed yourself over. No other politicians will work with you if any of them find out."

"The money was too good to pass up." A wry smile pulled at his chapped lips. "Besides, I ran the actual blackmail through Ellie. Conrad doesn't know I'm involved."

"And you actually did it? You told Conrad about the video and asked him to pay up?"

Sean puffed up his chest like he was proud of himself. "The first package of money arrived within the hour."

"When was that?"

"A few weeks ago."

"And you never stopped to consider what else the mayor might do to bury evidence like that?" If Conrad killed Ellie because of the blackmail, she was going to let Jasper eat this human-shaped garbage can. "How long after the payment did Ellie go missing?"

"Umm …" Sean screwed up his face, like thinking was hard for him. "It was right around the time the second payment was supposed to show up." He frowned. "You don't think she ran off with my money, do you?"

Dani's only answer was to drop her sword and punch the vile man in the mouth.

Nick called when Dani was halfway home.

"I have a lead," he said, and Dani agreed to go with

him. She waited outside Bloody Mary's for Nick's car —a nondescript gray sedan—and slipped into the passenger seat.

"Where are we going?" Dani asked when Nick pulled away from the curb. His driving was like everything else about him—careful, thoughtful, and safe.

"I'm meeting with Ricardo's fiancée." He reached across Dani and popped open the glove box, producing a case file.

Her stomach fluttered as he handed over the file, and she was hit with the sudden urge to reach out and touch him. To thread her fingers through his and forget about work for a moment. If the detective made the first move and let his hand rest on her knee, she'd let him. But Dani pushed all those thoughts aside. There wasn't time. Instead, she flipped through the paperwork.

"Julia Scott, thirty-two," Dani read aloud. Attached was the image of a white woman with golden hair and a soft smile. "Do you think she knows anything?"

Nick nodded once and inched into the intersection to make a left when the lane was clear. "I'm hoping she'll have more information on her fiancé's connection to the mayor."

"About that ..." Dani hesitated, debating whether to mention *how* she managed to get a meeting with the mayor. "I spoke with Mayor Conrad this afternoon."

"Why am I not surprised?" Thankfully, Nick seemed impressed at her initiative rather than pissed at her for stepping on his toes. He'd always respected her work, and her opinion, which made guilt niggle at the back of her mind as she relayed everything she'd learned during the meeting.

When she finished—excluding any mention of Raj —she continued with Ellie's good-for-nothing ex-boyfriend. "McGrath was blackmailing the mayor. He has a sex tape of him and Ellie."

Detective Hart knit his brows together. "And you trust your source?"

"Not as far as I can throw him," Dani said, though she could probably throw the skinny man a fair distance. "But he seemed genuinely distressed that the blackmail money had dried up. He cared a hell of a lot more about that than Ellie's disappearance." She paused, choosing her next words with care. "I think Conrad had something to do with Ellie going missing. He was shocked when I brought her up. And even if he didn't do anything directly, there's definitely *something* going on with him." *Something more than his normal necromantic dealings,* she thought to herself.

As much as it would simplify things for her, Dani didn't think she could tell Nick about her world.

While used to witnessing strange things at work, he always found a human explanation. There was no hint he suspected the existence of the paranormal.

"You know I trust your judgment, Dani. Always have."

"I'm sensing a 'but' in there."

"But," Nick said as he pulled the car into a driveway, "I can't do much with gut feelings. Especially if the mayor is into something nefarious, like your informant said. I need objective, physical evidence before I can do anything about it." He turned off the car, but he paused, the keys dangling from his fingers. "It is weird that he didn't say anything to the chief about the blackmail though."

"Maybe he was afraid someone at the police department would leak the intel. Every sleazy reporter in Blackthorn would fork over a nice chunk of change for that kind of story."

"I guess you're right. They'd be all over it like a rash." Nick leaned back in his seat and stared up through the sunroof. "I don't think I'll ever get used to these kinds of visits. I appreciate you coming with me." He reached for Dani's hand and traced her knuckles with his thumb. "It means a lot."

Dani's heart lurched, and she tucked a loose strand of hair behind her ear, exiting the car before her professionalism dropped and she did something embarrassing, like lean across the console to kiss the hell out of the detective. They were on a case after all. There would be time for kissing later. When they weren't about to speak with a bereaved fiancée. "Let's hope Julia can shed some light on things with Ricardo."

After years as a private detective, Dani's first instinct was to take the lead, but this was Nick's case. She fell back a step to let him knock on the door and introduce them to a puffy-eyed Julia Scott.

Julia Scott looked like she'd aged a decade since the photo in her file. Under normal circumstances, she must be a beautiful woman: clear skin, soft curves, and a pretty face. Now, though, her bottle-blond hair hung limply around her shoulders. Dark bags sat under bloodshot eyes, and her entire face was swollen and blotchy from crying. As it was, she looked on the edge of tears.

"We know you've been through a lot today," Nick said gently, "but if you could spare a few minutes for us, it could help our case."

Julia agreed and led them through the house, which was nicer than Dani expected for a local politician's campaign staffer. All of their furniture looked brand new—and expensive. A deep leather sofa and chair set was accented by solid-wood end tables, and a massive flat-screen was affixed to the wall. Dani and

Nick followed the fiancée into a formal dining room where they sat at a hand-carved cherry table.

"Can I get you anything?" Julia stood behind one of the chairs, crossing and uncrossing her arms like she couldn't find a comfortable position.

Nick took a seat across from her. "I'm fine, thank you. What can you tell us about Ricardo's work?"

"No one called him that." Julia pulled a tissue from her pocket and blotted her eyes. "Well, his mother did, but everyone else knew him as Ric." Her voice cracked on her fiancé's name, and she curled her arms around herself. "Ric worked long hours. We were always arguing about that, especially when the mayor called him in the middle of the night to run errands. I hated how busy he always was. I begged him to find another job."

So much for Conrad not knowing the guy. The mayor acted like he had never heard of Ric when Dani asked about him, yet here Julia was, talking like Ric was some kind of personal assistant to the man.

"You're sure it was the mayor himself calling?" Nick asked.

Julia nodded and finally settled enough to take a seat at the table. "I could hear his voice sometimes, when Ric answered the phone. I never heard much though. He would always slip out of bed to talk in private."

Dani wasn't sure what to make of this new information. "Did he try leaving the job, like you asked?"

"He complained about the mayor all the time, but he said the money was too good. We want—we *wanted* to have kids after we got married, and my family has a history of fertility struggles. Ric wanted to bank up as much money as possible in case we had a hard time too. He said as soon as we started a family, he'd find something else so he could be home more with our … with our kids."

At that, Julia lost what remained of her composure and broke down into heavy sobs. Dani felt for Julia, even if her own thoughts about children were still so tangled up and confusing. Julia's dreams of having kids with the man she loved had been ripped away from her.

Nick got up and sat beside the grieving woman, resting a comforting hand on her back as she cried. He glanced at Dani, who was trying to unravel the vastly different stories she'd heard that day. Someone was lying about the relationship between Nathaniel Conrad and Ricardo Nuñez.

And Dani had a strong opinion as to who.

While it was possible that Ric overstated his importance to the mayor to impress his fiancée, it seemed more likely that Conrad and his team were lying to cover up whatever demonic role they had in the man's death. Besides, even if Raj refused to do anything about it, he'd clearly picked up on the mayor's lies during their meeting.

Once Julia regained control of her emotions, and insisted she was fine on her own, Dani and Nick took their leave. In the privacy of his car, Dani shared her theories with him—minus the necromancer side of things, of course.

"I need facts, Dani. I can't accuse anyone, let alone the city's mayor or his staff, of murder without proof." He turned east, back toward her apartment. "Even if you're right," he said just as she was about to argue her point, "if I go in now, that'll just give the mayor time to hide any lingering evidence. We can't show our hand until it's unbeatable."

"What do you suggest, then? We need to do *something.*"

Nick ran a hand through his blond hair, his muscles snug against his suit jacket as he moved. "I never said we'd do nothing. Mayor Conrad is having a ball tonight."

"A fundraising gala," Dani cut in. "He mentioned that as we—as I was leaving his place." Dani mentally crossed her fingers that Nick wouldn't notice her slip or ask who she was with.

"Right. As part of the mayor's *tough on crime* image, he invited most of the police force. I don't think many are planning to go, besides those already on protection detail." He grinned conspiratorially at her. "But I have a plus one. If you want to go with me."

"Detective Hart, are you asking me on a date?" Dani asked, even though he technically already *did* ask her out. They just had to cancel.

But Nick shook his head. "This one is strictly business." He pulled over in front of the bar and took her hand in his. "When I finally get to take you out, Dani, you will be my only focus." He pressed a kiss to her hand. "I'll pick you up at eight."

Danika was drowning in silk.

At least, she thought it was silk. Having nothing suitable to wear to the fundraising gala, she called in reinforcements and ended up at Lana's house. Thankfully, the two women were close enough to the same size that Lana's closet transformed into Dani's fitting room. She had already tried on half a dozen dresses with mixed results.

"What about this one?" she asked, stepping out of the closet and into the bedroom where her gallery of critics waited. Dani wore a bohemian dress, the billowing fabric belted snuggly at her waist.

"Ooh, I like that one," Lana said. "It's so comfy."

Beside her on the bed, Spencer—who was now free from his hangover—scoffed. "It's suitable for visiting a farmer's market and not much else, Lan."

"I'm with Spencer on this one," Cassie, Lana's kid sister, quipped. It was hard to believe that Cassie was already sixteen. The girl Dani had first met—bald head and body weakened by cancer and chemo treatments—was gone. In her place stood a vibrant girl with color in her cheeks and blond hair that flowed past her shoulders.

Her feisty attitude, though, had only grown.

Dani usually loved it, except when it was directed at her own insecurities. And dressing up for a fancy affair? That was definitely one of them. She'd rather slay demons any day of the week.

"But it hides all my weapons." Dani twirled to face the full-length mirror. "See? You can't tell I'm armed at all."

"You look like a circus tent. I can't let you go out like that." Spencer sprang from the bed and ushered her back into the closet. "I'm picking the next one."

"Make her cute," Lana called after them. "She has a date."

"It's not a date!" Dani called back at Lana, but that didn't stop her from remembering the soft touch of Nick's hand and the promise of a real date sometime soon. She felt like an impulsive, hormonal teen, just like Cassie.

When she turned back to Spencer, he had a strange look on his face. "What?"

Spencer shrugged and resumed flipping through dress options. Lana had a *lot* of dresses, and Dani was fairly certain some of them were acquired back when Pam had full run of her body. They were gorgeous—and ridiculously expensive—if a little out of Lana's normal style. Low-cut necklines and sky-high hems that showed off way more skin than the bohemian dresses and professional suits Lana preferred.

"Come on, Spence. We've been friends too long for you to shrug and shut down on me." She rested a hand on his back, noting the tension there. "What's going on?"

Spencer opened his mouth to say something, but stopped. "It's not a fair thing for me to ask of you. Forget it."

"What are you talking about?" Now she was really concerned. But then Lana teasing clicked something into place for Dani. "Wait, is this about Nick?"

Spencer pulled a black satin dress from the rack. "What can I say, I'm still Team Raj." He held out the dress to her. "Try this one."

Dani accepted the gown and fussed over it to distract herself from Spencer's admission. "There's no way this will hide my gun."

"Give it a try, Dani," he pleaded, and Dani got the sense he meant more than the dress. "Please?"

"Fine. But when it doesn't work—"

"It will," he said, and slipped out of the giant walk-in closet.

Alone, Dani wriggled out of her current dress and hung it back up where she'd found it. She couldn't get Spencer's *Team Raj* comment out of her head. Lana was clearly Team Nick—he was kind and brave. Responsible in a way that felt safe and even a little sexy. He could give her a taste of normalcy amid all the demon hunting. Spence of all people should understand her attraction to that.

As she slipped the black dress over her head, she dreamed about what her life might look like if she let herself fall for the detective. He knew enough about her private detective work to understand her strange hours. He could provide the kind of stability she had craved all her life, and she couldn't deny her attraction to him. Even now, her heart beat a little faster thinking of the staged kiss they'd shared at the precinct to fool his boss.

It may have started out fake, but the way he held her, the way he kissed her had morphed into something real. Dani could be happy with Nick. Being with him would be simple. Easy.

Dani adjusted the fit of the dress and reached behind her for the zipper. Then there was Raj. It made sense that Spencer preferred them together. He and Raj had been friends since they were kids, and if

Dani and Raj got back together, all of them could spend time together again. Spence wouldn't have to bounce between them like the child of divorced parents.

But that didn't mean they worked. Necromancers and Ink Carriers had been enemies for hundreds of years, ever since the first Frost woman took on the Ink. Poe had taught her as much during her childhood of demonic history lessons. She couldn't trust Raj to hold her heart.

"All right," Dani announced. "How bad is this one?"

She stepped out of the closet, the soft fabric hugging her curves. Her weapons were hidden, but less comfortably so than with the last dress. When she made it to the bedroom, the room fell silent.

"Is it that bad?" She turned to the mirror and froze when she spotted herself. "Oh."

Dani had only ever thought of herself as a warrior. She was strong. Determined. Fierce. She had learned early on that makeup and fancy dresses were for other people, for those not destined to spend their lives cut open and bruised by demons. And growing up as she had, she'd never been to a school dance. She dropped out of school before she was old enough for prom.

But now, she looked—

"Stunning," Lana said.

Maybe strength and beauty could go together after all. As her friends fussed over her, Lana working on her hair while Cassie—who ran a rather successful makeup tutorial channel online—took care of everything else, Dani's mind flit back to Raj.

Like her, he didn't have a lot of choices growing up. His father put constant pressure on him, choosing powers for Raj—like the ability to spot an outright lie among other things—that would make him an asset to the entire Dasari family. He'd been groomed his entire life to take over as his father's heir.

Their stories weren't all that different, something Dani once thought brought them closer together. But as time went by, she came to realize that it pushed them apart.

Now, with his father gone, the entire family looked to Raj for leadership, for guidance. He was the one who kept their businesses running, made sure his extended family wanted for nothing, and babysat the demonic bargains. It was his responsibility to ensure no Dasari made a bargain that hurt the family goals. Raj was more of a necromancer today than he was when they first met. Both of them had embraced their fate, and Dani wasn't sure if they could ever rekindle what they once had.

As Cassie added a shimmering highlight to Dani's

cheekbones, she let herself consider what life would be like with Raj as he was now. With him, she could live in complete honesty. She wouldn't have to explain why she went out every night or why she came home with strange bruises and clothes stained with demon blood.

She wouldn't have to explain the scars on her arm.

Dani ran a hand over the raised lines on her skin. Her heart ached for Silas, the python spirit who had lived in her skin. Who fought alongside her.

Who she lost.

"I need gloves," she said at last, hiding the scarred skin against her stomach. "Elbow length, if you have them."

"Oh, I … I don't think I have anything like that," Lana said, but it was Spencer who took her hands in his.

"You don't need to hide them, Danika." He spoke softly, like they were the only two people in the world. "And if this detective is as good a man as you believe, he won't pressure you to explain anything you aren't willing to tell him."

Dani squared her shoulders. Spencer was right. She could do this. "Thanks, Spence." She squeezed his hands in hers.

But when she glanced in the mirror, she noticed one final problem.

"Cassie?" she called, and the teen sprang to her side. "Do you have anything that can cover my tattoos?"

Having her scars on full display was one thing. Walking into the mayor's home with bare arms, leaving the Ink out in the open for any demon or necromancer to see? Out of the question.

Cassie grinned. "I have just the thing."

A migration of butterflies fluttered through Dani's insides while she waited for Detective Hart to pick her up for their not-date.

She had texted him earlier with Lana's address, and now she stood on the front porch, backlit by the motion sensor light that kept flicking on and off. The night air was cool on her skin, and she wasn't accustomed to letting her arms be this bare.

Dani couldn't stop looking at her left forearm, where Cassie had hidden the image of Jasper on her skin. It was strange, being able to feel his spirit inside her but not seeing the black lines of his body wrapping around her arm. The Ink were an inextricable part of her, their spirits woven into her soul with unbreakable thread.

At least, she'd always thought it was unbreakable. Until Spencer's uncle tore Silas away from her.

Cassie had also touched up around her collarbone, where the tips of Poe's wings were visible, but she thankfully didn't have to cover much. The dress hid all of Kiva on her back.

When Nick's gray sedan pulled into Lana's driveway, Dani's stomach fluttered with nerves. She caught herself running her fingers along her scars and forced herself to stop. Touching them would only draw more attention.

She left the safety of the porch and aimed for the car, but Nick surprised her by getting out to greet her. His entire face lit up when he took in all of her, the places the black fabric hugged her hips and breasts, even as the fuller skirt concealed her weapons. "You look beautiful," he said, voice earnest and pitched with emotion.

Dani wasn't used to such naked and unabashed compliments. "You clean up nice yourself," she teased, but that was an understatement. Nick was a regular James Bond in the crisp tuxedo. The slim fit of the pants showed off powerful legs, and the jacket hung perfectly over his broad shoulders. She desperately wanted to reach for him but reminded herself that this was part of the job, *not* a date.

"Shall we?" He opened the passenger door for her

like some sort of gentleman from the 1800s helping his lady into a carriage.

"Why, thank you, sir," she said, playing along like it was some elaborate game of dress-up. But Nick's hand grazed the small of her back as she slipped past him, and all pretense fell away. Her skin warmed at the contact, and her earlier thoughts came rushing back.

A man like Nick could be good for her.

The detective closed her door and hurried around to the driver's side, slipping smoothly into his seat and reversing out of the driveway.

"You really do look beautiful," Nick said a few minutes later as he headed to the edge of Blackthorn. "I hardly recognized you when I pulled up."

Dani gently smacked his arm. "Are you saying I look horrible the rest of the time?"

"No, of course not!" Nick pulled to a smooth stop at a red light and turned to look at her, his blue-green eyes filled with an intoxicating heat. "You're always beautiful. It's just that you're usually the kind of beautiful that makes me think you could kick my ass rather than waltz around a ballroom with me."

"I could definitely kick your ass," Dani said, but she was smiling. "Even in these heels."

Nick laughed. "I don't doubt it." The light turned green, and as he eased forward, he cautiously held out his hand to her. Dani sucked in a silent breath, a furious debate raging in her head. Finally, she intertwined her fingers with his. His calloused hand was warm. Sturdy. She wondered how they would feel against other parts of her skin.

"I'd be happy to show you sometime," Dani said, trying to lighten the mood. Trying to distract from the newly erratic rhythm of her heart as the heat from Nick's hand pulsed through her. If this was Nick on a night he specifically declared wasn't a date, what would it be like when they finally went out?

Traffic picked up as they passed through the heart of Blackthorn, their progress slowing to a crawl.

"Can I ask you a personal question?" Nick said when they got stuck behind the same light for the third time.

Dani squeezed his hand. If she wanted there to be real dates in the future, answering a few questions was the least she could do. "Of course."

"Do you have any siblings?"

"What?" She wasn't expecting something so benign. "Why?"

Nick tapped the steering wheel with his free hand. "I just realized I don't know much about you outside of work stuff. I'm sorry if it's too personal."

"No, it's fine." Her voice came out in a rush. She

didn't want Nick to shy away. "And I don't. Have any siblings, that is."

"What about your parents?"

Dani watched the light flick green and chose her words with care. "I never actually met my father. I'm not sure if he even knows I exist."

"Oh. I'm sorry." Nick eased forward, and they finally made it through the intersection. "What about your mom?"

"Enough about me." Dani tried to keep her voice light, but thoughts of her mom tightened her throat until it was hard to speak. "What about your family?"

"My family is a bit of a cliché," Nick said. "My father was also a detective before he retired, and my mom's a nurse. They met after Dad got shot on the job." Nick chuckled, and Dani got the sense there was some part of the family story she was missing, some inside joke. "I have two younger sister, Tessa and Kate. Tess finished her doctorate this past spring and works as a physical therapist. Kate's only twenty-one, so she's still in college."

The normalcy of his family tugged at forgotten wounds. "What is she studying?"

"She's changed majors a few times." They finally passed through the downtown area, and the traffic picked up to a more normal speed. "The last time we spoke, she had settled on a double major of women's studies and human services."

"They sound great," Dani said, and she meant it. But as Nick told her stories of the last holiday the Hart family had spent together, a persistent worry dug at the back of her mind.

Could she really upend his world?

Nick believed in law and order. He cared about his job and worked hard to find justice for the victims on his caseload. He wanted the world to be far more just than it currently was, and he actually did something about it.

How could Dani shatter that illusion for him? How could she tell him about the real villains running Blackthorn under his nose? Would knowing that necromancers pulled most of the strings in the city break him? That he could only ever hope to clean up their messes instead of holding them to the law?

Dani liked Nick enough to know that she didn't want to cause him that kind of pain. But if she let herself fall for him, eventually she'd want him to know the truth of her. If they ever moved in together, it would only be a matter of time before he noticed something strange, if he hadn't already.

Once Nick knew about the demonic world, he could never *un*-know.

If she truly cared, wouldn't she leave him now,

before he could fall for her? The longer she delayed, the more it would hurt him. He deserved to find a normal girl, someone he could actually grow old with. Someone whose life's calling didn't leave them with a life expectancy of forty.

But it felt so nice to hold his hand.

"Are you ready for this?" Nick asked as they turned into the Conrad estate. The long driveway was already packed with cars, and a tremor of anticipation made goose bumps prickle along Dani's arms.

"There's something you should know about me, Detective," Dani said, as Nick pulled the car into a vacant spot. "I'm always ready."

Nick chuckled, and they exited the car. He offered his arm, and Dani slipped her hand around his biceps. He radiated heat, and as he led her into the mansion, she felt like a princess stepping into a fairy tale. The foyer had transformed since she'd been there that afternoon. The main lights had been dimmed to an intimate softness, and strings of twinkling lights were strung throughout the room.

Nick led her through to the grand ballroom at the back of the house, and they blended seamlessly into the well-dressed crowd. Dani's senses prickled, a clear sign that there were demons nearby, but so far, she didn't spot any with the crowd.

It made sense, that Nathaniel Conrad would keep

demons out of a party like this, but they were still close. Still a danger to all these people.

Nick leaned close and pointed out the politicians and other influential Blackthorn citizens by name. Dani knew most of them, many of whom were necromancers. It always shocked her, the reminder of how thoroughly necromancers had infiltrated the power structures of the city when she saw them together like this. Nick noted anyone they might want to question about Ricardo.

"Dance with me?" Nick asked, stepping away to hold out a hand.

Music swelled around them as the string quartet picked up the next song, and Dani let herself be carried away by the fantasy.

Until she saw Rajan Dasari laughing across the room.

With his arm thrown casually around Nathaniel Conrad's shoulders.

"Is something wrong?" Nick studied Dani's cold expression and turned to see what had caught her attention. "Is that the club kid from the morgue this morning? What's he doing with the mayor?"

"I have no idea." Dani's words came out harsher than she intended. She debated whether to storm over and find out, but Nick's hand came to rest against her back, and she let the irritation slide out of her. "You said you wanted to dance?" she asked, looking up at him.

Nick smiled, but a question still tugged at his brow. Dani rested her palm against his, her other hand at his shoulder while Nick adjusted his touch at her back. He held her close and led her around the room with an ease that surprised her.

"I didn't realize you could dance so well." Dani tipped her chin to watch the detective, who was still several inches taller than her despite the heels she wore.

"My sisters forced me to learn." Nick spun Dani in an elegant circle and brought her close again. "But I can't really complain. It's been a valuable skill."

"Oh yeah?" Dani asked. "Do you treat all your dates to fancy dance parties?"

"Only the special ones," Nick said, but there was none of the teasing Dani had in her voice. He wore sincerity like a badge of honor, so different from the armor Dani kept around her heart. "How do you know Rajan Dasari?" Nick asked when Raj came into view again.

Past Nick's shoulder, she watched Raj and the mayor. A thrill of something she couldn't name traveled her spine when Raj looked up and noticed her and Nick in the crowd. The smile fell from his face. His dark eyes smoldered.

Dani didn't particularly want to share her biggest mistake, but she already kept enough secrets from Nick. She didn't want to lie about this too. "We ... dated, a few years ago."

"Oh." Nick's body tensed beneath her fingers.

"It ended terribly." Dani shifted her hand from Nick's shoulder to the curve of his neck, her thumb tracing the line of his jaw. "He's nothing to me but a bad memory," she said, as much to assuage herself as Nick.

"As soon as this case is over," Nick said, leaning into her touch, "I'm taking you out for real."

Emboldened by the hurt of seeing Raj, Dani shifted closer until their bodies pressed tight together. Her hand slipped to the nape of Nick's neck and let her fingers twist through his soft blond hair. "This feels plenty real to me," she whispered.

Nick's eyes ignited with desire, and he tipped his head closer. It would take next to nothing to raise onto her toes and kiss him. Dani's breath caught in her throat and—

"Mind if I cut in?"

Raj's voice was like a bucket of ice water over Dani's head. With a sigh, she released herself from Nick and turned to face her ex. She didn't remove her hand from the detective's though, and a petty satisfaction filled her when Raj noticed their joined fingers.

"I don't think Danika wants you as a dance partner," Nick said, coming to her defense.

"Why don't you talk with the mayor?" Dani rested a hand on Nick's chest, and his heart beat steady against her palm. "I'll deal with this."

"Are you sure?" Nick didn't budge, a stubborn set to his strong jaw.

"Trust me. I can handle men like Rajan, no problem." She didn't bother lowering her voice, so she knew Raj must have heard her. She hoped her words stung as much as seeing him did to her.

Nick nodded and stepped away. "I'll be right over there if you need me. Say the word."

When they were alone, Raj scooped Dani into his arms, and they fell in step with the surrounding dancers. "You do realize he'll never know you the way I do."

"I don't see how that's any of your business." Dani didn't pull away—she didn't want to cause a scene before she and Nick got what they needed out of the mayor—but she angled herself as far away from Raj as she could.

Raj spun her, drawing her in closer when she returned. "It was once. It could be again."

Dani scoffed. "Keep telling yourself that." They turned through the crowd again, and when she spotted the mayor, he was feigning concern over Nick's questions. "How can you be besties with the mayor when you *know* he has something to do with my case?"

"Why do you always expect the worst from me?" Raj countered, and he actually seemed genuinely hurt. "You're not the only one who knows how to go undercover to get what you want." He looked her up and down, naked hunger in his gaze. "You're beautiful tonight, by the way."

Heat rose up Dani's neck, and Raj shifted closer. A thrum of pleasure bloomed from his touch, and she found herself entranced by his dark eyes. Somehow, the space between them had disappeared as they danced, and the heat of his closeness enveloped her.

When they had been together, every moment was electric, and the familiarity of his touch—of how much she *wanted* it—terrified her. It would be so easy to fall back into his arms. To accept his kiss. To melt back into the love they'd shared, doomed as it was.

But she couldn't.

She stepped away as dancers spun around the mismatched pair. A necromancer and the woman destined to destroy him. "You can't say things like that anymore, Raj. It only makes it worse."

"Fine." Raj crossed his arms, every line of his muscled physique accented by the expensive fabric of his suit. "Tell me you never want to see me again. If it's the truth, I'll leave. I'll leave, and I'll never contact you again."

Dani hated his confidence, hated the challenge in his expression. "What's stopping you from lying about whether I speak the truth?"

"Self-preservation." Raj ran a hand over his chiseled jaw, his hair slicked back and tied at the nape of his neck the way he knew Dani loved. "Trust me, no one wants to offer their heart for the slaughter with no chance of being saved."

His words—and all the things left unsaid—hung between them. Dani felt the implications echoing along her bones, chasing toward her heart.

He as good as said he still loved her.

"I can't do this. Not now." Dani shook her head, tears prickling at her eyes.

"Dani, wait—"

But she didn't wait. She turned and maneuvered through the crowd. She needed space. A moment to collect herself. God, she hated how easily Raj could unravel her defenses. *I'm the Ink Carrier, for fuck's sake.* She shouldn't be so easily rattled, not when she beheaded demons for a living.

Dani left the ballroom and traveled down a wide hallway in search of some place quiet to get herself back together. She still had to deal with the mayor. If Sean made Ellie the source of the blackmail, she had to find out what Nathaniel did to her.

Halfway down the hall, a pair of feminine voices caught her attention.

"… gets weirder every time. I'm telling you, one of them has a split tongue."

"That's nothing. Did I tell you about the guy with a

tail? I swear to god, if the money wasn't so good, I'd quit this freak show in a second."

Dani turned the corner and found two women touching up their makeup in a mirror. They both wore beautiful dresses, but the hems were much higher than Dani's and their breasts looked ready to spill out.

"I'm so sorry," Dani said, approaching them with her voice low. "Are you Sean's girls? I'm new and I'm late and lost and I …" She let a tear spill down her cheek that had nothing to do with her false predicament.

"Oh, darlin', you're okay," the taller of the two, a blond, said. "You're in the right spot."

"But you gotta keep it together," the short brunette added. "These weirdos are into some freaky shit, so if you can't hang, you should leave now."

"I'm good. I promise." Dani dabbed at her face, grateful Cassie had used waterproof mascara. She was going to strangle Sean for not telling her that he was still supplying escorts for the mayor. Piece of shit. "I'm just a little nervous. It's my first time somewhere this fancy."

The women appraised her. "Well, at least you clean up good, kid," the blond said. "Now, come on."

"We're not supposed to hang around the main party." The brunette linked her arm through Dani's scarred one. "There's a VIP room upstairs." She leaned close to whisper, "There's going to be a hell of an after party for the mayor's closest friends. If you play your cards right, you could make a killing tonight."

Dani smirked. She'd love to kill *something* tonight. "Lead the way."

The VIP room turned out to be full of the demons Dani sensed earlier, and the Ink stirred with hunger beneath her skin. Poe, Jasper, and Kiva were all eager to tear into their flesh and banish the demons from the human realm. Dani followed the escorts she met through the crowd, watching as they split off to give attention to the humans in the room. Dani recognized a few as necromancers—five years of slaying demons in Blackthorn had indirectly introduced her to dozens of them—but without the Ink free to sort the difference for her, it was impossible to tell how many of the other humans were necromancers too.

Acrid smoke curled through the air, casting room in a haze of ill intent. Despite his shithole apartment, Sean ran an impressive operation. Dani counted at least a dozen high-end escorts, including a few men, making their rounds. The mayor's friends eyed them like they were little more than playthings, and their clear desire for sex and power and control made her skin crawl.

As Dani made her way through the room, she drew more and more attention from the men and women around her. Though they wouldn't recognize her as the Ink Carrier with her tattoos hidden beneath Cassie's makeup, they could definitely pick up the strength of her not-quite-human power.

It didn't hurt that her dress was killer too.

She carefully avoided the men who approached her, playing coy and slipping out of reach. Dani wasn't going to let any of them touch her, not without meeting the bite of her blade.

Instead, she focused her attention on the escorts in the room. A curtain rippled to her left, and a man with a hazy smile exited. Before the opaque fabric swung shut, Dani spotted a half-naked woman lounging on a bed inside, her hair dyed a fiery red.

Before anyone else could sneak into the private room, Dani slipped inside and closed the curtain behind her.

The woman blinked up at her from the front of the bed, a slow, seductive smile spreading across her lips. "Girls are double."

"I'm just here for information." Dani glanced behind her at the sheer curtain and kept her voice low. "I'm looking for my friend, Ellie."

"Information is double too, sugar." The girl turned and sat up, arranging the sheets to cover the bits of exposed skin.

Dani could've kicked herself. "I don't have cash on me, but I'm good for it," she promised. "I know Ellie used to work these parties, but I haven't seen her in weeks. I'm hoping you can help."

The woman's painted lips pressed tight, and she mimed locking them with a key.

"I'm really worried about her," Dani pressed. "She used to be the mayor's favorite."

At that, the woman looked up. "She doesn't come around here anymore." A sly smile. "We've all been jockeying to be the mayor's new preferred pet. We're hoping he picks someone new tonight."

Behind Dani, the curtain ripped open, revealing a demon with amber eyes and a reptilian tail. The demon grinned, pointed teeth glinting in the half light. "Two for one? My favorite."

"Sorry to disappoint," Dani snapped, shoving past him. "I was just leaving."

"Suit yourself, hon," the redhead said behind her.

As Dani slipped back into the party, her senses were overwhelmed with the amount of sex and booze and smoke in the air. It pressed against her already heightened awareness until she wanted to climb out of her skin. Or start beheading demons. That would work too.

She scanned the room for another escort who might be more willing to talk to her. She didn't blame the redhead. If Dani had brought cash to the party, she would have paid her. The woman must have her own bills and debts to deal with. She was at work. Dani could respect that.

Even if it did nothing to help her case.

Across the smoke-hazed room, a demon with sheer black wings led another escort away from the party. The girl looked like she was barely eighteen, if she was legal age at all.

Maybe it was a sixth sense she'd gained from her Ink, or perhaps it was just experience from hunting them for years now, but Dani's gut told her the demon had more than sex planned for the girl.

Dani followed them out of the VIP room and down the hall. She kept her distance to avoid attracting the demon's attention, light on her feet even in heels. They turned a corner, and Dani hurried to catch up, peeking around the corner in time to see a door click shut.

Jasper wriggled anxiously inside her left forearm.

"Soon," she promised the Ink. "You'll have your fill of demons before the night is over." Even though Dani wanted to take down every demon in the mayor's estate, her rational mind knew that wasn't smart. Not with the sheer number of demons she'd be facing.

Not with so many humans in the house.

Humans like Nick.

Swallowing down the rush of conflicting emotions that came with thoughts of the detective, Dani inched toward the closed door. As she neared, her sensitive hearing picked up the voices within.

"… anything you've ever wanted," the demon was saying. "I only ask for a little something in return."

"I don't know," the young woman said, but Dani could hear the interest beneath her uncertainty. She wanted an easier life. Something secure and comfortable.

Dani wouldn't let the girl enter into a bargain she didn't understand.

"There must be something you're willing to give up," the demon crooned, and Dani had heard enough.

She reached for the handle but found it locked. Cursing under her breath, Dani turned and rammed her shoulder against the door. It crashed inward and sprayed shards of wood into the room.

The demon turned on her and let out a guttural hiss that vibrated through her bones. The young girl's pale face turned ashen and she inched away from her client.

"You should go," Dani said with as much compassion as she could muster. "The cost is always higher than the reward with creatures like this."

"Creatures?"

"Just go."

"I don't think so." The demon grabbed the girl by the wrist as she tried to walk past, preventing her from leaving. It growled at Dani. "Who the hell do you think you are?"

Moving faster than any other human could, Dani grabbed the demon's wrist and twisted it violently to one side with an audible *crack*. The creature screamed and lost its grip on the escort, and the girl made her escape.

"Fool!" The screeching demon grabbed hold of Dani, human arms melting away to reveal writhing tentacles. The suctioned grip tightened around her forearm, and the slime scorched her skin in chemical burns. "You'll pay for that."

"You first." Dani yanked her arm free and kicked the demon square in the solar plexus.

The demon fell back, but its translucent wings beat against the air, keeping it standing. It snarled, lip curled over sharp teeth, the illusion of humanity fading with each breath. Red eyes looked Dani up and down, catching on her arm. "Ink Carrier," it said on a growl.

Dani glanced to her arm. The demon's slimy grip had wiped away most of the makeup covering Jasper's inky form. She scrubbed the rest of the concealer away. "Guess the cat's out of the bag." A feral grin curled at her lips, and the Ink beneath her skin hummed with excitement.

Before she could pull the gun or hilt from her thigh, the demon bellowed and dove at her. With the extra speed from its wings, Dani wasn't able to dodge out of the way before the demon rammed into her.

They tumbled out of the room and crashed into the empty hallway. Dani landed hard on her back, the demon reaching for her throat.

"Jasper!"

The king cobra unfurled from her arm and slithered out in tendrils of ink and shadow. A second later, the fully formed Jasper sprang from the hallway floor and coiled around the demon's neck. Dani scrambled away, but her dress twisted around her legs, slowing her movements.

A tentacle wrapped around her ankle, pulling her up short. Dani lashed out, kicking with her other leg. Her heel slid clean through the demon's eye, and it screamed a blood-curdling cry. Somewhere deep in the house came an answering shout.

Dani's blood ran cold. This demon had a mate.

She needed to get the hell out of there before

every demon in the estate barreled down on her. Dani untangled her gown and sprang to her feet. The hallway was still clear—for now—and she called for Poe. The raven soared, and Dani reached through the slit in her dress for the hilt of her sword.

Look out!

Poe's voice screamed in her head, but Dani wasn't fast enough. Another demon slammed into her back and lifted her into the air. Out of her peripheral vision, she saw the same translucent black wings just as teeth sank into the tender muscle between her neck and shoulder.

She wouldn't give the demons the satisfaction of her scream. She bit back the cry and drove her elbow into the creature's abdomen again and again and again. The creature released the bite.

And then dropped her.

Dani fell, knocking her injured shoulder on the railing that separated the second-floor hallway from the drop to the ground floor below. She grabbed hold of the edge just in time to catch herself and a jolt of agony rang through her body at the impact. In the hall, Poe and Jasper fought the demons, giving her the time she needed to pull herself back over the railing and onto the second floor.

But her shoulder wouldn't support the weight. Not like this.

"Dani?"

The voice nearly stopped her heart, and she tried again to pull herself onto the landing. Her arms wouldn't cooperate, and then suddenly, Nick's face was staring down at her.

"What happened? You were only gone a few minutes." He reached over the railing and grabbed hold of her wrist.

She didn't have time for this. She didn't have words to explain what he was seeing. "Later, Nick," she said, groaning has he hauled her over the railing. "Down!" Dani yanked the detective lower as Poe and the second demon crashed through the air above him.

"What the hell?" Despite his confusion, the detective slipped into a fighting stance, ready to dive into a fray he wasn't at all prepared for.

"Close enough." Dani reached for the hilt at her thigh and pulled it free.

"Danika, wait. What are you—" His words died when Dani flicked the blade into place.

The first demon stood across from them, wings stretched to the limits of their span in an attempt to intimidate her.

Dani was injured. She wasn't dressed appropriately for a fight. And worst of all, the man she wanted to protect from all this stood ready to battle beside her. But Danika Frost was also the Ink Carrier, and she sure as shit wasn't going to let a little blood or inconvenience stop her from doing what she did best.

In one fluid movement, she charged the demon and arced her blade. The demon was fast—one of the fastest she'd ever faced. It struck with each of its tentacled limbs, using its wings as both shield and weapon.

Frustrated, Dani let the demon block her next blow and used the contact to press closer. "Eat knuckles, asshole." She smashed her fist into the demon's face and, when it was distracted, twisted her blade and pulled it free, slicing along its side.

Black demon ichor sprayed across the front of her, ruining her dress. But Dani didn't have time to care about that. Lana knew the risks to the garment when she lent it. Dani pressed forward, attacking again and again, but the wings were an added complication. One of the bony ridges caught her along the jaw, sending her sprawling across the floor.

Before Dani could call for more backup, Nick appeared at her side. He ducked under swinging tentacles and landed blow after blow on the demon's abdomen and face. His body moved like it was made to fight, all sharp jabs and fluid feints.

Dani pulled herself to her feet and called on her largest Ink. "Kiva!" She winced when the panther pulled from her skin, the pained sound escaping her lips.

Nick whirled around to check on her.

"Look out!" Dani called, but it was too late. The demon wrapped one of its tentacles tight around Nick's neck and squeezed. "Let him go." She tightened her grip on her sword.

The demon ignored her and yanked Nick close. He winced, eyes wild with fear, as the scent of charring flesh hit her nose.

Dani threw caution aside and dove full-speed back into the fray, Kiva on her heels. Careful not to injure Nick, she sliced into the demon, trying to sever its hold on his neck. She and Kiva moved in perfect synchronicity, and the two of them kept the demon on the defensive. It tried to take flight with Nick still in its clutches, but Dani's sword sliced through one wing while Kiva slashed the other with her claws. As it fell, Dani swung. Her blade sliced clean through the demon's neck, and the tentacle finally released Nick.

The detective slumped against the wall, losing his voice to a fit of coughs as he tore the dead weight of the arm away from him. Underneath, his fair skin had turned a bloody red from chemical burns.

Before Dani could ask if he was okay, the demon's mate let out a keening wail. Pain shot through her chest as Poe returned to her as a tattoo. Fear quickened her heart. For Poe to be forced back into her skin like that, the demon must have destroyed his solid form.

It comes, Jasper hissed into her mind. *Now.*

With full trust in her Ink, Dani turned and swung her sword. The other demon flew right into its path, severing its head just like its mate. But the demon's momentum carried it forward into her anyway, and Dani collapsed under the weight.

"A little help," she muttered. Kiva bit down on the demon's leg and dragged it off Dani.

Jasper slithered back into view and unhinged his jaw to consume the first demon's head.

"What the fuck is going on here?" a brusque voice demanded.

From her place on the floor, Dani surveyed the hallway. Nick was still sitting against the wall, one hand pressed to his neck, eyes wild with confusion. But he wasn't the one who spoke. He was focused on something to Dani's left, and she swallowed hard when she realized who was standing over the carnage.

Raj.

And Mayor Conrad.

"Well?" Mayor Conrad stared at Dani with murder in his eyes before shifting his attention to Raj. "How dare you bring the Ink Carrier—the *fucking Ink Carrier*—to my home."

"I—" Raj started, but the older necromancer cut him off.

"You lied to me, Dasari. You brought the enemy to my gate and then talked of alliance and friendship." He spit at Raj's feet. "You can forget everything we discussed. The Conrads will have nothing to do with you or yours again."

"Nathaniel—"

"Be grateful I don't kill you right now." Mayor Conrad whirled on Nick, who had made it to his feet but still looked completely out of his depth. "And you!

I will have your badge for this, Detective. Mark my words. Chief Martinez is a close personal friend, and he owes me *several* favors."

"Sir," Nick stuttered. "I …" But he didn't have anywhere for his thoughts to go. He flinched when Kiva snarled at the mayor.

Nathaniel addressed Dani next, the real source of his fury. "I assume your name isn't Danielle Winters."

Dani, who had also made it to her feet while the mayor was busy with the men in the hall, tipped her chin. "Danika Frost."

"Not even a clever alias," the mayor muttered, shooting another glare at Raj. He turned back to Dani. "Your days on this earth are numbered, Miss Frost. No one kills demons under my roof and gets away with it."

Conrad made to grab Dani, but Kiva snapped at his hand. He pulled back just in time. "Put these monstrosities away."

Please let me tear out his throat, Little Warrior, Kiva said, the fur on her hackles raised.

Dani stroked Kiva's back. "I don't think that's a good idea," she whispered. At either end of the hall, necromancers had gathered to serve as Nathaniel's backup. Dani and her Ink were grossly outnumbered, especially with Poe banished. The demon must have gravely injured him for the raven to be forced back into her skin.

"Put. Them. Away." A dangerous gleam entered the mayor's eyes, but she held his stare.

"Dani, please. Don't make this worse." If Raj were only angry, she would have refused, but the fear in his voice broke something in her.

She stared at her former love. "If he tries to kill me, I'm blaming you." She retracted her blade and called for Kiva and Jasper to return. Dani forced herself not to flinch, not to blink, as the Ink painfully returned.

Nick cursed colorfully, his face even paler.

As soon as the last of the Ink returned to her skin, Conrad struck Dani. Her mouth filled with blood, as both Raj and Nick protested. But the mayor didn't listen to either of them. He crowded closer into Dani's space. "You almost ruined everything," he said, voice cold and dispassionate. Somehow, that was more terrifying than his earlier yelling. "If your little stunt does anything to hurt my fundraiser, I'll have your head on a platter."

"Men like you don't scare me." Dani spit blood onto the expensive cream carpet between them, a declaration. A challenge. "I know Ellie was blackmailing you. I know there's more to Ricardo's death than you want me to find out." She stepped forward, pushing into his space now.

He stepped back.

"And I will keep pushing," Dani said, voice rising. She wanted them all to hear, wanted *Raj* to hear. "I will uncover every single one of your secrets, Conrad. And when I have them? I will *bury* you. I'll burn your entire campaign to the ground."

Several of the necromancers rushed down the hall toward them, the sickening current of their magic humming in the air like a thousand locusts. Mayor Conrad held up one hand, and they stilled. "Take them out of here. All of them. We can't risk a scene or kill her. *For now.*"

One of the necromancers grabbed Dani by the arm, and Mayor Conrad leaned close, whispering for only her to hear. "The next time we meet, Miss Frost, I will take great pleasure in removing your organs one by one."

A terrible chill froze Dani from the inside out, and she yanked away from the necromancer holding her.

"Enough, Danika," Raj snapped. This time, he was the one who clasped an iron grip over her biceps. "It's time to go."

Danika wanted to rage. To black out in anger and tear through Conrad and the demons he catered to. She wanted to burn the entire estate to the ground, but she caught sight of Nick, of the fear and panic on his face, and she let the fight bleed out of her.

She wasn't the only one at risk here.

The mayor's guards led them out of the house and stood like sentries at the door as they walked down the path to the cars.

Once they were out of earshot, Raj whirled on her. "You have to be smarter than that, Dani. A man like Nathaniel—"

"I don't want to hear it, Raj." She pressed her fingers gingerly into her bitten shoulder. The muscle was already stitching itself back together, but it still hurt like hell. "I'm so very sorry I embarrassed you in front of your bestie," she mocked.

"You don't have any idea what you've done, do you?" Raj ran his hands through his hair. "We dated for *three years*, Dani. How can you understand so little of my life?"

"I understand plenty. A man is dead. A young woman is missing, and both of them have ties to the mayor. Not to mention all the other bodies in the morgue. Those were *people*, Raj, and a demon used them up like they were a fucking snack."

Dani sucked in a lungful of the cool night air. Her entire body ached from the fight, but it was this fight —an echo of so many before—that weighed heaviest on her. "Their families deserve answers, so forgive me for not giving a shit about the expansion of your club or whatever the hell you and the mayor were planning."

"Why do you always assume that I only care about money?" Raj stalked over to his car, reaching into his pocket for the keys. "Nathaniel has every excuse to attack my family now. We're all at risk, because of you."

She felt his words like a blow. Anger and grief warred within her, twisting her insides. "Fine," she said, voice heavy with unshed tears. "The next time a demon attacks, I'll let it kill me. Then you won't have to worry about me ruining your life."

They both knew she was exaggerating, but her words still hummed like a threat between them.

"Get in the car, Dani." Raj pressed the button to unlock the doors.

"I'm not going anywhere with you."

Raj opened his own door. "And I'm not leaving you defenseless in front of the mayor's place. Get in." When she didn't move, Raj rested his forehead against the open door. "Why couldn't you have left Conrad to me? I had things under control." The anger had leaked out of his voice, leaving only desperation. Pleading. But Dani noticed all the things he didn't say.

I'm glad you're okay.

I don't want you dead.

I still love you.

She didn't even *want* him to say those things, but their lack hurt anyway.

"Dani, please. Get in the car. You're not safe."

"She's not alone, either." Nick stepped between them, and Dani had almost forgotten he was there. "I'll make sure she gets home safe."

Raj scoffed. "Fine." He slipped into the car, and it roared to life. The passenger window rolled down silently. "Good luck explaining all this to him."

And then he was gone.

"I do have a lot of questions," Nick said as they walked to the sedan, his voice harder than she'd ever heard from him before. He rubbed his injured neck. "And I expect *real* answers. The whole-truth-and-nothing-but-the-truth answers."

Dani wanted to rewind the entire night and erase the truth from Nick's mind, erase the *pain* he'd endured, but there was no sense wishing for the impossible. "I should probably drive. I don't need you crashing because you're in shock."

"You're injured."

"Only a little. And so are you." Dani held out her hand until Nick placed the keys in her palm. "The first thing you should know," she said as she eased into the car and slid the seat forward so she could reach the pedals, "is that I heal very, *very* quickly."

Nick's questions came slow at first, but each of Dani's answers birthed a hundred other queries. At first, Dani enjoyed the unburdening of her secrets. She told him about demons and necromancers. She explained the five families in Blackthorn and how they controlled more of the city than Nick could ever guess. It broke her heart to tell him how most of the cops were on various necromancer payrolls. It hurt to see his view of the world shattered.

"What about the creatures who fought with you? Are those demons too?"

Dani shook her head. "They're called the Ink. Many generations ago, my ancestors brought the Ink to our world to fight back against the rising threat of demons."

"But where do they come from?" Nick's forehead creased, a confused expression he'd worn for much of their drive. "Are you born with them?"

"No, though I was born with the ability to hear them. When they're in physical form, I can hear their thoughts as easily as the words you speak. Now that I'm the Carrier, it's like they're part of who I am. Their emotions echo through me even when they're within my skin."

Nick nodded, like somehow everything was starting to make sense. "Does it hurt when they come and go like that?"

"Every time," she said. "It's like a thousand burning needles pressing the Ink into my skin, just like if they were regular tattoos."

"That sounds excruciating." Nick's voice was heavy with emotion, and he reached for her hand.

Dani didn't say anything. She couldn't, not without all the pain and relief and regret of the day spilling out of her. When they made it back to Bloody Mary's, Dani parked behind the building, where the stairs led up to her apartment. She pulled her hand away to kill the engine. "Anything else, Detective?"

"I'm sure there's a lot I don't understand," he said, picking each word carefully, "but if you aren't born with the Ink, how did you get them?"

Part of her wanted to deflect, to avoid this part of her story, but she owed him the full truth, just like he'd asked. "Normally, the Ink passes when the current Carrier is killed." Dani blew out a breath. "I don't think any Frost women have died by natural causes in centuries."

One day she would die by the hands of her enemies too.

How much longer did she have left?

"Fuck, Dani." Nick tugged a hand through his hair.

She knew she should stop before she freaked him out any worse, but her tangled web of truths wouldn't be contained any longer. "Poe—he's the raven—he's been on me for years about having kids. If I die now, the Ink die with me. Then you're all fucked." She rested back against the leather headrest. "The demon you faced today is far from the worst of them. Your world needs protection, but how can I subject a child to this life?"

"Dani …"

"I need some air." Dani escaped into the cool night and sat on the trunk of the car. She didn't know what she wanted from Nick. Sympathy? Understanding? Solidarity? But she didn't want to risk disappointment. She couldn't handle that on top of everything else.

But Nick surprised her by joining her on the trunk. He offered his hand, and she leaned into him. They sat like that for a long time, taking comfort in the other's quiet presence.

"How old were you when your mom died?" His question was a whisper on the wind.

"She's still alive," Dani said.

"But you said—"

"That's what normally happens." Dani sat up and wrapped her arms around her shins, her knees tucked up to her chest. Her shoulder was fully healed now, though the muscle still ached. "She's been at Blackthorn Hospital for the past five years."

Concern pulled at Nick's brows. "What happened?"

"We had a fight." Dani rested her forehead against her knees. "I wanted to go to college, but she wanted me to stay with her. She said I needed more training before I took on the Ink."

Dani could still remember the fight like it was yesterday—first words, then a dagger in each of their hands. Andrea had challenged Dani to a duel. If Dani won, she could go to college. If she lost, she'd drop the whole thing and embrace her destiny.

"I stormed out of the house when I inevitably lost," Dani continued. "I ran into some kids from school, and they invited me to a club. I just wanted to dance and forget my future for one night. But then Poe appeared on my skin."

She shuddered. She hadn't realized what was happening at first. Her senses sharpened, and the sudden sensory overload was disorienting. But when the Ink came to her, she knew her mother was in trouble.

"With Poe showing up, I thought that meant my mother was already dead. That's how it always worked before. Instead, he told me that she needed help. I followed the Ink to a cemetery where I found her. I found her—" Dani looked to the sky in a failed attempt to stop the tears. Even though dreams from that night still plagued her sleep, she hadn't told the entire story in forever.

Nick didn't say anything, but he was there. He listened.

"I found a demon—a reaper—standing over her." Dani closed her eyes, and she could see every detail of that night. Her mom on the hard ground, covered in blood. Screaming. The tall man with bone-white skin and elegant features turning to look at Dani. His chilling smile as he extended a finger three times the length of her own. "He played with her mind, scrambled it until she couldn't tell reality from fiction. She lives in constant fear now. The hospital keeps her medicated, but drugs can only do so much against demonic influence. I've been trying to find him, to undo whatever he did, but the leads never go anywhere."

Tears slipped down her cheeks, and the guilt of that night threatened to consume her. It tried to drown out every good thing she had ever done, tried to convince her she was worthless. A failure. Unfit to carry the Ink. Unfit to know anything but pain.

"Hey," Nick soothed, brushing away her tears. "It wasn't your fault."

She looked up at him, at those blue-green eyes. "How could you possibly know that?"

"Because I know you," Nick said without a hint of irony.

Dani let herself lean into him. She always craved the comfort of touch after a hard battle. The Ink had always been there for her, but the years she was with Raj … Being with him when she was hurting helped numb the worst of it.

It had been two years since she'd had that kind of comfort.

Impulsive and hurting, she slipped off the trunk of the car and pulled Nick down after her. The second his feet hit the pavement, her hands were on his shoulders—careful to avoid his injured neck. "Kiss me," she begged, her lips a breath from his.

"Dani …"

She raised her face to his, stealing his words with a kiss. Nick froze, but a heartbeat later, his hands tightened at her waist. His lips parted for her, and then she was tasting him. Her body lit up like a goddamn Christmas tree as his tongue glided across hers. Her breath caught, and she wanted so much more. She wanted to forget everything that had happened since she'd taken on Ellie's case.

Since she'd taken on the Ink.

"Come inside?" she asked when she pulled away.

Nick placed his hands on her shoulders and separated their bodies. "I don't think that's a good idea."

"But—"

"Not tonight, Danika." Nick released her and tucked a wayward strand of hair behind her ear. "This was a lot. I need … I need time to process everything."

The rejection stung more than Dani expected. "Oh."

"Yeah." Nick rubbed the back of his neck and wouldn't meet her eye. "I'll call you."

Dani fought fresh tears and stepped back like his touch burned. "Right. Of course." She shouldn't have done anything. This felt so much worse, to almost have the connection she so desperately craved than to never have it at all.

"Good night, Dani."

And then Nick climbed into his car and drove away, leaving Dani alone in the dark, with only the streetlights for company.

The moon migrated across the sky, barely visible amid the light pollution of the city despite its fullness, as Dani stood behind her building. *Too much.* That was the thought that kept her rooted to the ground. The entire day—from seeing Raj at the hospital that morning to fighting demons at the mayor's estate to Nick's rejection—was too much. It felt like weeks had passed over the last eighteen hours.

She was done, wrung out, and so very alone.

The Ink was there, of course. They would always be there, but she couldn't stomach Poe's judgment or Kiva's soft support. Even the idea of Jasper's companionable silence grated at her exposed nerves.

Why couldn't her life be simple for once? Why was that too much to ask?

Maybe that's my problem, Dani thought as she finally turned and climbed the stairs to her apartment. Everything she wanted—to save her mom, to stop the demon tearing through Blackthorn unchecked, to find Ellie alive—was too much. She needed smaller goals.

She hoped a decent night's sleep wasn't too big of an ask for the universe.

Dani unlocked her apartment door and stepped inside, wearier than she'd been in months. She stripped out of the ruined dress, unbuckled the makeshift weapon holsters around her thighs, and stepped into the shower.

The hot water pounded against her sore muscles, and in the privacy of her apartment, she allowed herself to cry. She slammed her fist against the tiled wall again and again until her knuckles bled.

Red mixed with her tears and the water and swirled down the drain. Dani washed her skin clean and grimaced as the wounds closed, leaving behind unblemished skin.

Ink Carriers didn't scar—not usually. If she could, her body would be a map of all the pain she had endured over the years. Training mishaps when she was younger. A patchwork of bites and scratches all along her body where demons claimed pieces of her flesh before she banished them.

Instead, her skin with smooth. Perfect. Everywhere except the place Silas had lived in her skin.

She missed the python every day. Every single day for five years. The temperature cooled as she used the last of the hot water, and Dani traced the scar on her arm. Her mind filled with images of Raj. The pair of them naked in bed, his lips on her scars, his hands on her hip.

A bitter cold curled around her heart as the water turned to ice. If she hadn't let herself love him, he wouldn't have been able to hurt her.

They'd both been fools.

Danika shut off the water and wrapped herself in an oversized towel. In her bedroom, she found her phone on the nightstand where she'd plugged it in before going to Lana's house to get ready for the gala. It beeped, a reminder of missed notifications. She punched in her passcode and found two voicemails waiting for her.

She dressed in her comfiest pajamas and hit play.

"Hey, Dani! It's Lana. I'm sorry to bother you while you're working a case, but ..." Lana sighed. "That police scanner Spencer tinkered with picked up a call. There's been another body dumped. A girl." She paused. Took a deep breath. "The body matches Ellie's description."

"No." The word scraped over Dani's tongue, and

her whole night came crashing down around her. "No, no, no!" This was all her fault. More proof that she wasn't fit to Carry the Ink, that she never was. A girl was dead because of her. If she'd been better at her job, if she hadn't gotten distracted by Raj and Nick and everything else, she could have found Ellie before the coroner did.

Her phone automatically started the next recording. Muffled sobs filled the room. Dread coiled in Dani's stomach.

"I can't, John."

Dani recognized the voice as Anne Hughes. Ellie's mother.

"The police called." This time it was Mr. Hughes, his voice thick with emotion. "They found someone. They think … They think it's our Ellie. They want us at the morgue tomorrow. They—" He lost his words and the phone changed hands again.

"You said you would help us," Anne said through tears, fury overtaking her heavy heart. "You promised you'd find Ellie, but you didn't. She's dead. She's dead, and it's all your fault."

"Anne," her husband rebuked.

The line cut off.

Dani didn't blame them for hating her, even though she was fairly certain she didn't promise to find Ellie alive. She never promised those kinds of results, only that she'd try her best. Miserable, Dani climbed into bed.

She was nearly asleep when someone knocked urgently at her door.

"Why won't this day just *end*," Dani groaned, pulling herself out from under the covers.

The knocking came again, louder this time.

"I'm coming, I'm coming!" she called, but she still checked the window before unlocking the door. "Officer? How can I help you?" Dani wished her weapons were within reach. There was no telling whose payroll this woman was on.

"It's Detective, actually. Detective Olivia Cho." The detective held out her badge for Dani to see. "There was an incident at Blackthorn Hospital this evening."

Dani's heart stopped. "It's my mother, isn't it? What happened? What did she do?"

Detective Cho lowered her badge. "Andrea Frost was kidnapped."

Dani leaped from Detective Cho's car the second she slowed down in front of the hospital.

Flashing police lights bathed the night in blurs of blue and red and white. Officers stood in the lobby with doctors and nurses, taking statements. There were no friendly faces among the crowd. No Nick. No other officers she knew.

It didn't matter. Nothing mattered except finding her mother.

"Who's in charge here?" Her words lashed out, loud and full of command. She had changed from her pajamas into street clothes at Detective Cho's insistence, and as the lobby silenced and all eyes turned to her, she was glad for her jeans and leather jacket. "Who let this happen?" she snapped.

Detective Cho appeared behind her. "Take a breath, Miss Frost. As I already explained, we're doing everything we can to find your mother." She gestured down the hall. "This way, please."

Dani followed the detective, an Asian American woman with dark hair cut into a crisp bob. They stopped in the hospital's security room, where several techs were reviewing footage. "You said my mother was kidnapped." Dani had been too shocked to ask questions while the detective had given her the basics on the ride over, but now that she was in the hospital, now that she was there and her mother wasn't, all the questions rushed through her. "Who was it?"

"We're hoping you might recognize them." Detective Cho turned to the white man sitting at the controls. "From the beginning."

The man adjusted the video and hit Play. Dani watched helplessly as three men in long black jackets entered the hospital. Footage like this couldn't pick up demonic traits, but Dani could feel it in her bones. The trio wasn't human.

At reception, they didn't pause to sign in. The silent footage showed the woman behind the desk stand up and yell after them. The demons didn't stop, and the woman called for security. The footage paused, and the tech guy switched the feed to another camera angle. In this one, security approached the demons.

For a moment, the demons stopped. The one in the middle looked to its companions, and before the security guards could pull their batons or Tasers, the other two demons rushed forward.

Dani winced when the demons broke the men's necks.

"How many?" she asked, voice rough and stomach twisted with nausea. "How many did they kill?"

Detective Cho stood with her arms crossed, her attention never leaving the screen. "Five."

Five human souls destroyed all so the demons could … *what*, exactly? Why had they come for her mother? Was it payback for what Dani did at the mayor's party? Had they tracked Dani's real name to her mother? Were they setting up a trap for Dani, or did they want something with Andrea herself?

Trap or not, Dani would sacrifice everything to rescue her mother.

"This next part might be hard to watch, Miss Frost," Detective Cho warned.

"Show me."

The tech switched to yet another camera, this one outside Andrea's door. With keys they had stolen from the dead security guards, the demons were inside in an instant. Andrea fought back—six years with a tormented mind hadn't completely erased her former Carrier instincts. She broke one demon's nose with a vicious smash of her elbow. Kicked another between the legs. The third demon grabbed her from behind, and Andrea smashed her skull into his face.

She fought hard, but in the end, it wasn't enough. She was outnumbered and all alone in the hospital, likely doped up on sedatives too. Guilt ate at Dani's insides as she watched the demons posing as men drag her mother out of the hospital, killing anyone that got in their way.

"Do you recognize any of those men?" Detective Cho asked, and Dani shook her head.

This was all her fault. If she'd found the demon who hurt her mother faster, she could have saved her. If she was a good daughter, she could have found a way to keep Andrea safe at home with her. Kiva could have watched over her whenever Dani was working. She could have done something, anything other than leave her unprotected in a hospital for five years.

It was only a matter of time before someone came for her. She should have seen that before now. Back when she'd locked her mother away, out of sight, out of mind, because she couldn't cope. Because she was a terrible daughter. A terrible Ink Carrier.

"I know this is a hard time, but can you think of anyone who might want to hurt your mother? Does she have any enemies? Do you? Anyone who might use her to get to you?"

Dani shook her head. "It could be anyone." Her mind raced with suspects. It could be any of the five families—she even considered the Dasari family suspect now. Fuck, it could even be someone like Sean McGrath or any of the lowlifes who were pissed that she told their spouses about their affairs.

Her life was full of enemies, and very few allies.

"Anything at all, Miss Frost? Even the smallest thing could help."

But there was nothing—at least nothing she could tell the detective. Her mother was in danger, might already be *dead,* and Dani had no idea how to find her.

Several hours later, Dani woke in her mother's empty bed.

She had convinced the detective to let her see the room, and after the crime scene techs finished gathering fingerprints and other physical evidence, they left her behind. It had taken threats, and then Dani begging through tears, to get the detective to break protocol. As soon as she was alone, Dani climbed into her mother's bed and let herself fall well and truly apart.

Tears coated her face. Sobs wracked her chest. Finally, sleep dragged her under, giving her a brief break from her misery.

But Dani was awake now, and the brightness of late morning only shed further light on her desperation.

Before she'd left late last night, Detective Cho had promised to do everything in her power to find Andrea. The detective was earnest in her proclamation, but Dani knew, more than most, how little that promise meant. People promised to do their best all the time—the police, doctors, Dani herself—and their charges still died.

Girls like Ellie still died.

The young woman's parents were probably heading to the morgue right then to identify their dead daughter. Dani could still hear the grief that laced each word of their voicemail. And she had played her part in their grief; she had given them hope and then failed to deliver.

Now, her own mother might be dead too.

Her tears came again, closing her throat. Her entire life was one huge fucking mess. What was even the point anymore? For every demon she banished in this city, the five families raised a dozen more.

The scales were already tipped in their favor, and

Dani was a fool to think she could ever make an impact.

She wasn't sure why she even tried. What was the point of her power if she couldn't actually make a difference?

Dani cursed her ancestors. She cursed the Ink. She cursed herself for daring to believe she could fix anything. And when she ran out of people to curse, when she grew sick of her own self-pity, she finally dragged herself out of the bed.

With careful fingers, Dani picked through her mother's life. There wasn't much, and the lack tugged at Dani's heart. When she'd first placed her mother at this hospital, she tried to bring gifts, little tokens for her mother to remember her by. But so many things were a risk for Andrea, and the hospital wouldn't let her keep them—for their safety as much as her mother's.

The one thing the room had in abundance was Andrea's artwork.

Stacks of paper covered nearly every surface. Many of them had spilled during the fight, and they lay scattered across the floor. Dani picked up one from the desk, recognizing Kiva with a pang in her heart. The Ink were often the subject of Andrea's art. Poe in flight or sitting smug on a branch. Kiva and a young Dani lounging together under a tree.

Jasper and Silas, always together. Her heart ached anew.

Andrea didn't know she'd lost Silas.

But it wasn't just the Ink that Andrea was compelled to draw again and again. Dozens and dozens of pages contained little more than illegible lines and strange squiggles. Still, Dani paged through each one, wondering at the hellish world that was her mother's mind. The drawings were much like Andrea herself, spurts of clarity mixed with confusion and nonsensical ramblings.

Dani's fingers stopped flipping through the pages and turned back a few, something catching her eye. The stack of paper fell through her fingers and scattered across the floor as she clutched the single image. Her mother had scrawled a crescent moon with an arrow through it.

It looked uncomfortably familiar.

Dani got to her knees and rummaged through the other pages with renewed vigor, spreading them across the floor before her. She arranged the drawings like a puzzle, shifting each piece until the image took shape. With growing dread, she realized all the strange shapes weren't just the imaginings of her mother's tortured mind.

They were all part of the same image.

It took the better part of an hour, but Dani fit the

last piece in place and stood to examine her work. The symbol covered almost the entire floor, and Dani had to climb onto the bed to get a vantage point where she could see the entire thing at once.

It was a summoning sigil. One she'd seen before.

Dani pulled out her phone, ignoring all the missed messages from Lana and Spencer, and opened her photos. She compared the picture on her phone to Andrea's drawing on the floor three times before she could believe her eyes.

All this time, her mother had been trying to warn her, trying to send her a message. She had painstakingly drawn the sigil of the demon who had marked all those bodies.

Verloc Djurian Rlenheim.

Verloc Djurian Rlenheim.

Everywhere Dani turned on this case, the demon's name followed her like a ghost. The dead bodies. Ricardo. Ellie. Her mom. How was it all linked? What was this demon trying to do?

Answers to the rest of her questions could wait. First, she needed to rescue her mom, and to do that, she needed to find the necromancers who'd raised Verloc. If her mother was drawing the sigil, they had to be the ones who took her. It was the only thing that made any sense.

Dani left the hospital and hailed a cab.

On the way home, she texted Spencer and Lana, telling them to meet her back at her place. She explained that her mom was missing, that she needed their help.

Her friends were already waiting for her when the taxi dropped her off in front of the bar.

The three of them went up to Dani's apartment, where she immediately released the Ink. The force of their departure nearly sent Dani to her knees, but Spencer caught her at the last minute. Poe—who had fully recovered since being banished to her skin the night before—circled the apartment, agitated and ready to attack. Jasper slithered up Lana's leg, and Kiva pressed closed to Dani's side.

"How can we help?" Spencer sat on the edge of the couch. "Anything you need, Dani. We're in this with you."

What has happened, Little Warrior? Kiva asked, pressing the flat of her head against Dani's thigh. The Ink could sense her emotions, and they were on overdrive, thoughts and fears crashing against each other in Dani's troubled mind. They couldn't read her mind though.

She swallowed down the emotion in her throat. "Demons took Mom." The words spurred both her and the Ink into a frenzy of action. Her mind filled with the Inks' overlapping questions while Dani stockpiled weapons on her kitchen table.

When did they take her?

Who?

I'll rip out their throats.

"We'll find her," Dani promised, looking over her blades and firearms. It didn't feel like enough, but it was all she had at her disposal.

"How can we help?" It was Lana who asked this time, but it wasn't her Dani needed—at least not yet.

She turned to Spencer. Poe had perched on his shoulder, ruffling his feathers. "I need you to do something for me."

"Anything." Spencer stood, disturbing Poe. "Name it."

Despite his reassurance, Dani hesitated. "I wouldn't ask for this if there was another way. I wouldn't ask if they hadn't taken my mother."

"What is it?" Spencer closed the distance between them. "Dani, what?"

Dani worried at her lip. She knew what this would cost Spencer, but they didn't have a choice. "I need you to trace the sigil back to the necromancer who used it."

Spencer froze. His eyes went wide.

"I know. I hate myself for asking, but we can't trust Raj to do it. Just look." She pulled up a photo she'd taken of her mother's drawings and turned the screen for Spence. "Verloc is connected to my mother. I don't know how, but he is. We need to know who summoned him. Whoever is behind him is behind my mother's disappearance. I can *feel* it."

Silence fell in the cramped apartment—three humans and three ancient beings all succumbed to anticipation. Until finally, *finally*, Spencer spoke.

"Okay." The single word fell from his lips with all the resignation of a man who had accepted a terrible fate. Spencer had always said he never wanted to touch necromantic power again, how it coursed through his body like a poison. It took him years to purge it from his system the first time, and there was no telling how he'd react to the magic now.

He ran a hand over his face, his hair falling from a vivid violet back to his natural brown. "I'll need a few supplies from the office, and it can't be done before sunset."

He turned to leave, but Dani grabbed his hand. "I'm sorry, Spence. I'm so, so sorry."

Spencer pulled her into a fierce hug. "You'd do the same for me." He stepped back and brushed the hair from her face with all the tenderness of a favorite brother. "This kind of magic is more dangerous than you know. I'm counting on you and Lana to keep me off it once this is done."

"Of course," Dani promised. She'd do whatever he needed.

"Good." Spencer smiled and went to the door.

When he pulled it open to go to the office, Nick stood on the other side, his fist poised to knock. "Uh, Dani?"

But Dani was already moving to the door. "Nick, what are you doing here?"

Nick shoved his hands in his pockets, and Spencer excused himself, taking Lana with him to the office to gather supplies for the ritual. Nick shifted on his feet, tracking the movement of the Ink behind her until he brought his full attention to Dani. "I heard about what happened at the hospital."

Dani nodded. "Come in."

The detective shut the door behind him, but he hovered close by as the Ink tracked his every movement. "Do they know I'm a friend?"

"They won't hurt you," Dani promised, shooting a meaningful look at Poe.

Don't look at me, the bird squawked in her mind. *If you won't take Raj, he'd be a suitable match to make an heir.*

God, even in her direst moments, the feather-brained fool still had a one-track mind. "Can I help you with something, Detective?" Dani hadn't forgotten the way he'd left her last night, standing alone in the cold. "I thought you needed time to think."

"I do." Nick's fingers brushed over his badge, like it was a talisman of the past Dani had destroyed when she inadvertently introduced him to the demonic world. "I may not understand what you're up against, but I care about you, Dani. I'll do whatever I can to help get your mother back."

The detective started to reach for her but seemed to think better of it, cupping the back of his neck instead. "And I'm … I'm sorry for leaving the way I did. If I had stayed, I could have gone with you to the hospital."

Dani nodded, unsure of her ability to say anything about her mom without breaking apart. "Did you hear about the girl they found last night?"

"Ellie's parents are scheduled to visit the morgue this afternoon, yes." Nick took in Dani's apartment, his first time being there. "That's a lot of firepower. What are you planning?"

She ignored his question. "Do you know if she was marked like the others?"

"I didn't get a chance to examine her. One of the other officers brought her in." Nick rubbed his temples. "How can I trust the other officers now that I know half of them work for wizards?"

"Necromancers," Dani corrected. "Trust is a funny thing in my world, Detective. I'm sorry you got dragged into it." She sat down at the table and kicked out a chair for him, wishing she could bring herself to reach for his hand. "I never meant for you to find out."

Before Nick could respond, Dani's front door swung open to reveal Spencer and Lana, each with an armload of supplies. Dani hurried over to help them bring everything inside. They cleared the table of Dani's weapons and laid out the items for Spencer's ritual.

Salt to create a protective field around Spence as he cast. Chalk to draw the sigil he was about to trace. At least a dozen candles, and a long, slender knife.

Nick watched them work in silence, taking it all in.

The wait for sunset was agony, but there was nothing any of them could do until they knew who raised Verloc. Nothing but pace the small apartment and triple-check that Spencer had everything he needed for the spell.

"Are you sure about this?" Lana asked as the sun finally dipped below the horizon, and Spencer checked his supplies one last time. "Isn't there another way to—"

"I'll be fine, Lan. Promise." Spencer arranged the candles around three edges of the table and opened the jar of salt. "You made up your mind and let us bargain with Pam. Let me do the same." He ushered them away from the table. "Before I panic and change my mind."

"Spence," Lana protested, but Dani shook her head.

They didn't have a choice.

Spencer carefully poured a circle of salt around the table, sealing himself—and the magic he was about to use—inside. When the circle was complete, he lit the candles and chanted incantations under his breath that Dani couldn't understand. It was a demonic language, some bastardization of Latin, and it set her teeth on edge.

Dani wished there was another option. She hated to put Spencer through this, hated to see the tremor in his usually steady hands. Asking him to do this was like giving drugs to an addict.

She was a terrible friend.

Candles lit and the circle sealed, Spencer closed his eyes and took several deep breaths. "Dani, send me a photo of the sigil." He held his phone as he waited for Dani's text, and when it went through, he pulled up the image and set the phone on the table. "Here goes nothing."

Dani, Lana, Nick, and the Ink all took a step back, watching and waiting in the little apartment.

Spencer picked up the white chalk and traced the demon's sigil into the kitchen table before him. He chanted as he worked, voice a deep growl that rose and fell in unpredictable currents. A malevolent energy charged the room, making the Ink restless. Dani recalled them to her skin, wincing as they bled into her, but her focus remained on her friend.

The chanting rose to a fever pitch as Spencer completed the final line of the sigil. His pupils expanded to blot out the soft brown of his irises, expanded past the edges to consume some of the whites of his eyes. He dropped the chalk and picked up the long knife, setting the edge of the blade along the back of his forearm.

"He's not going to—" Nick began, but Dani hushed him. They couldn't afford to distract from the ritual.

Spencer's voice was no longer his own, several octaves lower than normal and filled with sounds of shredding metal and crunching gravel.

With a quick jerk of his arm, Spence drew the blade across his skin. Blood spilled along the long line and dripped over the sigil. Acrid smoke curled into the air, winding in deliberate circles around Spencer's head.

A scream of pain and terror tore from his throat, and he gripped the table's edge for support.

"Spencer!" Lana rushed forward, but Dani caught the back of her shirt and hauled her away from the salt line.

"We can't interrupt him now," Dani said, holding her friend. "He's so close."

Spencer's head fell back until he stared unseeing toward the sky, his entire body rigid and the power in the room suffocating. Then in a rush, it all stopped. Dani's ears popped from the sudden change in pressure.

And Spencer collapsed to the floor.

Dani and Lana rushed forward as one, sweeping away the salt with their shoes until they could cross the barrier. Dani lifted him into her arms, grateful for her enhanced Carrier strength.

She brought him to the couch and laid him on the soft cushions. His entire body trembled in violent muscle spasms.

"Nick, grab the ice pack from the freezer. A kitchen towel too." Dani knelt beside the couch as she directed her team. "Lana, can you grab him a glass of water? He'll need that soon."

Lana and Nick left to get the items she requested, while Dani stroked Spencer's hair out of his face. "I'm sorry," she whispered, again and again. "I'm so, so sorry."

The muscle spasm slowly calmed, and Dani accepted the ice pack from Nick. She wrapped it in the towel and pressed it to Spencer's sweat-slicked forehead and neck until the former necromancer's eyes pried open.

"You okay?" Dani pulled the ice away so she could see her friend better.

"My head is pounding, my body feels like it was run over by a truck, and my stomach has seen better days." He pushed himself up to lean against the armrest. "But I'm okay."

"Did you see who raised the demon?" Dani asked, failing to keep the desperation out of her voice. "Was it the mayor?"

Spencer shook his head, wincing and pressing a hand to his temple a second later. "Fuck me," he groaned and reached for the water Lana held, draining half the glass in one go. "It wasn't just the mayor," he said at last, voice strained. "It was the entire Conrad family."

She couldn't believe it.

Dani paced the living room, dread and determination filling her in equal measure. "The entire family?" she asked Spencer again, and he nodded. "Fucking hell." They were in deep shit, deeper than Dani had ever guessed. If it took the entire Conrad clan to raise Verloc, he was more powerful than anything they had faced before.

The whole family wouldn't work in tandem to raise a demon unless there was no other way. Unless the demon was so strong that it required their united power to raise it.

But Dani didn't care about any of that. The Conrads had her mom, and she was going to get Andrea back. Now.

With new determination in her movements, Dani

shrugged into her shoulder holster and fit each of her handguns—loaded with the banishing bullets Spencer had made for her—on either side.

"Dani?" Lana's concerned voice followed her into the kitchen as Dani tightened the modified hilt for her bladeless sword around her waist. "What do you think you're doing?"

"I'm getting my mom back." Dani tugged her leather jacket on to conceal her small arsenal of weapons.

"But you don't even know where she is," Lana argued.

"The hell I don't." Dani checked her weapons one more time, making sure they wouldn't alter her maneuverability. "I'd bet my life they have her at their manor."

The estate was a fortress, and the only place large and secluded enough to perform a ritual with the entire Conrad family. They must not have fully raised Verloc yet though. Dani—and especially the Ink—would have noticed if such a powerful demon was there during the party.

"Dani, if you charge into a place like that without backup, you'll be risking your life." Nick stepped into her path and blocked her from the door. "I know you're hurting, but you need to be smart about this."

"I have to do this." Dani easily shoved Nick out of the way.

"Not on your own, you don't." Nick blocked the door again, seemingly unconcerned with how easily Dani had maneuvered him, how much stronger she was. "At least let me come with you. I may not understand everything that's happening, but I'm a good shot."

"I'm coming too," Lana said, rising from the couch. "Well, Pam can go. She can be helpful when my body is on the line. Plus, she'll want to make sure our end of the bargain is complete so she can have her fun."

Dani looked from Lana to Nick and back again. She didn't want her friends to risk themselves, but she couldn't deny that backup was probably a good idea. And Pam always loved a bit of chaos. "We can't leave Spencer alone. Not when he's like this."

Still shaky and too pale, the former necromancer pushed himself into more of a seated position. "I'll call Adrian. He loves to play doctor." Spencer tried for a smile, but sitting up alone left him weak. He slumped against the back of the couch with a wince. "Detoxing from magic like that is a bitch."

Fresh guilt stabbed Dani's heart. Spencer had been free of necromantic magic for so many years. She hated that he had relapsed because of her.

"Cassie can come over too," Lana added. "I'm

surprised she hasn't blown up my phone yet, demanding dinner. I'll have her bring over food. Spencer will be well cared for, Dani. Let us help you."

"Fine," Dani agreed, an uneasy feeling tugging at her gut. "Call Adrian. The second he gets here, we're gone."

It took Spencer's boyfriend thirty minutes to fight traffic before he arrived at Dani's apartment. Adrian took one look at the scene before him and nodded to Dani. "Go. I'll take good care of him."

Dani motioned for Nick and Lana to head out, but she paused at the threshold. "I'm sorry about this, Adrian. Cassie will be over a little later. She can get you anything else you might need."

The tall, graceful man smiled. "Spence is fully capable of getting himself into trouble, Dani. He'll be fine."

She wanted to argue, but Spencer cut her off. "Go on, Dani. Save the world. It's what you do best."

"Feel better," Dani said, and disappeared out the door.

Lana and Nick waited for her in the small parking lot behind the bar, loitering by Nick's sedan. They piled into the car and fine-tuned their plan on the way to the mayor's house.

Dani had Nick park a half mile before the compound where the car wouldn't be seen by any of the mayor's staff or family. Dani and Nick checked their weapons one last time.

"Take this. Your gun will be useless against demons." Dani gave Nick one of the guns Spencer had spelled for her, plus an extra magazine of banishing bullets. "A head shot with these is the only way to get rid of them."

"How will I know who the demons are?" He accepted the weapon, holstering his standard-issue Glock.

"They'll be the ones trying to eat you." Dani turned to Lana, who was fiddling with her amulet. "Are you ready?"

Lana bit her lip, but she nodded. "Keep this safe for me?"

"Always," Dani promised.

"Here goes nothing." Lana paused and turned to the detective. "The demon who possesses me is a succubus. She will try to seduce you, but please don't let her. It'll make things really awkward between us after."

"Possesses you? What—"

But Lana lifted the amulet and passed it to Dani before the detective could finish. Her eyes rolled to the back of her head, and when her awareness returned, Lana was gone.

"Ooh la la," Pam crooned, smiling at Nick. "What

do we have here?" She reached out and trailed a finger down his where his abs would be down the buckle of his leather belt.

Nick stepped out of reach. "Your life is incredibly strange, Dani."

Dani couldn't deny his words, so she focused on the task at hand. Namely, explaining their situation to Pam. "Lana assured us you would be on board for this. Can we count on you to be helpful?"

Pam twirled a lock of hair around her finger. "Lead the way, Ink Carrier."

So, she did. The three of them moved silently through the trees to the Conrad estate. Halfway there, Dani released the Ink. Poe soared into the air, and Dani gave him instructions to destroy any CCTV cameras on the property. Kiva prowled alongside Dani, and Jasper rode on her shoulders.

At the edge of Mayor Conrad's property, a wrought iron gate separated them from the premises. "Once we're inside," Dani whispered, "we split up. Nick and Pam—you'll slip along back to the gardens and enter through there. Kiva will go with you for protection. *And* to keep Pam in line."

Dani wasn't about to leave Pam alone with Nick. The demon was a succubus after all. She was likely to try to seduce Nick or trick him into a bargain without proper supervision.

"What about you?" Nick asked, looking out over the estate.

"Jasper, Poe, and I will enter through a side window. We'll sweep the first floor and meet you outside the ballroom. Between Pam and me, we should be able to sense where the greatest power in the house is."

"I don't think you should go in alone," Nick said.

Dani reached for Jasper and caressed her fingers down his scaled body. "I'm not alone." She waited for the all-clear from Poe, then reached for the wrought iron and heaved with all her strength. Inch by inch, the metal gave way.

"You really could kick my ass, huh?" Nick asked, sounding part amused, part excited by the prospect.

"Only if you ask nicely," Dani said, the tension before the fight masking all her worry and fear. She slipped through the new gap in the bars, and her team followed suit.

They approached the house and split up as planned once they neared the massive estate. Pam, Nick, and Kiva veered left around the back of the house, while Dani and the rest of the Ink headed for a secluded window surrounded by shrubbery that would keep her out of view.

Dani reached for the window but found it locked.

She cursed, trying to decide if the speed of smashing in the window was worth the noise it would make.

I can dissolve the frames, Jasper hissed, already sliding from Dani's shoulders. He bit into the window casing, injecting the wood with venom. It bubbled up, the supernatural venom eating through the organic material until it was little more than pulp.

"Nicely done, Jasper." Dani shoved up the window, and Jasper absorbed what was left of his venom through his scales. There were definitely benefits to the Ink being ancient spirits rather than true replicas of the animals they mimicked.

Dani squared her shoulders and touched the weapons strapped to her body. "I'm coming, Mom. Hang on."

But before she could slip through the window, someone grabbed her arm and yanked her back.

Dani put all her strength into an elbow jab and aimed right for her assailant's abdomen.

The man behind her let out a startled wheeze and released her. "Dani, wait."

But she didn't wait. She whirled around, her fist already arcing in a perfect right hook. The man ducked under her fist just in time, backing away with his hands up.

"Dani, it's me." He lowered her hands, revealing a face Dani knew all too well.

Rajan.

Her anger boiled at the sight of him. At his chiseled jawline and full lips. It was him all along. It had to be. Why else would he be at the Conrad estate in the middle of the night?

"How could you?" she demanded, not giving him any space to retreat. She lunged, trying to distract him with a quick jab so she could sneak in a vicious uppercut. But she and Raj had sparred often during their three years together, and he drew frantic sigils in the air, summoning protective barriers.

"Stop it, Dani. Listen to me," he said, breathless as he traced more runes to replace the ones Dani had already smashed.

"Listen to you? After you've betrayed me again and again?" Dani smashed through the next barrier hard enough that her momentum carried her forward and she caught Raj across the chin. "How long have you been working for Conrad? Did you send the demons to the hospital yourself?"

"The hospital? What are you talking about?" He seemed genuinely confused, but Dani didn't trust it. Raj drew another barrier and used it as a battering ram, shoving Dani back toward the house.

"Then what are you doing here?" Dani tried to slip around the barrier, but Raj knew her too well. He sidestepped in time to keep the barrier in place and pinned her against the side of the house, right beside the window she'd opened. "Poe? Jasper? Where the hell are you?"

Poe swooped toward them, but he came to rest on Raj's shoulder. *Listen to him, Dani.*

Betrayal coursed through her. The Ink were supposed to be on her side. Always. They weren't supposed to agree with the enemy, with the man who hurt her every chance he got. She held on to her rage to bury the unspeakable grief that rose like the tide. "Why are you here?" she demanded again.

"I couldn't stop thinking about the sigil we saw at the morgue," Raj said. "After our meeting with the mayor, I knew he was hiding something. So, I tracked the sigil back to the entire Conrad family." He paused, clearly waiting for Dani's show of surprise. When it didn't come, he raised an eyebrow. "You knew? How?"

Dani was too ashamed to admit that she had asked Spencer to break his vow to stay away from necromantic magic. "If you knew then, why didn't you say something sooner? Why buddy up to Conrad at the fundraiser?"

"Because sometimes, Danika, it's easier to draw out the truth if people think you're an ally." He glared at her, his expression distorted slightly from the magical barrier between them. "If I drop this, are you going to try to hit me again?" He gestured to his hands, held out to keep the shield in place.

"Maybe," she muttered, earning a scowl from Raj and a disappointed head tilt from Poe. "No."

Raj lowered his hands and the energy shield faded

to nothing between them. They stood there, in the shadow of the mayor's grand estate, with their shattered trust laid before them like an offering. "I was going to tell you at the fundraiser," Raj said at last, "but you caused all sorts of trouble before I had a chance. And then you wouldn't stop fighting me about every last thing. You always see the worst in me."

Dani felt smaller than she had in a long time. "Raj. I—"

"If you had just gotten in my car, I would have told you everything." He ran a hand through his dark hair and stared up at the darkening sky. "I thought there was a part of you that still trusted me. I guess I was wrong."

"Raj—"

"Forget it, Dani," he said, cutting her off a second time. "Whatever Conrad's doing in there is big, much bigger than either of us should handle alone. We might as well finish this together. Once it's done, you'll never have to see me again." He rubbed his jaw where she'd hit him. "You still have a hell of a right hook."

"They took my mom." Dani hadn't planned to tell him, and it wasn't an excuse—not really—but she had hurt him. It was more than the fist he caught with his face, and she needed him to know she was sorry, even if she couldn't say the words.

"The hospital ..." Raj pieced her earlier accusations together. "You thought I had something to do with them taking Andrea?" He didn't sound angry anymore, only hurt. Like she'd torn out his heart.

"I didn't know what to think. All I know is that she's gone, and that she's probably here. And then you showed up and I—" Dani squeezed her eyes against the tears. "We can't keep delaying. I have to get in there and save her."

"What's the plan?" Raj approached the window she'd fizzled through with the help of Jasper's venom.

"Simple." Dani gripped the windowsill. "Get in. Grab Mom. Get out."

"You do realize it won't be that easy, don't you?" Raj watched Dani haul herself up until she was sitting on the ledge. "Whatever's happening in there is incredibly powerful. Can't you feel it? The mayor's plans won't be good for anyone—not even the other necromancers in town."

"Of course, I feel it," she snapped, irritation rising again. The power was even stronger now that she sat on the windowsill. It pressed heavily on her like stacks of limestone, a coldness like slipping under a frozen lake.

Dani into the mansion and reached out an arm to help Raj follow her inside. His hand fit perfectly into hers, and she felt herself grinning despite the horrors that awaited them.

"It's a good thing I carry a big sword."

Silence rested over the first floor of the estate like a blanket of fresh snow. They had entered into some kind of sitting room with straight-backed chairs and expensive throw rugs, but the room was empty of life. Empty, yet the air felt charged with power.

Dani grasped her hilt and slid the blade free. As much as she preferred a sword in one hand and a gun in the other, she couldn't risk the noise ruining their element of surprise. Not with the stakes this high.

Besides, her sword did a damn good job at decapitating demons.

Jasper slithered through the open window and Poe flew in behind him. The king cobra flicked his tongue. *The air is thick with the stench of demons.*

Poe landed on the back of one of the stiff chairs. *Some of it's old, from the guests last night.* He tilted his head left, then right, then left again. *This way.*

The bird flew out of the room, leaving Dani and Raj to hurry after him. At least Poe wouldn't complain about Dani avoiding her *sacred duty* for a few weeks after something this big. The uneasy feeling crawling along her skin told Dani there was a lot of demonic energy in this place. She just had to find it.

And hope it wasn't too much for her small crew.

Poe soared ahead and turned a corner. A man shouted and Poe's indignant caw replied. Dani raced forward, but by the time she arrived, the pair of necromancers who had been guarding a set of doors were on the ground with blood-covered scratches swiped across their faces. They held their hands protectively over their heads and Poe swooped at them again.

Dani raised her sword, but Raj held out a hand. "Let me." Faster than Dani could object, Raj traced intricate patterns in the air, fingers moving with perfect precision. Energy shields shot forward and bound the necromancers in little prisons against the wall.

"This way." Raj reached for the door and yanked it

open, recoiling as the demonic power intensified. The air was thick with it, making it hard to breathe.

They were definitely heading in the right direction.

Dani reached for Jasper, who had coiled up her body to rest around her shoulders. He nudged his head into her palm, and she felt her own fear reflected back at her. She and the Ink were made for this, sure, but there were limits to their strength.

Dani was, after all, only mortal.

In another part of the house, someone screamed. A low growl rumbled toward them, and then a wet *squish*. A moment later, Kiva appeared, trailed by an overly pale Nick and a delighted succubus. Pam had transformed Lana's fingernails into long claws, which now dripped with blood.

"That explains the squish," Dani said, reaching for Kiva. Her fingers slid through the panther's soft fur, and the strength of having her remaining Ink all together gave her a shot of courage. "Ready?"

Nods all around. Nick put a little more distance between him and Pam, but his hands were steady on his gun. "Dasari," he greeted Raj, hiding any confusion he might feel at seeing the necromancer at Dani's side.

"Detective." Raj rolled his shoulders and cracked his neck, already tracing shields into the air with his long, elegant fingers. Pam approached Raj, licking her lips. She must recognize him from the first time they met five years ago. The succubus was desperate to jump his bones then, and she wasted no time now, leaning in to press herself against his body.

Before Dani could intervene, Raj whirled on the succubus, pressing her between energy shields. He leaned close and whispered something into Pam's ear, too quiet for even Dani's enhanced hearing to pick up.

"Should we …," Nick said beside her, nodding down the stairs.

"Yeah. Raj?" Dani paused at the threshold to the stairs. "You good?"

Raj dropped the shields holding Pam and nodded.

"All right, then." Dani squared her shoulders. "Stay close. Whatever's down there is strong."

Poe dove below first, and Dani hurried after the bird. Nick came next, Kiva and the others following behind. At the bottom of the stairs, the basement hallway broke off in several directions, low chanting echoing off the stone walls. Flaming torches lined the path, casting dancing shadows all around them.

"Which way?" Dani asked the Ink.

"Down here," said Raj, and they all followed. With each step across the musty dirt floor, the pulse of necromantic magic grew stronger, raising all the small hairs on Dani's arms and neck. Kiva growled.

"Who's there?" An unfamiliar voice echoed toward them, bouncing off the uneven stone. "Billings, is that you? Did you check the CCTV? The feeds are still out."

Raj held up a hand to stop the group, and Dani adjusted her grip on her sword, easing to the front of her team. A guttural sound pierced the air, definitely demonic in nature.

"Here we go," Dani whispered. She took off like a shot and raced around the final corner. Jasper sprang from her shoulders the moment the second set of guards came into view. The small battalion of necromancers and demon-possessed corpses made the two guards upstairs seem like kittens. Eight—no, ten—guards protected huge double doors, solid stone monstrosities covered in demonic symbols.

Her sudden appearance spurred the guards into action, and then it was a clash of metal against claws, pincers, and barbed tentacles. Dani ducked under a demon's dagger-length claws and brought up her sword in a vicious arc. The blade sliced through skin and muscle and bone, severing the arm clean off. Demonic ichor sprayed across her face, but she didn't have time to care about that. She spun, blade ringing through the air, and aimed for the demon's neck.

But a blade met hers, a necromancer parrying her blow. His wide boot shot toward her stomach, but she backed out of reach, only to crash into yet another guard. Except when she turned to defend herself, she found Raj staring back at her, his hair falling into his face. Despite the chill, his skin sheened with sweat.

Around them, the hallway was in chaos as Dani's team tried to breach the stone doors. Gunfire echoed through the chaos as Nick shot with an expert aim. Poe slashed with his talons and stabbed with his beak. Kiva snapped her wide jaws around a necromancer's shoulder and tugged him into the air until he screamed and his shoulder dislocated.

Raj dove back into the fray, using shields as battering rams.

Something tightened around Dani's wrist, wrenching it until her sword clattered to the stone floor. She looked away from Nick, reloading the gun she'd given him, in time to see the tentacled demon drawing close.

She pivoted, throwing all her weight behind a sharp blow with her elbow. But the demon barely seemed to feel the impact, twisting her wrist until she fell to her knees to relieve the pressure. With her free hand, she grasped at her gun, yanking it from the holster at her ribs.

"Eat lead, squid brain." Dani squeezed the trigger,

but another tentacle burst from the demon's chest. It curled around the gun before she could get off a shot. The pressure at her wrist tightened, her bones grinding together painfully.

A gun went off behind her, and Dani ducked from pure instinct. The bullet struck the tentacled demon between the eyes, and it dropped to the ground, its suctioned grip releasing from Dani.

"Thanks." Dani glanced over to find Nick lowering his weapon. He smiled at her, letting his guard down for just a moment. The necromancer Kiva had bitten surged up, his fingers tracing sigils in the air. Nick grasped his throat and fell to his knees. "Nick!" Dani shoved the tentacles away, searching for her gun. She was *not* going to be the reason Nick died today.

Raj split the skull of the demon beside him, leaving Kiva to go in for the final kill. Jasper had already bitten a demon and injected it with his potent venom, bringing it a fast and painful death. Nick squirmed in the necromancer's magical hold, the veins on his neck bulging as he choked and gasped for air.

Dani abandoned her search for the gun and lunged forward with a war cry. She ducked under the weapons that swung toward her and rammed her shoulder into the necromancer stealing Nick's breath.

They fell to the ground in a heap, and Dani let out

all her rage at the Conrads and her fear over her mother and her need to protect Nick and Pam and her Ink. She landed blow after blow against the necromancer's jaw and nose until she heard Nick gasp and inhale behind her.

But she wasn't done. Her rage couldn't be quelled. She gripped the necromancer's head and slammed it into the ground until he fell unconscious.

A hand appeared before her, brown skin spattered with red. Dani accepted Raj's help, and he pulled her back to standing. The floor was littered with bodies, the path to the wide stone doors clear. Dani surveyed their group.

"Where the hell is Pam?" She picked through the mess, reclaiming her sword and her gun.

Raj shrugged, and Kiva nudged Dani's leg. *Don't worry about the succubus, Little Warrior. We must hurry. The power grows.*

"Everyone good?" Dani waited for their confirmation before crossing to the double doors. "Be prepared for anything."

The noise of their battle should have alerted everyone inside of their presence, so the necromancers must have had their hands full raising Verloc since no one came to assist the guards. Regardless, the element of surprise was no longer theirs to wield, so

Dani flung open the doors and strode in like she owned the place.

Past the stone doors, a wide, cavernous room opened before her. Gone were the dirt floors and rough stone walls, replaced with floor-to-ceiling black marble that absorbed the light. Shadowy, hooded figures moved in her peripheral, and a fresh rush of fear swept through her. There were at least three dozen necromancers surrounding the edge of the room.

At the center, a single figure stood before a glowing summoning circle. Though the circle was easily ten feet across, it was still dwarfed by the grandness of the mansions underground level.

At Dani's approach, the figure tipped back his hood, revealing Nathaniel Conrad. His pupils had blown wide from casting, the black taking over everything else.

"Nice of you to join us, Miss Frost." Mayor Conrad smiled, and there wasn't an ounce of concern on his face. "Allow me to introduce Verloc Djurian Rlenheim. *You* may know him as The Reaper."

The mayor stepped aside to reveal a wickedly handsome creature standing within the summoning circle. Skin as pale as bone, features elongated until they toed the line between beauty and horror. Its fingers stretched to a needle's point, three times the length of Dani's.

A cold chill sucked all the air from her lungs. She did know this demon.

It was the same one that took her mom's mind.

"Hello, Ink Carrier," the bone-white demon cooed, its voice sliding around Dani's brain. She remembered that voice, remembered the glowing red eyes that last time were hidden behind a corpse's baby blues.

There was no corpse this time. Not yet.

This was Verloc himself, a demon drawn into her world but still awaiting its host, something to keep it held fast in the human realm once it stepped outside of the glowing sigil. Otherwise, it would be sucked back into its own demonic world.

Verloc smiled, and the air cooled around them. The room stank of sulfur and sweat and freshly dug graves.

And Dani couldn't bring herself to move.

She trembled—with rage and fear and a bone-deep sense that only one of them could leave that room alive—and remembered every terrible moment in the graveyard six years ago. Verloc's finger penetrating Andrea's skull. The way he'd tasted Dani, his vile tongue on her cheek, and proclaimed her the last of her line.

Though she'd cut off his hand and driven him away, it was too late. Andrea never recovered. Dani took on the Ink too young. Both of their lives had been altered forever.

"What's the matter, Ink Carrier?" Verloc's red eyes flicked to where Kiva stood with her haunches raised. "Cat got your tongue?"

Kiva growled. *He's not fully in our world yet, Little Warrior. The sigil keeps him here. He's still feeding from the necromancers in the room. There's time.*

"What are you doing, Nathaniel?" Raj cut in before Dani could react. "This is madness. You can't raise a reaper."

"Watch me." The mayor gestured to the necromancers along the walls, and seven hooded figures darted forward.

Raj released a frustrated yell and turned to cast magic barriers against the necromancers. Nick raised the gun Dani had given him, shouting for the necromancers to halt. Dani wanted to join them, to protect them, but Kiva's voice shouted in her mind.

We have to break the sigil! Hurry!

Though it hurt to turn her back on the men who had come with her, Kiva was right. They had to banish the reaper. Already, power radiated off Verloc in pulsing waves. If the necromancers provided him with a human host, she might not be strong enough to stop him.

Dani launched herself forward, Kiva and Jasper at her heels while Poe soared ahead. The space between them and the sigil shrank to almost nothing before Mayor Conrad raised a hand. They slammed into a solid wall of energy. It tossed them back, and Dani landed hard on her side, the cold marble floor tearing at her skin.

"I wouldn't try that again if I were you," the mayor said, calm in a way that terrified Dani. He pointed behind her, and she whirled around to see what new horror he had in store for her.

Raj and Nick had fallen to the Conrad necromancers. Three men held Nick in their grasp. Blood dripped down his face, and his gun was in pieces on the floor. The other four necromancers had pulled Raj to the other side of the room and forced him to his knees. The tallest of the men kicked Raj each time he tried to pull free.

But that wasn't the sight that stole Dani's voice and upended her entire world.

It was her mother.

A large, heavily muscled man dragged Andrea forward, a knife held tight to her neck. Dani staggered to her feet, careful not to get too close to Verloc's sigil. If she crossed the line, he'd be able to attack her or inhabit her body.

"Danika? Baby, is that you? What's going on? Where are we?"

Her mother still had on the pajamas she wore when Conrad's demons had abducted her, her hair a wild tangle of confusion to match her glazed eyes and furrowed brow as her troubled mind tried to make sense of the situation.

"It's okay, Mom. Everything's going to be all right." Dani ground her teeth and turned her attention back to the mayor. "Let her go. Now."

"Drop your weapons," Nathaniel Conrad countered.

Her failed ambush of the sigil had brought her mere inches from the mayor. Now, he stepped past her, crossing the room to her mother. He motioned to the necromancer, and the man dug his blade deeper into Andrea's throat. A line of red slipped down her skin.

Her mother cried out, calling Dani's name, her voice full of fear and pain.

"Stop!" Dani dropped her sword. "Please, stop."

Nathaniel flashed that politician's smile. "All your weapons, Miss Frost."

Dani relieved herself of her gun and took a dagger from her left boot. When she stood, the mayor gave her an unamused looked. "Fine," she said with a sigh, pulling a final dagger from her waist.

"The animals too, Miss Frost." Nathaniel scowled. "I'm not running a petting zoo."

She froze, remembering the last time a necromancer held her hostage with the Ink trapped inside her skin. Trapped with no way out. She couldn't leave them helpless like that. Not again. If she lost any more of them, she—

It's okay, Little Warrior. Kiva nudged her head into Dani's hand. *Trust that you're not alone.*

Dani released a shuddering breath, but she recalled the Ink to her, wincing with their return. Wincing as the disappearance of the Ink further terrified her mother, who raved about demons and begged Dani to take her away.

She had to shut out her mother's voice if she wanted to keep breathing. "Why are you doing this?" she demanded, voice shaking with adrenaline.

"You haven't figured it out?" Nathaniel laughed, pacing a short path in front of her mother. Powerful men *loved* to brag about their perceived accomplishments. "I guess it's too complicated for a simple girl like you to understand. I did a little digging after we *officially* met, Miss Frost. Poor thing, didn't even finish high school."

"Get to the point," Dani snapped, but his words were like salt in a wound that never quite healed. High school was the last of her worries when she was forced to flee east with her mother after Verloc's attack.

Conrad sneered at her. "I have big plans, Miss Frost. Presidential plans." He paused to let that sink in, but Dani wasn't overly surprised.

"Let me guess, you made a bargain to make that happen." Typical necromancers, never satisfied with the power and wealth they had. They always wanted *more.*

"Eight years from now, I *will* be elected president of the United States." Nathaniel paused, letting out a self-satisfied sigh. "President Conrad. It just sounds so *right,* doesn't it?" He paused again, his focus shifting to something behind Dani.

She turned to see what had caught Nathaniel's attention. Verloc paced his magical cage, his power still growing. He seemed more solid now. More substantial. With a sickening wave of realization, Dani knew what the mayor had bargained away.

The sheer enormity of power and influence required to buy his way to the presidency was not something a common demon could provide. What were the Conrads using as their bargaining chip to secure their delusions of grandeur? How much were they willing to sacrifice? What would a demon as old and strong as Verloc want in exchange?

"You're pulling him through to our world." She turned to face the demon who ruined her life. "You're not looking for a human host. You want to pass through into this world completely."

"Very good, Ink Carrier." Verloc flashed a wide smirk of pointed teeth. "I've entered this world many times over the centuries, but your foul family always sends me back. This time, I'm bringing all my power with me. Once I've risen, no one will be able to stop me."

"How is that possible?" Dani traced the scars on her arm. Maybe there was a way to bring Silas back to her too.

"It took my entire family," Mayor Conrad said, motioning to the dozens of necromancers in the room, necromancers still chanting to bring forth Verloc's final form. "Several human sacrifices too."

"All those marked bodies in the morgue …" The disparate puzzle pieces fell into place, and Dani looked to Nick to see if he'd come to the same conclusion. Verloc wasn't inhabiting those bodies and burning through them like most demons do—

Nathaniel Conrad had sacrificed them to raise the reaper.

Nick pulled against the necromancers who held him captive. "Is that what happened to Ricardo? Was he one of your sacrifices?"

"Ricardo knew the risks," Conrad snapped at the detective. "He was more than willing to help with the ritual, and he was paid handsomely for it. All he had to do was round up the unwanted ones in our city, people with no family to care if they went missing."

"So, what happened then?" Nick asked, the investigator in him still seeking answers despite the strangeness of his circumstances. "Why murder one of your own staffers?"

Mayor Conrad shrugged. "One of the men he found was stronger than expected. Ricardo shoved the man past the sigil line, but the man had hold of Ricardo's jacket, and they fell in together."

Verloc's toothy grin widened. "There was more to him than the others." He groaned, like he missed the taste of such energy. "I bet the Ink Carrier's life would be enough to finish the ritual."

"Don't touch her," Raj shouted and tried again to rise to his feet. One of the necromancers standing guard punched him hard across the face. The force knocked Raj forward, and the other necromancers pinned him to the marble floor.

Conrad laughed, the sound shredding the last of Dani's composure.

"What about Ellie?" Dani asked, ignoring the way Verloc smacked his lips at her like she was some tasty treat. "Was she one of your sacrifices?"

A shadow passed over the mayor's features. "I wish. I haven't seen that blackmailing bitch in weeks."

"Then who killed her?" Dani shook her head. There wasn't time for Ellie right now, not with her mother standing *right there* in her cotton pajamas with a knife to her throat. She had to get them out of there. "If you're so close to raising your demon and winning your elections, why take my mom? Why not just let us go?"

"It was part of the bargain," Nathaniel said, the muscles in his jaw clenching. "A late addendum once Verloc heard of your presence at my party."

"But why?" Dani pressed. The mayor stayed quiet, and Dani realized it was because he didn't *know* why. She whirled on the reaper. "What do you need her for?"

Verloc pressed the tips of his needlelike fingers together and studied Dani. "I don't *need* anything, young Carrier. I *desired* retribution."

"For what? You already took everything from her."

"This isn't the first time I've tried to take my rightful place among your world. One of your ancestors sent me back to the underworld. I was so *close* to rising, and she took it all away!" The demon shook with fury and tried to approach Dani, but the lines of the sigil kept him contained. For now. "I vowed then that I'd end your insufferable line of Ink Carriers. It was easy enough to find your mother. I wanted her trapped in her own mind—and her Ink trapped with her—until I could fully ascend."

"You didn't know the Ink would pass to me." Dani wasn't surprised. She didn't know it was possible either until it occurred. According to Poe, it had never happened before. In her family's history, the Ink had always moved to the next generation after the current Carrier died, most of the time during battle. Never before had something like Andrea's fate happened.

Yet the Ink passed to Dani as soon as Andrea became unfit to wield her magical tattoos, practically deeming her as good as dead as far as her duties were concerned. Andrea could no longer carry out her job, and so the responsibility moved to the next in line.

No one had counted on that. Not even Verloc.

"You survived that night by sheer luck." Verloc flashed another of those fearsome grins. "Neither of you will get away this time. You'll be my final sacrifices."

Dani had gotten lucky that night six years ago,

managing to slice off Verloc's hand, which had since grown back. Given her current situation, she feared her luck had run out.

Two men rushed Dani, but she wasn't going down without a fight. She didn't need a blade. Her entire childhood, Andrea had honed her body into a weapon. She ducked under the grasp of the first man, weaving in close to smash her elbow up into his nose.

He screamed, but there wasn't time for victory. The second man grabbed Dani from behind, wrapping his large arms around her and squeezing the breath from her lungs. She gasped for air, but she'd trained long enough that her body reacted faster than her mind. She sank into her legs and tossed the man over her shoulders.

Before she could stand, another necromancer tackled her from behind. Then another. And another. She lost count of her opponents, lost count of the blows they dealt. Boots and fists cracking against her ribs, back, and skull. Blood in her mouth. Bones cracking until a scream tore from her throat. Fresh panic closed in. She couldn't breathe. Distantly, she was aware of voices shouting her name. She needed help. She needed the Ink.

"If you call those vile creatures," Conrad said, his voice cutting through the haze of her thoughts, "I'll slit your mother's throat myself. Throw her over the line!"

Several more blows landed against her battered body before they finally stopped. Dani lay against the floor, unable to move. Her lungs refused to inflate.

Strong hands hauled her to her feet, and all the pain shifted to settle into a new place. Her knees wouldn't hold her weight, and stabbing fingers dug into her arms. The necromancers shoved her forward, toward the edge of the sigil. Toward Verloc.

Toward death.

"Conrad, wait!" Raj's voice lashed out, full of authority despite his position on the ground. "You can't do this. It's against our laws to raise a demon like this. The reaper will kill us the second it's free. None of the families will be safe."

The men shoving Dani forward stalled. She fought through the pain to turn her head, desperate to see what was happening.

Nathaniel Conrad stormed across the room to where Raj was still pinned to the floor. He motioned for his family to drag Raj to his feet. "Just because you're too weak to control a demon, Dasari, doesn't mean I am."

"You control *nothing*. You foolish, arrogant—"

The mayor struck Raj hard across the mouth. "Insolent whelp. You've been intolerable since your father died. My power is beyond your limited comprehension. I will rule this country like I've ruled over Blackthorn."

"The only thing you'll rule," Raj said, pausing to spit blood onto the floor, "is your own demise. Raising a reaper is madness."

"From where I stand, you don't have much of a choice in the matter." Conrad gripped Raj's chin and forced his face upright. "Maybe I should throw you to the reaper before the Frost women. Fancy an appetizer, Verloc?"

Raj grinned, his teeth stained with blood. "Do you really think the head of the Dasari line would come all the way out here without backup?"

Conrad's head whipped around, searching the room. All was quiet. Still. "I'm not afraid of your family."

Raj tilted his head back and let out a bellowing laugh that echoed off the bare walls. "Lying doesn't suit you, Nathaniel."

The mayor backed away. "Throw them to the reaper. Now!"

Dani struggled against the strong men gripping her arms, her broken body not yet healed enough to stand on her own. "Now would be a great time for that backup, Raj."

"Now, Pam!" the Dasari leader called out, not a trace of fear in his voice.

The door Dani and her team had entered through burst open. Light streaked through the room in wide arcs, illuminating at least two dozen Dasari necromancers.

Dani spotted Amara among the crowd and grinned.

Raj had summoned his cousins.

26

Danika Frost had never been happier to see necromancers in her life. The Dasaris swarmed the room, and everything erupted into pure chaos.

"Kiva! Poe! Jasper!" Dani called the Ink, and they burst from her skin and entered the fray the moment they were corporeal, Kiva pouncing on the man at Dani's left, while Poe attacked the face of the man at Dani's right. The other necromancers scattered as the Dasaris attacked.

The air grew heavy with magic as the two families faced each other, pierced by Pam's gleeful laughter soaring above the sounds of battle. Though she worried about her friends, Dani didn't have time to focus on Nick or Raj or even the Ink. She had her own list of priorities.

One: Save her mom.

Two: Stop the mayor.

Three: Destroy Verloc.

And she couldn't afford to waste any time. Dani dove out of the way of a necromancer racing toward her, but her body protested the movement. She managed to catch herself in a roll, but pain tightened her muscles and she was too slow to get back to her feet. The necromancer lashed out, his boot connecting with her ribs. She screamed, and the man laughed as he stepped on her neck, crushing her airway.

A sudden burst of energy tossed the necromancer several feet away.

"You okay?" a familiar voice asked, and then a hand came into view.

"I've been better," Dani said, accepting the offer of help. When she was on her feet, she finally saw her rescuer. "Thanks, Amara."

Raj's cousin grinned and raised her hands. Tiny flames burst to life above her palms. "We're going to talk about the whole you-being-the-Ink-Carrier thing later, but for now, the succubus said you needed a little firepower." And then she was gone, chasing after the necromancer she'd tossed aside.

Dani grabbed her sword from the ground and searched the room for her mom. *There.* The necromancer who held Andrea hostage was pulling her toward the exit. Andrea was still a Frost, though, and she fought like hell against her captor.

But it wasn't enough. The necromancer wasn't giving any ground.

She had to act quick. Dani tried to run, but her body wouldn't cooperate. She wouldn't be fast enough, not like this. Not unless—

Dani raised her sword over her head and gripped it in both hands. Pain throbbed and burned throughout her torso, but she could do this. She could bear anything to save her mother. With a quick prayer to a god she wasn't sure existed, Dani launched the sword with all her strength.

The sword whistled through the air, blade over hilt, crossing the expanse between Dani and her mom faster than she could run. And she did run, a broken stride that felt like moving through molasses.

But her aim was true. The blade met the necromancer's face, piercing straight through and lodging into his skull. He dropped, leaving her mother screaming but safe. Dani finally reached them, one hand resting gently on her mother's arm while she gripped the hilt and drew her sword free with the other. She hated to take human life—even if they were necromancers—but desperate times called for desperate measures.

"It's okay, Mom. I've got you." Dani pulled Andrea into her embrace despite the agony of her body, and the former Ink Carrier shook with fear.

"There're demons," Andrea said, voice high with panic. "Demons and monsters overrunning our world."

"I know, Mom. I know, but I'm going to fix it."

Danika, look out! Poe's voice screeched in her head. She whirled, raising her sword in time to block an incoming blow from a snarling demon. Past the creature, she saw a ball of energy collide with her raven, reducing him to smoldering feathers before he burst into Ink and returned to her skin.

Dani screamed and smashed her sword against the demon's tough scales, but the blade glanced off. She pushed her mother aside, but she was too slow to avoid a slash to her stomach. Blood spread across her shirt, but Dani wouldn't let the creature near her mother. She pressed forward, looking for a way to pierce the hard scales while keeping it as far away from her mother as possible.

The demon swung a heavy fist at Dani, and she ducked to avoid the blow. From her crouched position, she noticed a spot that wasn't covered in scales, a bit of soft flesh at the underarm. *Perfect.*

Dani shifted tactics.

She let herself fall back, let herself give in to her

injuries. The demon had to stretch to reach her as she retreated, and with each move, she ducked and parried with her sword, memorizing the way the monster moved, noting which angles would give her the best advantage.

With a warrior's cry, Dani leaped into the air. The demon reached for her, but she twisted at the last second, driving her blade deep into the demon's body through the soft spot under its arm. The demon collapsed to the ground, unable to breathe with the punctured lung. A flush of victory warmed Dani. She raised her sword to deal a final blow, but Jasper's panic rang through her mind.

She spun, searching the crowded marble arena. Verloc laughed from behind his sigil line while a pair of Conrad necromancers grabbed hold of Jasper and tore him in two.

Dani screamed as Jasper's soul twisted around her left arm.

The loss of another Ink wiped away every feeling of victory, and Dani saw the fight with new eyes. There were more Conrad necromancers than she thought, outnumbering the Dasari family at least two to one, and that didn't include the handful of demons causing havoc. Raj was covered in demon ichor, fighting back-to-back with Amara. Pam was busy seducing the Conrad necromancers, draining away their life force when they kissed her, leaving a path of dead, dried-up bodies with delighted expressions in her wake. It wasn't going to be enough, not when Nathaniel Conrad stood beside a still-rising Verloc, barking orders at his family.

"Kiva!" If Andrea didn't panic at the sight of the panther, Kiva could take her to safety. "Kiva, I need you."

Coming, Little War—

Dani found Kiva in the crowd, just in time to see one of the necromancers run her beloved friend through with a spear. Her heart lurched as Kiva burst into smoky ink and braced for the pain of her return. Kiva pierced into Dani's back, and she arched away from the pain, but she couldn't escape it. She was alone.

Nick, she thought suddenly. *Where's Nick?* She returned to Andrea's side and searched the crowd for the detective. If he was dead, she would never forgive herself.

At Dani's two o'clock, a scrawny necromancer went flying through the air. Nick stepped into view, strangely calm now that the fighting had started. His blond hair was dulled by dust and demon ichor, and blood had sprayed across his shirt. Yet he had rolled the sleeves to his elbows and seemed to be holding his own.

"Nick!"

The moment the detective spotted her, he ran, dodging around fighting necromancers to come to her side. "Are you okay?"

"I'm fine, but I need your help."

"Anything."

"I need you to take my mom and get the hell out of here."

Nick shook his head. "No way. I can't leave you here alone."

"You have to. I can't fight them if I'm worried about her." She sucked in a breath, testing the impact on her ribs. Her body was healing, but she needed it to heal faster. "Please, Nick. Get her out of here and keep her safe. I'll be fine."

She didn't feel fine, not with her Ink banished and the Dasari necromancers shifting to defense, but she couldn't let her mother get hurt. She faked a confidence she didn't have and hoped it would be enough to convince him.

Nick looked like he wanted to protest, but he shook his head. "Okay. I'll handle it. Just promise you'll get yourself out as soon as you can."

For a brief, exhilarating moment, Dani thought he might kiss her. But Nick simply squeezed her hand and turned to her mother. "Miss Frost? I need you to come with me." He spoke in gentle tones, but Andrea backed away.

"I don't know you."

"He's a friend, Mom. He's safe." Dani urged her mother toward Nick. "He'll protect you."

"Does he know about the demons?"

"Yes, ma'am. I do. I believe you." Nick guided Andrea toward the door, and this time, she went willingly.

The second they were out of sight, Dani whirled on the room. Raj and his cousins were no longer trying to destroy the spell that was raising Verloc. They were simply trying to stay alive. Dani counted at least three dead before she stopped herself. She couldn't let their sacrifices be in vain.

She couldn't be the reason any more of them died.

Dani tested the feel of her healing body. It would be hours before she was back to her full strength, but she could fight. She could do this. She just needed to find her target …

There.

The room blurred around her as she rushed the head of the Conrad family. Nathaniel was still barking orders when she came upon him, but he noticed her in time to draw a shield, just like the ones Raj conjured.

Luckily for her, she had fought alongside Raj enough to know the limits of such power.

Dani attacked the shield, searching for the edges, testing for weak spots, unrelenting, as she smashed it again and again and again.

"You're an embarrassment to the Ink Carriers. Your mother too." Nathaniel Conrad sneered at her and pressed the shield forward, putting more space between them. "I'm going to enjoy watching the reaper scramble your brain and consume your soul."

"Why?" Dani asked, smashing into the shield again. "Afraid you can't kill me on your own?"

Conrad roared something unintelligible. She didn't recognize the language, but his family clearly did. Two necromancers broke off from their current battles to attack Dani.

"Fucking cheat," Dani snapped at Conrad. She turned to face the oncoming assault, but Raj got there first.

He pummeled the first necromancer with a shield the size of his fist, knocking the man unconscious. She was about to thank him when something cold pierced her abdomen.

"Dani, no!"

Someone laughed in her ear. "The Carrier's death is mine."

The piercing cold twisted in her gut, and Dani

looked down, searching for the source of her pain. A spear of ice protruded from her lower stomach, rotating before the man behind her drew it back out again.

Dani fell to her knees as Raj screamed. His eyes, his beautiful brown eyes, turned to black as his pupils overtook everything else. His most terrible power exploded within him, consuming the man she loved and leaving behind only a vessel of destruction.

"Raj, don't." Dani tried to reach for him, but the pain was too much. She pressed her hands against her wound. Blood poured through her fingers, but that fear was nothing compared to what this power could do to Raj.

Summoning Death always left a mark.

"Raj, please," she begged, but it was too late. The Conrad necromancer behind her was already scream-ing. She'd seen this power only once before, knew how it turned its victims' minds into the perfect torture devices, forcing them through their worst fears, subjecting them to impossible pain. The man collapsed beside Dani, blood pouring from his nose as he screamed. When the man fell still, when he was dead, Raj didn't return to himself. The oppressive heat of his power grew, and he stumbled away from Dani. Headed back into the fray.

Fresh screams echoed through the room. It was too late.

"Raj, come back! I'm okay!" Dani pressed her hand against her wound and found the skin was already stitching itself closed. She pulled herself to her feet, but Raj would have to wait. She refocused her attention on the mayor. "You'll pay for this. For all of this." She slammed her sword into the shield over and over, putting every ounce of her depleted strength behind it.

Nathaniel only laughed. "You'll never break through."

"Oh, I know." She had only a second to delight in the mayor's confusion. She hit the shield one more time, then backed up several paces. Using every last bit of strength and stamina she had left, Dani sprinted forward and leaped into the air, flipping over the top of the shield. She barely made it over the edge, and the movement was far less graceful than normal, but it was the best she could do given her injuries.

"How—"

"You idiots never remember to extend the shield high enough." Dani spun, using her momentum to smash a vicious roundhouse into the mayor's face. Behind her, the mayor's family screamed as Raj infected the room with Death itself.

If she didn't hurry, Raj's soul could be lost forever.

The mayor tried to draw fresh shields, but Dani fought close, not giving him enough space to cast. Mayor Conrad caught hold of Dani and spun her around, one arm clamped around her neck while the other pressed hard where the spear had pierced her flesh. She screamed in agony as the wound reopened.

"The stories about you and your family are over-rated," Nathaniel hissed in her ear, sour breath hot on her cheek. He dragged her toward Verloc, who stalked inside his sigil prison, seeming desperate to be involved in the action. Fear coalesced in Dani's veins. "I'll be remembered forever as the man who ended the Ink Carrier line."

Nathaniel pushed Dani forward, and the sigil line drew dangerously close.

Five feet.

Three. Two.

One.

At the last moment, Dani grabbed Conrad's arm, the one holding her neck in a vise grip. With every iota of remaining strength, she hurled the mayor over her shoulder.

Nathaniel toppled over her with a fierce cry and landed hard at Verloc's feet.

Inside the broken sigil line.

27

The ground shook in violent tremors that cracked the foundation under Dani's boots. Behind her, necromancers screamed as Raj's power infiltrated their minds and tore them apart from the inside. Nathaniel Conrad was screaming too.

He hurled profanities at Dani. "Do you have any idea what you've done? The ritual is ruined!" Part of the sigil at the mayor's feet had been wiped away as he fell, breaking the spell that tethered Verloc to this world. With the ritual incomplete, Verloc wasn't long for this world.

"That sounds like a *you* problem."

"You foolish, pathetic …" Nathaniel's voice died when Verloc stepped into view, the demon's bone-white face contorted into a hungry scowl. The mayor's entire demeanor changed in an instant. "Please, Verloc. We can work this out. I'll find a body for you. We can still destroy the Ink Carrier. We can still—"

Verloc shoved his long finger into the back of Nathaniel's skull, piercing into his brain. A pulse of demonic power shot out of the broken circle, knocking Dani off her feet. She scrambled away from the circle as the mayor screamed. Loud *cracks* sounded all around her, and when she turned to look, wide fractures crawled up the walls as the entire house shook.

With a vicious thrust, Verloc jammed his needle-like finger clean through the mayor's head until it protruded between his eyes. The demon laughed, his body breaking down into little more than mist and glowing red eyes.

"If you'll excuse me for a moment, Ink Carrier." Verloc pulled his finger—the last solid part of him—from the mayor's head. Nathaniel Conrad swayed on his feet until Verloc's translucent form stepped forward, melting into the necromancer's dying body.

And then they were one, the mayor's dead human eyes blinking to red.

"Much better," Verloc said, now in full possession of Nathaniel's body. He flexed his new limbs. "A poor replacement for my own form, but it'll suffice."

"The hell it will." Dani raised her sword, prepared to banish the demon no matter the cost, but the ground beneath her tremored. The ceiling above split.

"Dani!" A familiar voice called her name, and then Amara was at her side, pulling Dani away from the broken sigil. Chunks of stone rained from the ceiling, blocking her view of Verloc. "Raj needs you. Now!"

"Where?" But Dani saw before Amara could answer.

Raj stood over a pile of corpses, Conrad necromancers who'd lost their fight to Death. His eyes were still fully black, and thick blood dripped from his nose. Banishing Verloc could wait—if the demon even survived the crumbling estate.

Amara got to Raj first as Dani came up behind her. His cousin reached for Raj's hand and tried to pull him away. A chunk of the ceiling landed less than five feet behind them. "Come on, Rajan. We have to *go.*" The fighting had ceased, necromancers from both families—the ones still standing—bolting for the exit.

But Raj didn't budge. He shoved his cousin aside and clenched his fists. The blood dripping from his nose ran faster as more of the ceiling crumbled around them.

"Get the rest of your family out of here," Dani shouted at Amara. "We'll be right behind you."

"But—"

"Go, Amara!" Dani pushed the necromancer toward the door and turned back to Raj. It hurt to see him like this. She knew it hurt him too. He couldn't control this power. He knew better than to use it. Dani touched her abdomen, the skin healed over but still tender from where she'd been run through. He must have thought he had no choice. He probably hadn't *thought* at all, just reacted.

"Listen to me, Raj." Dani spoke in hushed tones, afraid to even touch him in this state. It was risky to be this close, but she refused to leave him there to die, not when he had done so much to help her. Not when seeing her hurt pushed him to this. "It's time to go."

His black eyes trained on her, and the beginnings of a terrible pressure built inside her head.

"It's me, Raj. You're safe." Cautiously, Dani reached for the man she had once loved—the man a part of her would *always* love—and let her hands come to rest on his chest. He was warm beneath her skin, his body trembling and his brow slick with sweat. But he didn't pull away. The pressure in her head faded. Dani reached higher, tracing her thumb along his jaw. "Come back to me."

Another hunk of ceiling fell beside them, tiny bits of debris scratching against exposed skin.

"Raj, *please*." Dani raised onto her toes and wrapped her arms tight around his shoulders, her fingers tangling in his hair like they had so many times before. She searched his black eyes, looking for some sign that her Raj was still in there. "Don't leave me. Not like this." Dani released every hurt that had ever existed between them. Every argument. Every fact about their lives that had driven them apart. She let it all go …

And she kissed him.

Her lips brushed his cheek. The corner of his scowl. His forehead. Until finally, she drew him close and kissed him with every ounce of love and passion they'd once shared. She needed him to know that he wasn't alone in this world. That someone cared deeply for him, enough to stand in the basement of a building that was about to collapse.

And then she felt it, the sudden shift in his back. His arms came around her waist, and he kissed her like she was life itself.

Another chunk of ceiling fell next to them, and the pair flinched apart. Raj gasped for breath like he'd just come up for air, and Dani whispered, "You're okay. You're okay," over and over like it was part promise, part spell. "Come on. We have to go." Dani held out her hand. The black in Raj's eyes receded, leaving behind the rich brown of his irises.

Raj placed his hand in hers and stumbled forward. The first steps were tentative, like he was getting used to his body again, but Dani urged him on until they were running. Up the stairs, the steps crumbling away as soon as they passed. Out into the hall where valuables had fallen and smashed across the floor.

Another shot of demonic power exploded from the basement, pushing them along. The house made a terrible sound, cracking and groaning and splintering. Dani tried to drag Raj to the front door.

"This way is faster," Raj said, voice rough and breathless.

Dani didn't argue. She followed Raj down the hall to the right, and they passed into a kitchen. Raj released her hand and raced forward to open the door. The walls were shifting, and the door was stuck closed.

"Forget the door." Dani pushed him toward a window that had shattered. "Let's go."

Raj cupped his hands to give Dani a boost up. She didn't want to risk leaving him behind, but there wasn't time to argue over who went first. She took the boost and slipped through the window, wincing when the broken glass sliced through her back as her shirt rode up, but then she was out.

She turned to help Raj, but he was already dropping out of the window. "Come on." Dani took his hand again, and they ran, putting as much distance between them and the now-possessed mayor's estate.

Another pulse of energy shot out across the lawn, throwing Dani and Raj off their feet. They fell to the ground, hands still clasped.

And then the entire house collapsed and burst into flames.

As she stared at the remains of Nathaniel Conrad's crumbled, burning home, Dani indulged in a moment of victory. The mayor was dead, Verloc had seen to that, and even with Verloc in possession of Nathaniel's body, there was no way either of them could survive the fire raging through the remains of the estate.

And without a functional body to inhabit, Verloc's demonic spirit would have no way to remain on the earthly plane.

It was over.

"Dani?" Nick rushed to her side and crushed her in a fierce hug. When he stepped back to take her in, his face paled. "Where did all that blood come from? What—"

"I'm fine, Nick. I promise." Dani lifted the edge of

her torn shirt, where her puncture wound had faded to fresh pink skin. "See?"

"What am I looking at? Were you impaled?"

"She's fine, Detective," Raj cut in, his hands still trembling. "Our Dani bounces back quicker than the rest of us mere mortals."

Dani ignored the warm feeling that rose within her at his use of *our*. There was still too much to do. "Nick, where's my mom?"

"She's fine. She's with Pam."

"Pam? Why is the succubus watching my mother?" Dani followed Nick toward the edge of the property where Andrea sat on a short stone wall, wrapped in Nick's jacket. Pam, much to Dani's shock, stood guard.

"Mom." Dani's voice broke, and she hurried to her mother's side. Her heart couldn't contain the relief at seeing her mother alive and unharmed. Tears slipped past her lashes, and she brushed Andrea's hair from her face. "Everything's going to be okay now," she promised, hugging her mother tight. "You're going to be all right."

"Danika? Is that you?" Andrea Frost pulled from her daughter's embrace, confusion etched across her face. "Why are you crying?"

"Just relieved, Mom. That's all." Dani wiped the tears away and tried to ignore the sting of failure.

Verloc might be gone, but his effect on Andrea hadn't lessened.

"I'm sorry to interrupt," Nick said, stepping back into view. "But the police will be here soon."

"Thanks." She rubbed her arms. The last of the injuries she'd sustained inside the estate—including the cuts from the window—were healing over. "For everything," she added, reaching for Nick's free hand. "You didn't lose your shit in there, Detective, and you had every reason to run away and never look back."

Nick interlocked his fingers with hers. "I don't scare away easily." He faltered suddenly, and Dani wondered if he was thinking of last night, when he declined her advances. "At least … at least once I've had a second to wrap my brain around everything."

Dani released him and reached for her mom, who still looked thoroughly confused about what was going on. She was calm though. Thank god for small favors. "Thank you for keeping my mom safe. I don't know what I would have done if something had happened to her."

"Anytime, Dani." Nick placed his hands on his hips and turned to face the smoldering remains of the Conrad estate. "I don't know how the hell I'm going to explain this when the fire department arrives."

"Faulty wiring?" Dani smirked when Nick shot her

an exasperated look. "You'll think of something. I have faith in you."

"That makes one of us." Nick ran a hand through his blond hair, covered in dirt and bits of demon ichor like the rest of them.

Dani rose onto her toes. "You'll do great." She pressed a quick kiss to his cheek and turned away before she could see his reaction. Sirens wailed in the distance.

"Come on, Mom." Dani helped Andrea up, offering her arm like they were off to a fancy party. "We need to get you somewhere safe."

The Frost women picked their way across the lawn toward the road. As they neared a row of immaculately pruned bushes, close to where Dani had torn a hole in the wrought iron fence, Raj stepped into view with a squirming Lana.

No, not Lana. Pam.

Dani hadn't noticed Pam or Raj slip away, too caught up in her reunion with her mom. The succubus was back to her old tricks, pulling against Raj's grip. He held her arms tight behind her back.

"But I did just like you told me to," she whined, trying to grind her ass against Raj. "Please don't lock me away."

"Demon," Andrea growled, coming to a stop. "Monster!"

"Shh, it's okay, Mom. I'll get rid of her." Dani reached into her pocket for the amulet Lana had entrusted to her. "Wait here."

Dani left her mother a few steps behind, listening to make sure she'd hear if Andrea tried to bolt. When she reached Raj and Pam, Dani separated the necklace chain to lift over Pam's head.

"No, wait! What about our bargain?" Pam dropped her usually seductive tone and resorted to full pleading.

"Bargain?" Raj asked, an emotion crossing his face that Dani couldn't read. "I thought the Ink Carrier didn't make bargains?"

Dani ignored him, even though his words made her feel like a hypocrite. How many times had she berated him for the bargains he made and facilitated? Her hands paused with the amulet dangling in front of Pam's face. "You only get the three nights once Verloc is banished."

"And he is! He must be!" Pam pulled again in Raj's grip, but he held strong. "The whole house came down on him. The ritual failed because I brought in all those pretty necromancers to save you. I earned this."

"If the terms of the bargain were met," Raj cut in, "Dani won't be able to put the amulet on you. There's no harm in letting her try."

"Exactly," Dani said, though part of her felt bad for what she'd done. Even if the morals of duping a demon were dubious. She raised the amulet and slipped it over Pam's head. The succubus collapsed in Raj's arms.

"Wait." Raj shifted Lana's weight. "Does that mean Verloc is still on Earth? Is that what the bargain was for?"

"Not exactly," Dani said. "I did promise Pam three nights of control if she helped us banish Verloc, but I never said *when* we'd have to pay out those nights. That's for Lana to decide." Besides, letting Pam run free for three nights required a *lot* of extra planning to make sure she didn't get into too much trouble.

"I'm impressed. Seems you learned something from our time together after all," Raj said, but his attempt at teasing fell flat. They were both too raw for jokes about their past. He nodded toward the street. "My car is just down here. Let me take you and Andrea home. We can drop Lana somewhere safe too."

Dani reached for her mother and held tight to her hand. A part of her wanted to argue. Wanted to bid Raj good night and find her own way home. But Andrea needed her, and she was tired of fighting.

So, she led her mother to Raj's car and headed home.

Dani sank into the soft leather and tried to relax her muscles. Despite her fast healing, her body was beyond exhausted. Everything ached, down to an atomic level. Her mind was just as weary. There was still so much to do. Lana needed looking after. Dani had to get her mom back to the hospital …

Dani twisted in her seat to watch her mother. Andrea had curled up into a ball, and she stared out the car window with wide eyes. Lana, for her part, seemed to be resting comfortably, but an old guilt rose from the dead.

A part of Dani wanted to take her mother home with her, wanted to care for Andrea herself instead of taking her back to the hospital. But they'd tried that. Between her investigative work and demon hunting, Dani couldn't watch her mother around the clock, and that was the kind of care Andrea needed. The hospital was the safest place for the former Ink Carrier, at least until Dani found a way to undo whatever Verloc had done.

It hurt that banishing Verloc hasn't done anything to help her mother's condition. She shouldn't be surprised; banishing him hadn't done anything last time, but it was still the hardest blow she'd taken all night. At least now she knew which demon was responsible, and she vowed to find a cure for her mother, no matter the cost.

Still, she wasn't ready to say goodbye. Not when she had just gotten her mother back.

"Should we go to the hospital first?" Raj stopped at a red light, a sign on the street indicating the hospital on their right.

"I want to be with her tonight," she said, leaning her head against the cool glass.

"Dani …"

"Just for one night, Raj. I'll take her back in the morning." Dani turned in her seat to face him, taking in all that he was. Dark, bruise-like circles under his eyes. Bits of dried blood on his face that he wasn't able to wipe away. The hollows of his cheeks more pronounced. "Are you okay?"

He quirked a smile at her, just the right side tipping up. "I'm fine, Dani. Where are we going?"

"Umm … one sec." Dani pulled out her phone and dialed Spencer. He answered on the third ring. "How you feeling, Spence?"

"Like ass," he replied, voice weary even through the phone. "What happened? Is everyone okay?"

"We're fine. Lana just needs a little extra care tonight. Does Adrian have time for one more?"

"Yeah, bring her over to our place."

"Your place? I thought you were at my apartment?" Dani covered the receiver and whispered to Raj, "They're at Spencer's. Can you head there?"

"You live in a one-bedroom and have shit for food in the house," Spencer said. "Of course, we came back to my place. Now, tell me everything."

Dani used the drive to explain what had gone down at the mayor's estate. Spencer must have put her on speakerphone, because Adrian and Cassie chimed in with their commentary too. By the time they got to Spencer's, Adrian was waiting outside for them. He lifted a still half-asleep Lana into his arms.

"We'll take good care of her," he said through Dani's open window. "I'd better get her inside."

They said their goodbyes and were suddenly alone.

"Where to now?" Raj asked as Dani rolled up her window and they set off.

"My place?" Her words came out like a question, and Dani hated how unsure she sounded, how unsure she felt. She pictured it then, the stark reality of her mother in her sparse apartment. Waiting—hungry and exhausted—until the Ink had recovered to watch over Andrea while she picked up food from Bloody Mary's kitchen.

"Counteroffer."

Dani raised a brow as they stopped at another red light.

"Stay with me tonight. Andrea can have her own room, and I'll make sure it's completely safe. No one will be able to get in or out except you and me." Raj watched the signal like he was afraid to check Dani's expression. "You know she'll be safe with me."

Objections clawed their way up her throat—reflex more than anything—but in the end, she couldn't deny the truth of his words. His place was better protected than hers, covered in wards to keep out unwanted visitors. They would be safe. She could actually relax.

"Just for tonight."

Dani let the city lights wash over her in a blur of yellows and whites and reds. She must have dozed off, because the next thing she knew, Raj was kneeling beside her open door. "Come on," he said, offering her a hand. "Let's get you cleaned up."

"Not until Mom—" But when Dani glanced in the back seat, Andrea wasn't there.

"I already brought her inside," Raj said before the panic could rise up like a familiar foe. "She's resting."

"Thank you," she said, realizing just how many times she'd had to thank Raj in the past few days. After years without seeing him, suddenly it was like their worlds orbited each other, gravity pulling them together. Inescapable. Inevitable.

Raj's house was as impressive as ever, from the

soaring ceilings adorned with crystal chandeliers to the marble floors that sparkled underfoot. She followed him to a guest room with an attached bath where he provided a soft towel. "I think I still have a few of your things. I'll leave them in the bedroom for you."

He slipped away before Dani could offer thanks or surprise that he had kept her clothes after all these years. Alone, body stiff from the battle and the injured Ink using some of her energy to heal themselves, Dani slipped into the shower and let the hot water wash over her. She'd learned during her time with Raj that his place never ran out of hot water, so she stayed well past when her shower back home would have run cold.

Fingers pruned and skin glowing a soft pink, Dani cut the water and wrapped herself in the towel Raj had left behind. She remembered these towels, the ridiculous luxury of the soft, fluffy fabric against her skin. In the bedroom, Dani found a small pile of clothes on the bed. She hadn't realized she'd left so much behind. Bypassing the nicer items, Dani dressed in a pair of black leggings and an oversized gray sweater, and tied her hair back in a single braid.

"Dani?" Raj's voice followed a gentle knock.

She opened the door to a freshly showered Raj, his wet hair raked out of his face. Like Dani, he was dressed down, in heather-gray pajama bottoms and a white T-shirt. This wasn't the Rajan Dasari who owned Obsidian and led an entire family of necromancers, a man who wore expensive tailored suits like armor. This was Raj—her Raj. A man who wore his emotions on his sleeves. A man who had loved every part of her, even if they were doomed from the start.

"Everything okay?"

"Yeah, of course." He ran a hand through his hair. "After a day like today, I thought you might want something to drink."

"That would be great." Even though she knew the way, she let Raj lead her to the kitchen. He picked through the wine options, and Dani reached for a pair of glasses. She set them on the counter as Raj uncorked a bottle of red.

"You remembered where the glasses are," he said as he poured the first glass and handed it to her.

Dani sipped the wine and wished alcohol had more of an effect on her. What she wouldn't give to dull the edge of longing creeping around her heart. To smooth the awkwardness from her tongue. But her body was exhausted, and she was tired of games. "I remember a lot of things, Raj."

He set the bottle on the counter and lifted his glass, watching her with naked sadness spread across his face. "I know the past few days haven't been easy for you." Raj placed his wine on the counter without taking a sip, his thumb tapping an anxious rhythm against the base of the glass. "But I can't deny that part of me is glad this happened. I've missed you so much."

Raj's words hung between them, heavy with emotion. Heavy with hurt and regret and a longing Dani knew only too well. Her rational mind told her to leave. To bid him good night and slip away. Instead, she found herself setting her glass on the counter between them. Reaching for his hand and sliding her fingers through his.

He shuddered as their skin pressed together. His breath caught, and he shifted until the length of his arm grazed against hers.

"I wish ..." Raj stared at the ceiling like he was trying to stop tears and pull himself together. "Please don't leave again, Dani." He turned to her then, the full weight of two years of separation glittering in his deep brown eyes. "There has to be a way this works."

"Raj, I—" Dani meant to push him away, but the soft fabric of his T-shirt and the warmth of the muscle underneath undid something in her. Instead of creating space, she erased it, running her hands up his shoulders and wrapping her arms around his neck to pull him close.

The moment she touched her lips to his, they were past the point of no return. Kissing Raj felt like coming home, and when his tongue slipped along hers, fireworks obliterated every last bit of reason reminding her that this was a terrible idea.

His hands found her waist and tugged her closer. She bit his lower lip, drawing a deep moan from deep inside him that set her on fire. But it wasn't enough. Now that she had part of him again, she needed everything.

Dani released Raj long enough to lift herself onto the counter, and then she pulled him close, tearing at his shirt. She couldn't stand the idea of the thin fabric keeping his skin from hers. Raj pulled the shirt over his head and kissed Dani hard and fast, pulling away to press his lips to her neck and jaw while his hands slipped under her shirt.

"Wait," Dani said, breathless. Panic settled across Raj's features, but she had only meant her shirt. She removed the offending bit of fabric, and then Raj was back, lips on her breast, hands splayed across her back as she arched into him.

Yet it still wasn't enough. Dani wrapped her legs around Raj's waist, pulling his body against hers. His erection pressed against her inner thigh, separated by the soft fabric of the bottoms they both wore. Dani reached for Raj's waistband and let her hand slip inside. But this time, Raj stopped her. He whispered a choked "Bedroom. Now," before lifting Dani and carrying her to his room, where they stripped free of the last of their clothes and fell into the bed they used to share.

Raj cherished every inch of her, first with his fingers, then with his mouth, until Dani couldn't stand to spend another second without him inside her. She drew his lips back to hers and kissed him like their lives depended on it. Then she reached between them, curling her fingers around the length of his erection before guiding him where she wanted him most.

They spent hours wrapped up in each other, and when their bodies gave out in a mind-numbing explosion of pleasure and release, Dani fell into the most restful sleep she'd had in years, nestled in the arms of the man who had always loved her.

The first light of morning spilled past the curtains and pulled Dani from sleep. For a moment, the soft sheets left her disoriented and confused, but then Raj shifted behind her in bed, his arm draped across her naked torso, and Dani remembered *exactly* what happened last night.

She needed to get out of there. Now.

Carefully, Dani eased from Raj's grip, replacing herself with a pillow nestled under his arm. The last thing she wanted to do was talk about their night. It had been a magical, toe-curling encounter.

It was also a mistake.

Moving silently through the massive house, Dani made it back to the guest room where she *should* have spent her night. There was so much to do, but she needed to look somewhat put together for it. She grabbed her phone where she'd abandoned it on the bed and called the hospital. They were apologetic about what had happened to her mother and relieved to hear that Andrea was okay. Dani asked if they were prepared for Andrea's return, and the hospital administrator promised they would be ready within the hour.

Which meant there was time for a quick shower.

Dani tried not to think about Raj as she scrubbed herself clean, but her mind kept flashing there anyway. His dexterous fingers holding on to her hips. His full lips trailing kisses along her skin. The way he explored every inch of her with relish and abandon as he reacquainted himself with her naked body.

She should have stayed in her room when he asked if she wanted a drink. She should have slept alone in an unfamiliar bed rather than let herself get tangled up in his sheets.

She *really* had to stop thinking about it.

After her shower, Dani dressed in more of the clothes Raj had left behind—this time jeans and a plain black T-shirt. She was braiding her hair, since she didn't have time to do anything more elaborate, when her phone beeped to remind her of a new voicemail. She punched in the passcode and finished up her braid as she listened.

"Hello, Miss Frost, this is Malinda Bailey. We spoke a few days ago regarding—"

"Heading out?" Raj asked, appearing in her doorway. He was dressed in jeans and a thin sweater rather than the soft pajamas he'd worn only briefly last night. "I don't suppose you have time for breakfast?"

"… willing to meet with you this afternoon. Give me a call back when you get this and we'll set a time."

Dani paused the voicemail and slipped the phone into her pocket. "I have to get Mom back to the hospital, and I still have to deal with my clients' dead daughter."

"Right. Of course." Raj shoved his hands deep into the pocket of his jeans. "It was Ellie, right?"

"Yeah." She tried not to let her surprise show. She'd only mentioned Ellie by name a couple times in front of Raj, if that. Yet, he remembered.

"I'm sorry about what happened to her. I hope you find whoever's responsible."

Dani nodded, but she didn't know what to say. Tension filled the air between them, the small room filled with years of things left unsaid. Neither was willing to make the next move until Dani's phone buzzed again in her pocket. She sighed, tied off her braid, and checked her phone. This time it was

Spencer, asking if she wanted him to open the office for the day. "I'm sorry, Raj, but I really do have to go."

"Let me drive you and Andrea back to the hospital." He remained in the doorway as Dani approached, his expression tender and pleading. "It's the least I can do."

"It's really fine. I'll have a car pick us up." She selected the app on her phone to set book the ride.

"Dani …" He said her name with such hurt and hope that the simple pair of syllables was filled to bursting with all the things she could tell he wanted to say. Raj didn't want her to leave. He wanted things to go back to the way they were before. If all the hints Spencer dropped over the last two years were any indication, Raj had wanted that the second she left him.

But she couldn't do that. It wasn't fair that he could stand before her, holding out his heart in his hands. Her only option was to lock her own heart away, hide it in a drawer and hope she didn't lose it. She wished she could tell him that he meant nothing to her, but that lie would never hold up.

So instead, she told as much of the truth as she could bear. "Look, Raj." She forced herself to meet his gaze, damning the depth of his dark eyes. "Last night was … amazing, but we both know that this whole 'you and me' can't happen again. Our worlds are too different. We'd be better off—"

"As friends?" Raj finished, hurt crinkling his forehead before he smoothed it away behind a mask.

"No, not friends either." She slipped past him into the hall, her heart in her throat as a hot, sick feeling coursed down her limbs. "I don't think we should be in each other's lives. At all. It'll be easier that way."

"What are you saying?"

Dani leaned against the wall for support, her back to Raj. "I'm saying you should lose my number. Move on. Find someone who fits into your world."

Raj fell quiet for a long time. In the distance, a clock *tick-tick-ticked* as the seconds passed by. Finally, he cleared his throat. "If that's what you want—"

"It is." This was for the best. For both of them. She couldn't keep him on the hook forever, even if it hurt more than she would ever say to cut him out again. "I just need to get my mom. Then I'll be out of your hair."

"Of course." Raj's voice was different now. Cold and distant in a way that sent chills down Dani's arms. He walked past her with the mechanical precision she had only ever seen at Obsidian, dealing with unruly but influential demons. The truth of her reasoning didn't make the situation any less painful. Even though she knew it was for the best.

Even though it broke her heart all over again.

***

Practice was the lifeblood of Carrier training. Running got easier the more Poe made her do it. Punches and kicks got stronger and more accurate. For most of Dani's life, repetition made her work easier.

Leaving her mother at the hospital never got easier.

Andrea's cries followed Dani out of the hospital. Her pleas to go home with Dani, her frantic worries about demons coming for them both. Her mother's pain weighed heavy on her shoulders, and Dani needed a distraction.

The voicemail from Malinda Bailey—the one Raj had interrupted—niggled at her mind. She recognized that name from somewhere, and Malinda said Dani had called a few days ago. Who had she—

The memory crashed into Dani, and she yanked out her phone. Malinda ran one of the women's shelters in Blackthorn. She'd called about Ellie days ago. Dani hit redial without bothering to listen to the message again.

Someone picked up on the second ring. "Hello?"

"Malinda Bailey? It's Danika Frost. Is Ellie there? Is she alive?"

The woman on the other end of the line sighed. "Millennials these days. Don't you listen to your voicemails?"

"Malinda, please." Dani rushed toward the street and hailed a cab. "Is she there?"

"She is. She's willing to meet."

"Oh, thank god." Dani slid into the cab that stopped before her, renewed purpose filling her body. She hadn't fucked up everything. Ellie was still alive. Dani's outreach had paid off. "Where is she?"

Dani passed on the address to the cab driver and couldn't stop fidgeting the entire way there. When the driver dropped her off, she tossed a twenty at him and sprang from the car. The building was unmarked, but it looked just like Malinda Bailey had said it would. The women's shelter couldn't afford to advertise their location. They couldn't have abusive partners tracking women there.

Women like Ellie. Ellie, who was alive.

Dani signed in at the front desk and was buzzed through a second set of locked doors. Inside the main part of the building, Dani spotted Ellie sitting at one of the small tables. Ellie's brown hair was pulled back into a low ponytail, and she wore jeans and a plaid shirt, the sleeves pulled halfway down her palms. She fidgeted as she waited, like she was nervous.

"Ellie Hughes?" It took all of Dani's restraint not to crush the girl in a hug. She'd never been so relieved to locate a client, not since she'd saved Lana all those years ago. "I'm Dani. Your parents hired me to find you. Can I sit?" After a brief nod from Ellie, Dani took a seat across from the timid young woman. "I know you've been through a lot. I know about Sean, and the things he made you do. I know about the blackmail."

"What do you want from me?" Ellie leaned away, searching for an exit.

"I don't want anything." Dani reached for the other girl's hand. "I'm here to help."

Ellie remained wary of Dani's presence until Dani explained everything she'd done to find her—minus all the demonic pieces, of course. Once she was sure Dani was legit, Ellie's story flowed out of her.

"I never wanted this life. The sex. The blackmail. Any of it." Ellie's words came out in a rush. "I knew it was a bad idea, but I thought Sean cared about me. He was the first guy who ever said he loved me, you know? I wanted him to be happy, and it was just all these little favors at first. But then they got more and more … illegal. I was so wrapped up in things, I didn't realize how deep I'd fallen until we'd already black-mailed the mayor. I didn't know what to do except run."

Dani's heart went out to the younger woman. Her story was unfortunately common, especially in a city like Blackthorn. Men like Sean knew how to woo and manipulate women, how to make them feel safe and important, cutting them off from their support systems until the women had no one else to turn to when things went sideways.

"What am I going to do?" Ellie buried her face in her hands. "I blackmailed the *mayor* of a city. Did you know that he threatened to kill me? How am I going to come back from this?"

"You can, Ellie, I promise." Dani reached for Ellie's hand across the table and held it until Ellie met her gaze. "You have parents who came all the way here to look for you, parents who want you to be safe and loved and okay."

"But Mayor Conrad—"

"Won't be a problem anymore," Dani promised. "There was a fire at his home last night. It hasn't hit the news yet, but he's dead. He won't bother you ever again."

"Really?" For the first time, a note of hope entered Ellie's voice. Her eyes sparkled. But then she deflated again. "What about Sean? He'll want the blackmail money. He won't let me leave town."

"I can handle Sean." Dani's free hand curled into a

fist. She'd be happy to pay that creep a final visit. "Are you ready to leave Blackthorn? I know your parents would be happy to take you home."

"God, my parents." Ellie dabbed away the tears spilling silently down her cheeks. "How am I supposed to tell them what happened? They'll never look at me the same if they know … if they know about everything that happened with the mayor."

From what Dani could tell, the mayor wasn't the only *client* that Sean set up for Ellie either. "You get to decide what they know. If you want to tell them it was just a shitty boyfriend who scared you, that's all I'll tell them. They aren't entitled to the whole story. They just want to know you're alive and okay."

"I think I'd like that."

"And if you decide you want them to know everything," Dani said, leaning into the feeling in her gut, this worry that Ellie was carrying around shame she didn't deserve, "that's okay too. No one can fault you for the things you did to survive. Nothing that happened makes you any less deserving of love or happiness."

Ellie nodded, but she didn't say anything for a long time. She just held tight to Dani's hand as the tears fell. Behind Ellie, Dani noticed a short Black woman dressed in a charcoal suit with a flowy maroon blouse. She nodded at Dani, and the name tag, readable only because of Dani's heightened senses, read Malinda Bailey. She returned the nod.

"Can I take you to your parents?"

"Yes."

Together, they gathered the few things Ellie had with her and climbed into the cab Dani had waiting for them outside. They drove in silence to the hotel where John and Anne Hughes waited for information, and Ellie kept a tight grip on Dani's hand the entire ride over.

Dani texted John Hughes, and he and his wife stood out front of the hotel when the cab pulled up. "Deep breaths," Dani coached Ellie as she reached for the door handle. They emerged from the car, and Ellie's mother burst into tears at the sight of her daughter alive.

Ellie dashed forward to hug her mother. "I'm so sorry, Mom."

This was always the best part. Dani paid the cab driver and asked him to wait for her. She wouldn't linger, just long enough to make sure Ellie was okay, and collect her check. A pang of jealousy sat heavy in her gut as she watched the tearful reunion. She would give anything to have the same moment with her own mother. Dani really needed to visit Andrea more often.

And find a way to free her mother's mind now that Verloc was gone.

John Hughes broke away from the rest of his family and approached Dani, where she stood beside the cab. "Thank you, Miss Frost. For everything. I'm really sorry about the voicemail the other—"

"Don't mention it, Mr. Hughes. It comes with the territory."

John reached into his pocket. "Ellie says she's coming home. We couldn't have done this without you." He handed over a check, and Dani's eyes bulged at the amount.

It was double her usual fee.

"Mr. Hughes, I can't—"

"You earned it, Miss Frost. Your city is lucky to have you." John Hughes shook her hand and went back to his family, wrapping his wife and daughter in a wide embrace. That pang of jealousy flared again. Dani rarely cared that she didn't know who her father was, but moments like this always made her curious.

What might her life have looked like if she came from a normal family, if she was raised to be a daughter instead of a successor?

Dani shook the thought away and climbed back into the cab. It didn't matter. She would never know the answer anyway.

"Where to?" the cabby asked.

"Golding Street. South of Pickering," she said, ignoring the cabby's concerned look in the rearview. She still had one loose end to tie up.

***

Dani called her Ink and kicked open the door.

The wood shattered, and the door swung forward, making a satisfying *crunch* when it slammed into the inner wall.

"Seriously?!" An exasperated voice shouted from within. Glass bottles crashed to the floor and shattered. "I *just* put that in!"

Dani strode into the disgusting apartment and found Sean in the living room dressed only in boxers and a dingy T-shirt. Beer pooled at his feet where he had dropped his bottle.

He had the audacity to glare at her. "What the hell did I do now?"

"Oh, I don't know," Dani said, picking her way through the apartment. "How about supplying escorts to the mayor and letting Ellie take the fall for the blackmail *you* orchestrated?"

Sean shrugged. "A man's gotta make a living."

"Not by exploiting women and keeping most of

the profit for yourself." Dani whistled, and Poe swooped into the room, landing behind Sean on the coffee table. He squawked loudly and ruffled his feathers.

"What's this?"

Dani grinned. "A warning. Kiva?" The panther strolled in and came to rest beside Dani, baring her huge teeth. "Actually, let's call it a threat. A threat seems appropriate, don't you think?"

Sean stumbled back, his entire body trembling. "What the hell is this?"

"Oh good, you're scared. You should be." Dani stepped forward, and Kiva matched her pace. The panther growled, the deep sound reverberating through the room.

"I'll leave," Sean stuttered. "I'll disappear and never come back to Blackthorn."

"Nope. Try again." Dani didn't want Sean slipping away, where he could find a new city and new people to exploit, somewhere Dani wouldn't have time to find and stop him. "No ideas? Here, I'll help. You are going to stay in Blackthorn, where my friends and I can keep an eye on you. I want a list of everyone working for you and every bit of dirt you've been holding over them to keep them under your thumb."

"Why? So you can take over my business? Not a chance."

Kiva roared, and Sean flinched.

Dani glared at him. "Of course not. I'm going to bury the blackmail and free each of them from your influence. If they want to continue their services, it'll because they choose to do so. Not because they're afraid of their secrets getting leaked. As a bonus, they won't have to share any of their profits with *you*."

"But—"

"And if I find out you've started pimping again or selling drugs or anything *remotely* illegal ..." Dani paused and let her gaze drop to the floor, where Jasper had slithered toward Sean. He flicked his tongue against Sean's bare leg. "Well, let's just say there won't be a body for the police to find."

"You—"

"Will let my friends eat you? Yes, yes, I will." Dani flashed her most cheerful smile at the creep, delighting in the pallor of his skin. "Do we have an understanding, McGrath?"

Sean nodded, his greasy hair flopping into his face.

"Good." Dani turned and headed for the door. She paused at the threshold, Kiva and Jasper on her heels. "Oh, and one more thing. If you ever try to contact Ellie Hughes again, I'll run you through with my sword and *then* let my friends eat you."

Poe screeched and took to the air. Sean ducked,

but the sudden movement threw him off balance. He slipped on the spilled beer and landed in the puddle of liquid and glass.

"Have a shitty life!" Dani called as she disappeared into the hall.

<hr>

Bloody Mary, in her signature six-inch heels, delivered a tray of burgers, fries, and onion rings to the little corner booth. "Anything else, dolls?" she asked, voice a husky baritone.

"Another round?" Dani lifted her beer bottle to her lips and took a quick swig of the cold liquid.

"Coming right up," Mary said, and wiggled away to grab more drinks.

Lana sat beside Dani, dressed in a cozy navy sweater and a pair of jeans. Cassie, tired of playing doctor all day, was spending the night with a friend. Across the booth, Spencer leaned into Adrian. He was still shaky from the magic he had performed the day before, and his fingers trembled as he reached for a fry.

Dani owed them all so much more than burgers and beer, but at least it was a start.

"I don't know what I'd do without you," she said, more earnest than she meant to be.

"You'd probably rush into danger with even less of a plan than you do now and get yourself killed." Spencer dragged his fry through a pool of ketchup. "Luckily for you, we're not going anywhere."

"I'm serious," Dani said, resisting the urge to swat his arm. When Spencer and Adrian had arrived at the bar, Spence had moved through the space like every part of him hurt. She didn't want to add to that. Especially when it was her fault he was in pain. "And I'm sorry. To both of you. I hate asking for so much."

"At least Ellie is safe," Lana said, swiping an onion ring from the shared plate at the center of the table.

"Plus, the mayor's dead," Spencer added. "All in all, I'd say it evens out."

Mary returned then with another round, and the four of them fell quiet as they ate. Bloody Mary's made the best damn burgers in Blackthorn, but even the perfectly crispy bacon on top couldn't keep Dani from thinking about the failures dragging down the bright spots of victory her friends mentioned.

Sure, Ellie was alive, the mayor was dead, and Sean was scared shitless of Dani, but people had died. Members of Raj's *family* had died. And then she'd gone and slept with him. As if that wasn't a ticking time bomb waiting to blow up in her face.

Even worse, she'd made new enemies. Enemies who knew her name. Her face. Enemies who wouldn't hesitate to track her down. Even though Nathaniel Conrad was dead, another Conrad necromancer would rise to fill his position at the head of the family. The Conrads knew who she was now.

The Dasaris did too.

Which meant it was only a matter of time before all five families came knocking on her door. Raj might try to put a lid on her identity, but people still gossiped. Word would get out.

Speaking of Raj … Though he seemed normal enough last night, the lives he took in that basement would haunt him eventually, and there was no telling what other lingering effects he might face for wielding Death for so long. His family would have questions too. Chief among them? Why he'd risked their lives—why he'd made enemies of the entire Conrad family—to protect the Ink Carrier. Hell, why he'd even dated her in the first place.

"Are you sure we can mark this week in the win column?" Dani asked when her burger and fries were gone. "We made enemies, nearly got killed, and half of Blackthorn knows I'm the Ink Carrier now, including Nick."

Adrian raised one eyebrow. "Who's Nick?"

"That detective who has the hots for Dani," Lana said, nudging Dani with her shoulder. "He seemed to take things well. Any chance that date of yours will get rescheduled?"

Dani groaned. She hadn't told her friends about her night with Raj, and she didn't plan to. "I don't know, Lan. Things are complicated."

"They're always complicated. That doesn't mean you should abandon any hope of a love life." Lana took a swig of her beer—she was still working on the first one—and grimaced. "Speaking of love life … remember the woman whose cheating husband became demon food?"

That case felt like it happened ten years ago. "Yeah?"

"Her check bounced."

"Seriously?" Dani stuffed an onion ring in her mouth. "That's it, I'm calling it. This week officially blows."

"Hey, now," Adrian said, his arm resting around Spencer's shoulders. "We're all still alive. I passed my exams, *and* you said Ellie's parents basically gave you a 100 percent tip. I'd call that a win."

Spencer lifted his beer and held it up to toast. "I'll drink to that. Cheers."

"Cheers," they all said and clinked bottles.

Dani sipped her beer and sat back as her friends moved on to new topics. Maybe the guys were right.

Maybe things were adding up in their favor after all. She knew at least one thing for sure.

She had the best damn team—the best *friends*—a girl could ask for.

The rest would fall into place in time. She'd make sure of it.

Meet Dani: Street smart. Fiercely loyal. Carries a big sword.

All Danika Frost wanted was to lead a normal life and go to college. Too bad destiny had other plans.

After her mother is brutally attacked, Dani inherits the family business: protecting the world from things that go bump in the night. with the help of the Ink, ancient spirits who live in her skin as tattoos, Dani

must hunt down demons and the necromancers who
raise them.

Alone in the dark city streets of Blackthorn, Dani
meets a young girl named Cassie. Her sister is
missing, and Dani recognizes the tell-tale signs of
demonic possession. Now, it's up to Dani to track
down Cassie's missing sister before the monster
inside hurts someone. Trouble is, Dani needs the help
of an enigmatic and sexy stranger who may or may
not be a necromancer…

**Chosen is the exhilarating prequel novella to the
Danika Frost urban fantasy series, perfect for fans
of high-octane action, riveting romance, and
unforgettable characters.**

**Get your copy today and delve into the binge-
worthy series everyone is talking about:
books2read.com/u/4DyOYk**

Thank you so much for reading INKED. We hope you enjoyed it!

We have so much more coming your way. Never miss a release by joining our free VIP club. You'll receive all the latest updates on our upcoming books as well as gain access to exclusive content and giveaways!

To sign up, visit www.connorashley.com/dani-vip

Thank you for reading INKED! If you enjoyed the book, we would greatly appreciate it if you could consider adding a review on your bookstore of choice.

Reviews make a huge difference to the success or failure of a book, especially for newer writers like us. The more reviews a book has, the more people are likely to take a shot on picking it up. The review need only be a line or two, and it really would make the world of difference for me if you could spare the three minutes it takes to leave one.

With all our thanks,

Connor and Charlotte

www.ingramcontent.com/pod-product-compliance
Lightning Source LLC
Chambersburg PA
CBHW061040190726

48286CB00006B/1548